SCABLANDS
A WASTELAND ADVENTURE NOVEL

BY NATHANIEL DOSWELL

Part 1
Under the beach, the paving stones!

An explorer of yore, upon seeing the New World laid out before him, and having a savage underfoot, wrote that civilization was to succeed barbarism. He had it backwards.

The boy raised his hands to the dim fire, searching to find some warmth from the cold night's air. His father returned and fed another log into the flames, sending out a cascade of embers. "Where was I?" he asked, settling in beside his son.

"You were going to tell the tale of the Wolf and the Beast."

"Ah yes, the Wolf and the Beast."

"It's my favorite, Papa."

"I know," said the man. "And it's a true story. Let's see. Not many years ago, at the dawn of the New Age, there roamed an untouchable band of raiders, feared by all and afraid of none. The man who led this gang was the fiercest, most ferocious corpse-maker the wasteland had ever seen. The Great Beast of the Lakes was the name set upon him, and nightmares gathered in his wake. There was a fire in his eyes and a lust in his blood. The champions to a thousand lawless raids, he and his clan wrought havoc on the people, a clan of only ten. Each of these ten were monsters of renown in their own—skilled handymen in Cain's trade. Four of them once slaughtered an entire village, simply for the leisure of it. They burned the town and the dead, taking nothing of value.

"Bountymen came from all over, the scalp of even his weakest man being enough to retire on. There once, I recall, came a renowned tracker from the Southland. He brought with him a kill squad of twenty skilled hunters, and the promise of the Beast's skin. Off went his men, to hunt down the clan. For forty days they scoured the scablands, but only three returned, two of them badly gored. The illustrious tracker was forced back to his homeland in shame and defeat. Men like him came and went. It looked to be the devil himself who protected this clan. For years even the Rangers were powerless."

"But not all of them, Papa."

"That's right," he said. "There was one Ranger, a packless wolf, who brought about the end to the reign of the Beast. He sniffed out the clan and confronted them in their own den. He sauntered in, slaughtered them as you would sheep, and then he sauntered away."

"How'd he do that?"

"The wolf is a beast in his own right, a king among his kind."

"And where's the Wolf gone to now, Papa?"

"That, I don't know. But what I do know is certain and known to all. Wild dogs don't die of old age."

***

He entered the bar through the cliché swinging saloon doors and approached the Saturday-night counter. It was packed end to end. He asked if anyone wanted to offer him a seat. A number of people stood up, some out of respect for what he had been, others out of fear for what he could become should he be provoked.

Ashur Stanton was a disillusioned conqueror with more days behind him than in front. He walked with hunched shoulders and a low head. Most days this made him appear as a thief, but other

2

days he looked like an animal on the prowl. As of late, he had spent his life in the footsteps of an expeditionary soldier, an XP, working primarily for Tavern Springs, a small town at the end of the world.

The bartender, Lulu, approached as Ashur took his place at the bar. She was a dark-skinned woman with a washcloth slung over her shoulder, and the bubbly personality of someone twenty years younger. "I don't know how you do it," she said, pouring his usual drink. "But even in a suit you look disreputable."

"It's a family trait. My uncle was a used-car salesman."

"I assume you were meeting with the mayor again?"

Ashur nodded. "I told him I was going to leave town for a week or two," he said, taking a sip. "I'm tired of waiting around for something interesting to blow in. My work's dried up here for the moment. I'm about willing to pay the Master-at-Arms to run a drill, just for the sake of doing something."

"And how'd the mayor take it?"

"Same as ever: 'Very well. Use caution. May God speed your return' and the rest."

Lulu poured a drink for another customer and returned. "What happens if the town needs you and you're not here?"

"The Master-at-Arms is more competent than I give her credit for. Even if she wasn't, the boys could handle it without my guidance."

"Where are you off to then?" asked Lulu.

"Wellshire. I've heard some runners talk about raids out that way. They're looking for some muscle."

"That sounds like your kind of work."

He bowed his head. "I'm gone tomorrow."

"You're my best customer so I feel obligated to tell you," she said. "Don't get yourself killed. And don't get off your motorcycle to play lawman. Just cruise on through till you're in Wellshire. You hear?"

"You have my word as a valued customer. I will not get off my bike."

***

Ashur killed the bike's motor and got off. He holstered his sawed-off shotgun and drew the road goggles off his face. He had just gotten into an altercation with some road bandits in a buggy. They hadn't fared well. The buggy had rolled a number of times before coming to rest, upside down, in the center of the dusty road. The front left wheel had yet to stop spinning and bright red flames poured out of the engine, kicking out black smoke. The owners of the contraption had been smart enough to layer metal plates around the chassis, but left the tires exposed, allowing Ashur's shotgun to shred one of the rear wheels.

He didn't have to finish the job. He could have stayed on his bike and kept on the road. But he rather enjoyed doing away with highwaymen and other badland scum. He was still a Ranger at heart. Now out in the field, and out of his cheap suit, he appeared as though he could carry himself. He dressed in borrowed glory, like a soldier who hadn't heard the war was over—a field jacket, chop-finger gloves, and combat boots. Miscellaneous bits of tackle and gear dangled about his body. Aside from some soot and blood, he was clean-cut. From what was visible, he carried three different guns as well as a hunting knife.

Approaching the vehicle, he found the driver decapitated and the passenger bloodied but semi-conscious. He drew his .45 pistol and ripped the man from the wreck. The blood pouring out of the bandit's forehead obscured his face, but it was obvious that a few of his teeth had been swallowed. Once outside, the man became livelier and began to struggle. He began groaning and spitting out gibberish, clawing for Ashur's hands. Ashur lugged him a few more feet before pistol-whipping him and dropping him into the dirt. Red droplets trickled from the end of his gun. He cocked the weapon, aimed it at the man's head, and put him down. This was the everyday for those who chose to leave the high walls of a township.

Ten years had passed since the Collapse. But there had been enough bloodshed and famine in that first year alone to satisfy a thousand lifetimes. Before societies took shape and tribes emerged, the death toll was incalculable. Not only was the population devastated, but their technologies, our cultures, the kingdoms of creature and plant were all but eradicated. The Earth had become a desert. A decade into the Earth's last great mass extinction event, and Death had become a siren—a merciful goddess in her endless summer dress, wandering barefoot amongst the ash and offering a daylily to the passing wayfarer. This is the only spirit worshiped here.

Spitting distance from the wreck was an old construction site. It was an unfinished office complex fenced in by a faded tarp melted to chain links. There were rows of concrete cylindrical sections, ash-caked trailers, and the seared skeletons of work vehicles blanketing the area—the bleached bones of the world before. A nearby sign read, **Coming Soon To This Location: Charming Ruins.**

An explosive wave of light and heat rolled over him, blasting his ears. The buggy's engine fire had reached the gas tank, burning up the rest of the foul-smelling crude-fuel in a matter of seconds. Ashur dove away from the vehicle, landing face down in the ash. He rolled away from the wreck as shards of debris fell to the earth around him. He kept rolling until the chain link fence of the con-struction site stopped him. He laid there, his boots in a puddle of glass, and took a deep breath. The scene was quieting now. As the debris stopped and the wreck settled, a whispering breeze came through and kicked up some dirt. The particles of sand and ash rubbed against his skin. He held his sleeve over his eyes as the eddy settled.

He sat up. Then he stood up. He tried to find his bearings. His ears were ringing and his body ached. Anywhere that wasn't numb was throbbing. Somewhere on the back of his head he had sustained a cut. He could feel the warmth of it running down his neck and into his shirt. Ashur had travelled all day towards the remote town of Wellshire. Now he was only a few miles from the edge of town but the sun was setting. If the bandits he had just fought off were an indication of what lay ahead, he didn't want to go into a warzone, bleeding and in the dark. The explosion had taken it out of him and he decided it would be better to rest than to continue travelling.

He thought about making camp there at the construction site but knew it wouldn't be safe. A fresh wreck would attract scavengers and the bandit's friends may come by looking for their missing comrades. He'd seen a few houses some miles back and thought he could find shelter there for the night, so he backtracked.

He found the quiet cul-de-sac he had passed on his route and stopped at the neck of it, where it opened into the street. Watching the windows, he revved his engine so that the sound echoed throughout the dead end street. But no one came to the windows or out the doors. As the seconds grew into minutes, he saw no motion—no one sprang from the rubble, no one rushed him with a lead pipe, or screeched a tribal battle cry. It was silent.

One of the houses in particular looked less likely to collapse on him than the others, so he parked his bike out front and approached. It was a two story brick structure with a small porch and a one car garage. At one point the shutters had been green, but now, like the rest of the house, it had turned a withered earth tone. With his hand gun drawn, Ashur tried the door and found it un-locked. He announced himself before entering and then patrolled the halls and rooms. The upstairs was especially hazardous. There were holes in the floor and large sections of the ceiling had given in. But the house was indeed vacant.

He rolled the bike into the garage and went to lock the front door. From the front door, there were stairs leading up and a hallway which opened to the kitchen and living room. He made camp there in the living room. Years ago it probably held a television and a couch, maybe a coffee table. It was probably decorated to the owner's taste with paintings or pictures, knickknacks and art, but now it was empty, completely barren. The only other things in the room with Ashur were a half-burnt log in the fireplace and some graffiti on the wall. Throughout the rest of the house he was able to locate a few pieces of leftover furniture he could break down for firewood—a footstool and the legs off a table. There were a few chairs in the kitchen so he brought one into the living room to sit on while he stoked the fire. The sun went down shortly after he got it going and it didn't take long to put out his bedroll.

He washed himself up with some water from his canteen and cleaned the wound on the back of his head. There had been a small metal shard embedded in his skin. When he was done, he played solitaire in front of the fire and had a light supper of canned food. With the day's journey and the confrontation with the roving bandits, he was eager to get some shuteye. He removed any other gear he hadn't yet and made himself comfortable on his bedroll.

***

He awoke to the sound of a door closing. The light from the fire had dimmed and night had not yet passed. Light, slow footsteps were coming down the hall towards him. He grabbed his handgun and a flashlight and sprung up from where he slept. He had removed his boots before lying down and so his footsteps were silent as he approached the hallway. When the footsteps made their way into the kitchen, he turned on his flashlight and raised his gun.

"Don't move!" he shouted. "I've got a gun."

Stock-still in the beam of his flashlight was a teenage girl. She wore a dingy University of Wisconsin hoodie, a rucksack, jeans, and a belt that had missed every pant loop. She was using it

7

as a holster for a revolver. Her hand was on it but she had not drawn it. He could see both of her hands had bandages wrapped around them. There was something almost dainty about her presence against the backdrop of the decrepit house. She was slim with curved hips and peroxide skin. Her gingery hair had been pulled back into a bobtail, except the few strands free around her temples. They covered a little of her freckled face, but not enough to hide the bruises she had recently gotten.

"You're hurt," he said. He shined his light out of her face and down towards her hands. "How did you get in here?"

It took her a moment to find her voice. "I—I have a key," she stammered. "I come here sometimes." She didn't look like a threat. On the contrary, she looked terrified.

"If I put my gun away will you take your hand off yours?" he asked. They stood there like statues. It was all too quiet in the room.

"I'll decide after," she said.

He put his gun in his shoulder holster and put up his right hand, palm towards her. She was standing about six paces away from him. "You're safe here," he said softly. "My name's Ashur. I used to be a lawman. I stopped in here for the night and—"

"Do you have a badge?" she asked. She still had her hand on her revolver.

"No. I turned it in when I left the Rangers." People didn't typically carry papers any more. There wasn't anyone left to check them. Though right now, he wished he had his. He wished he had anything with his name on it. "Why didn't you lock the door?" he asked. "When I got here the door was unlocked."

"There's nothing in here worth taking. If I locked the door someone might think there is and break it down. Then I wouldn't be able to lock it while I'm sleeping."

"You're pretty smart," he said. "Listen. I won't keep you here if you want to leave. You're free to go but nothing else in this neighborhood looks safe. We can share the living room if you need to stay.”

“I don’t know,” she said. “I don’t know you.”

He wasn’t sure what to do next. “I have some medical supplies if you like. You should let me take a look at you.” He took a step towards her and she drew the revolver from her belt.

“Don’t.” She said.

He stopped where he was, his flashlight still trained on her gun, his right hand still palm out towards her. “Okay,” he said and stepped away. He grabbed a nearby chair from the kitchen and brought it into the living room. “I’ll get the fire going again. Please come sit.” Normally Ashur wouldn’t be so trusting with a stranger he met on the road, but obviously she’d been here before, and Ashur didn’t think she would use that gun unless she needed to. He could tell she didn’t want to. Even then, with her hands bandaged up the way they were, she might not be able to.

He ignored her and focused on stoking the flames. By the time he’d got the fire going again, she had come into the living room but kept her distance. “What’s your last name Ashur?” she asked.

“Stanton,” he said. “I’m Ashur Stanton.”

“Like the one they tell stories about Ashur Stanton? Like the Ranger and expeditionary?”

He smiled at her and stood up from the hearth. “Do people still tell stories about me?”

“My family used to,” she said as she put her rucksack down on the floor. “The people in my town did…years ago.”

With his history as a lawman and current status as an expeditionary soldier, Ashur was well known to some people. It was one of the few things he enjoyed in this lackluster waste of a world. And while being blessed with public esteem brought the promise of work, it also put a target on his back.

He placed the two chairs in front of the fire and sat in one.

"Come warm up," he said. "Let's talk a bit."

She made her way across the room and stood behind the empty chair so that it was between the two of them. "What's there to talk about?"

"Can we start with your name?" he asked.

"Rose."

"What are you doing here, Rose?"

"Travelling."

"You're leaving Wellshire?"

She shifted her weight from one foot to the other. "Yeah," she said flatly.

"Are you headed to Tavern Springs?"

Her destination wasn't difficult to pick out. The four city-states in the area were connected by the main trails, which carved a diamond shape out of the badlands: Wellshire on the west point, Tavern Springs to the south on Lake Winnebago, Irongrass to the north at Greenbay, and Medway to the east on coast of Lake Michigan. A few treacherous shortcuts ran through the middle of the wasteland, though not many travelers attempted to brave the Interior. It belonged to bandits. They even had a little village dead center in the chaos of it all called New Valley. Cutthroats spent most of their time there, working on cars, thieving, drinking, raping, killing each other—having a wonderful time.

"What are you doing here?" she asked.

"You're running out and I'm running in. People in Wellshire are offering pay for some extra security right now. I thought I'd lend a hand, make a little money."

She exhaled sharply through her nose before coming around from the behind the chair and sitting down. Her revolver was in her lap. "It's worse than that," she said. "We've been able to fight off raids before but this is different. Every day it's another massacre. And they don't care who they kill…Half the town has already been burned to the ground and Mayor Anderson said our only chance is to abandon the place. So I did. There's a few old-timers digging in but everyone else is packing up."

"And your family?" he asked. But she did not respond. "How do you know about this place?"

She leaned in towards the fire a bit. "I came here sometimes when I wanted to explore," she said. "It's about the farthest I've been away from home."

"Your family would let you come out here by yourself?"

"Oh they hated me for it. The things they'd put me through when I'd come back…I feel worse for it now but…I've always liked exploring."

"Don't feel too bad. It's helping you out now," he said. Ashur shined his flashlight at the graffiti on the living room wall. "Did you do that?"

She did not turn her head to look at it. "Are you gonna book me for tagging now?"

"I just wondered where you heard it."

She shrugged. "Maybe I just read it somewhere. I'm a copycat."

He tracked the writing on the wall with his light. "And all the while everyone wants to breathe," he read. "But nobody can and many say 'we will breathe later.' And nobody dies—"

"—because they're already dead," she finished.

"What's it mean?"

There was a crisp, crackling sound coming from the fire now. An occasional pop would send embers out into the living room. "When I'd ask my grandmother why I couldn't leave town she would say, 'We all spend our lives doing things we don't want to. We have obligations, restrictions, rules.' It means we all put off living until our lives have passed over us. For one reason or another."

"Did she look after you? Your grandmother?"

She shook her head and cleared her throat. "Let's not talk about it."

"Okay," he said. "How long has it been since you changed those bandages on your hands?"

She looked down at her hand and turned it over. The side covering her palm was a dark color. "Well over a day. I've been on foot this whole time. I couldn't grab many supplies."

"I can rewrap them for you but I'll need you to put the gun away."

"Get your supplies then," she said finally. Ashur went out to the garage and retrieved a small red box from one of the saddlebags on his motorcycle. When he came back inside she was still sitting there in front of the fire, gun in hand, poised in her lap. He moved his chair closer to hers and sat down with the kit.

"Now your turn," he said.

She shook her head no and stuck her free hand out towards him. "Do one at a time," she said.

He smirked and took her hand in his own as he began unwrapping the bandage as gently as he could. She winced a bit when the last part of it was peeled away from the skin. The wounds were fairly deep and there was a little bit of fresh blood.

"Is the other one just as bad?" he asked.

She nodded. "I had to stop a knife."

He grimaced at the wound. "There's no sign of infection yet but I need to stitch them up properly before I rewrap them. These aren't going to heal like this."

She groaned at this. "Can you do that?"

"I have what I need here," he said. "I'm adequate with a needle but I'm going to need both hands to work. You'll have to hold the flashlight." He was asking her to put the gun down again.

She took a deep breath and stared at him, chewing on her upper lip as she did so. "I can't."

He locked eyes with her and softly massaged the backside of the hand he was holding. "I know you're scared and you're tired. But I put my gun away in good faith…Please let me help. This needs to be treated and I can treat it for you."

She eyed him over once more but he was right. She tucked the gun in her belt, said "This is stupid," and then took the flashlight from him.

"It won't hurt as much as getting stabbed but it will hurt," he told her. He cleaned the wound with some rubbing alcohol before he began suturing it shut. He wrapped it up after cleaning it once more and then moved on to her other hand to repeat the process. She was remarkably stoic about the whole thing, not making much of any noise other than breathing deeply.

When he finished with her second hand, the only thing she said was, "Fuck," under her breath, followed by, "I think I'd like to go to sleep now."

"You've earned that much," he said.

She promptly stood up, went to lock the front door, and then retrieved a blanket and bedroll from her rucksack. She made a spot on the floor near the fire as Ashur had done and they laid down to sleep. The last conversation they had that night was short and one-sided. She said, "Thanks."

The following day, he woke up before she did. The sun was coming in at an odd position for the morning so Ashur checked his watch. He must have been exhausted. It was just past noon. He laid there a while, thinking. After about an hour, he stood up to go relieve himself and Rose began to stir.

"Keep sleeping," he said before walking to the kitchen, through the hall, and out the front door. He stood in the front yard and observed the cul-de-sac as he relieved himself. Ashur imagined the neighborhood in full repair, with green grass and lush trees, houses with young couples and new families. He thought back to the family he'd once had. And then it all came crashing back to the way it was, the fallen-in single-family homes, the trees like burnt match sticks, the rusty tricycle in the yard with him. He zipped up just before the front door opened behind him.

When he turned around, Rose was standing in the doorway. She had her shoes on and her pack with her. "Are you leaving?" she asked.

He smirked and began walking up the steps of the porch. "Do you want me to?"

"Well no…I just mean…" she said as he walked past her and back into the house. She didn't immediately follow him inside. He went back into the living room and packed up his things and brought them into the garage to store them on his bike. When he reentered the living room she was standing there, apparently looking for him. "Wait. Listen," she said. "I know you said you were going to Wellshire but…it's really bad. It's going to take more than you to do any good. And I know you don't know me…And I don't have a lot of money but…"

"You want me to take you to Tavern Springs."

She stared at him, wide-eyed and apprehensive. "Could you?"

"I *could*," he replied.

"But I mean, would you? It would take me a week to get there on foot, on roads I've never traveled before. I could pay you what I ha—"

"I thought you liked exploring."

She sighed. "You could leave me at the gate," she suggested. "Please. I'd never ask you for anything again I promise. I just…" She stuttered. "I'll give you anything okay?"

He looked her up and down. "You don't have anything I want, sweetie."

Her speech became rushed. "Then I'll work for you or something. I'll get a job and pay you back. Please. I've got a chance of surviving if I can get a lift with you. I know you've got a bike. I know you can handle yourself on the road. What do I have to do?"

He put his hand up. "Stop," he said. At that, he could see the worry and defeat growing in her face. He saw the sinking feeling of genuine desperation begin to overtake her as he stared her down. He wasn't a bleeding heart. He never had been. If she had been anyone else, he would not have had an issue leaving her there. But she reminded him of someone. "You will not steal anything. From me or anyone else. You will not wonder off. You will not lie to me. And when I start giving orders, you follow it first and ask questions after." He could see the dread in her changing into something else. "Run that back to me," he said.

She inhaled and wiped her nose on the sleeve of her hoodie. "I won't steal anything. I won't wonder off. I won't lie and I'll do what you tell me to."

"I didn't say you couldn't lie. I just said you couldn't lie to me."

She tried to force a smile and then stopped. "So you'll take me?"

"Yeah I'll take you," he said. "If you're ready to go. We wasted half the day sleeping so we won't make it there by nightfall. But I know a place we can stop."

Chapter 2

That evening they pulled into a hotel for the night. Emerson's Inn was hidden away, tucked up underneath a standing freeway which had shielded the structure during the Collapse. Large walls made out of scabland trash had been set up in fortification of the place, and many people had taken to gifting them with graffiti, some promoting the botched revolution of the world before, others being simple nonsensical road messages left by travelers. One such wall had, **THE RAPTURE HAS ARRIVED! JESUS SAVES!!!** scrawled on it. He remembered it for the most part because underneath it, some unarguably brilliant simpleton had responded with, **but Gretzky scores on the rebound!**

It was seconds before dark when they approached the front gate. Upon arrival, two inn guards brandishing AK-47s ordered the bike to a halt, demanding the duo's hands in the air—standard welcoming procedure.

The area they entered could be classified as a foyer. It cleanly separated the scablands from the inside courtyard and the rest of the motel. It contained a storage shed and a smallish trailer at the far end.

"Stanton, you dirty mother, how are ya?" Sal greeted before the kickstand had even touched dirt. Ashur was happy to see Sal, always was. With his nutty disposition and natural hospitality, he never failed to make a great host.

"Hey, Sal, how goes it?"

"Whoa now, hold on just a second. Who's the young miss?" He playfully investigated Rose's presence. In a ritual that had inexplicably managed to survive the Collapse, she gave him a kind smile, spoke her name, and then offered a hand.

"Sal Emerson. I own the place."

"Nice to meet you," she said, afterwards breaking handhold.

"We need a room for the night, know where we can find one around here?" Ashur asked.

"Well 'course. It'd be my pleasure to lend you a room," he responded with a smile that was missing a few teeth. He was not the prettiest nor the cleanliest man alive, but he was neighborly, and that was something unique enough to make him a rarity.

"What's it going to cost me?" Ashur asked.

Sal thought for a time, gazing up at the waning moon as he did. "Um…well, actually I could ask a service instead of trade."

"Got a job for me?"

"Full as a fat lady's sock I got a job for you," he confirmed. Rose cracked a tiny smile at Sal's comparison before he continued with the job description. "My regular courier got 'imself killed last week and I still don't got a replacement. So if you're on your way to Tavern Springs, you could drop off a package for me and I'd consider your stay paid for."

"I only need to know what I'm carrying and who it's going to."

"A man you prob'ly know. Eugene Vanderbilt."

"Yes. I know him."

"Excellent! You'll know where to find him then," Sal said, full of joy.

"And what's the package?"

"Oh…you know…nothing dangerous I'm sure."

"You don't know?"

"It ain't mine. Some scav looking fella dropped it off and gave me a silver piece to get it to the Springs. 'Sides, it's too small to be anything harmful." Sal made a shape with his hands.

"Anthrax? Flash bomb? Hell, I could get a block of plastic explosive in something that size if I had to."

"If it was any of those, would it stop you?"

"Do you think it would?" Ashur asked.

"Nope. I bet you'd just take it for yourself and use it on some poor bastard."

"Does it happen often? People dropping off packages I mean."

"Very occasionally. But it was enough to where I got…er…had myself a courier come by when his work ran light."

Ashur nodded. "All right. I'll pull the job."

"Great!" Sal exclaimed. "And with that settled, we can get y'all a room, but you know the rules." The two guards who had been slouching on either side of Sal came to attention.

"Yeah, I know, Sal." Ashur began to remove the lever action rifle from his back.

Before letting outlanders in, Sal tried to strip his customers of all their weaponry. It was the same precautionary safety measure that the nicer towns used. It never worked. Ashur unclipped his hunting knife and unloaded his pistol, rifle, and shotgun before handing everything over to the guards. Anytime someone relieved him of his guns, he emptied them, that way the they couldn't swipe his bullets and later argue that the guns had been empty the whole time. He had seen it happen, more than once. Nowadays, ammunition was more than just defense. After coinage, it was the most widely accepting bartering chip.

When it came time for Rose to give up her weapon, she hesitated. After both Sal and Ashur assured her that her weapons would be returned, she unloaded her gun and turned it over. Then the guards frisked them. They started with Ashur and during the search found a set of brass knuckles. No trouble evolved from the discovery though. Everyone tried to hold out on guards. It was commonplace.

Then they moved on to Rose. They were rougher with her. Before long, they took a butterfly knife off her and the both of them were declared clean. The guards opened the gate to the courtyard and Ashur raised the kickstand on his bike.

"Now before I let y'all in, you should know that there is a kid in there looking for an Ashur Stanton. Is that gonna be a problem?"

"No problem, Sal." Ashur walked his bike into the compound, Rose at his side. He saw a campfire and the three figures sitting around it. The motel had once been two stories, painted in a white and green striped design. It was now soot-grey with most every windowpane gone or boarded up. Two more guards, rifles slung over their shoulders, lounged against the wall while they watched over the courtyard. Ashur saw that one of them carried a Tommy Gun, the iconic drum magazine along with it. He parked his motorcycle and grabbed his pack from the saddlebags.

Sal led them to their room to make sure they had the right key. "And there you are," he said, swinging the door open before wandering off.

It didn't look welcoming, but at least it had a bed. Rose dropped her rucksack in the entryway and studied the room with Ashur. The ceiling sagged and cream paint peeled from the walls. Portions of the carpet had been removed, but with how ugly the fabric was, it didn't bother Ashur. There was a closet near the door, a bathroom at the back, and next to the nightstand lay the only bed. When Rose noticed this, she glanced at him and then at the mattress and then back at him.

He set his bag down. "Better grab it before I do."

She trotted a few paces and jumped face first onto the springy cushion. She smiled and lolled about, playing with the pillows.

He cleared his throat. "So what's the story with the raids on Wellshire?"

She stopped playing and sat up. "Uh…the raids started a few weeks back when our mayor cut off trade with New Valley and the rest of the Interior dregs. They killed a few of our people in a fight over protection money. That's what started it. We were able to defend ourselves for a while, but it didn't last."

He was surprised anyone would be dumb enough to cut off trade with the cutthroats. For one, however crude, they were quite the economic asset, and second, if trade was cut off, it was only logical that they would resort to taking things by force. Medway was the only place with walls big enough and doors strong enough to lock out the untouchables. Wellshire, on the other hand, was far smaller and more isolated. It barely registered as a dot on the map.

"Fucking idiot," Ashur muttered. She looked up from her nails. She had been cleaning the dirt out from underneath them. "Your mayor," he clarified.

She shrugged. "I didn't vote for him." She left the bed and walked across the room to read something someone had scribbled on the wall. "Is it exciting?" she asked. "The work you do."

"It's not quite like what you hear around the campfires. But no two days are ever the same, if that's your definition of exciting."

She finished reading the graffiti and came back to sit at the foot of the bed. "So where are you supposed to sleep?"

"The floor," he said, not thinking much of it.

"Cool." She nodded faintly. "Now what?"

Ashur scratched at the side of his neck. "You can either hang out here or come out to the fire pit. Your choice." She followed him out of the room. The courtyard had once been the motel's parking lot. Part of it still was. They made their way over to the campfire and the circle of white plastic chairs. Two gentlemen sat next to each other, chatting. The area around the fire pit was barren save for an office table and a boom box.

"Holy hell, is that Johnny Cash?" Ashur asked as they approached.

"You betcha," said the man with glasses. He was older. His skin was beginning to wrinkle. Ashur placed him somewhere in his sixties. He had hair like steel wool and a beard with a birthday.

"Who's Johnny Cash?" Rose asked as they pulled up chairs.

"He was a ways before your time," Ashur told her. "Before mine even."

"So who might you two be?" the other man asked. He was about the same age as the other but rather lanky and sported a slouch hat.

"Gordon." Ashur gave a name and then looked at Rose. To his surprise, she took to the act and followed the model—just not to spec.

"Daisy," she said.

"I'm Morris," said the bearded man. "This here's Jake."

"There's a keg under the table there. Complementary. Help yourselves," Jake invited.

Rose thanked him as Ashur wandered over. She wasn't far behind. When they returned to their seats, "The Man Comes Around" faded away, and the radio began to speak.

"This is the federal emergency management agency's emergency radio broadcast system Wisconsin...but you know it better as Radio Free Newaukee, with me, Yeoman Swain, your disc jockey. I'm coming to you over the waves, sending you what's choice. What's choice? Whatever I can find. Enjoy." A single from Credence Clearwater Revival was next in the DJ's lineup.

"Wonder where Sal got the radio," Ashur said.

"It's mine actually," said Morris.

Ashur noted the frayed cuffs of their soot-loaded outwear.

"Are you scavs by trade?" he asked.

"Scavengers? Yup," Morris confirmed. "We found that piece while rooting around on the Medway side of the Interior."

Ashur saw a door to one of the many motel rooms open. Someone stepped out and moments later, the fireside club had a new member. A young male with a red do-rag took the chair on the other side of the fire. "Who's this?" he asked.

Jake lifted a finger at Ashur. "That's Gordon, and the little ma'am's name is Daisy."

The boy couldn't have been older than twenty—a scruff of hair upon his chin, slight but defined build, and a studded, leather jacket. "Hey," he said. "I'm Keith. Nice to meet you."

"Nice to meet you," said Rose.

"Yeah," Ashur said. "It's a pleasure."

The group sat around for about half an hour, listening to the radio and drinking. In that time span, Jake and Morris told an exciting tale or two, revealing that they were old scavenging buddies. Keith on the other hand was an up-and-coming bounty hunter, a hatchet man hoping to make a name for himself. He'd just added a few kills to his name.

Ashur had crafted new stories for himself and Rose. Daisy was Gordon's daughter and Gordon was Emerson's new courier. Daisy came with Gordon on some of his deliveries, and the two of them had just returned from a job in Wellshire.

A tune belonging to Billy Joel died away. *"Now before I go and leave you in the dark, here's some news from the top. This is News Peak. Tonight we have your traffic, weather, and sports. Racing season is starting late next month, with the grand prix to be held at the Medway Amphitheater in eight months' time. Top-Driver, Danny 'The Dirty' Danworth, says he's going to, quote, 'Take his brandy lap, with a glass of victory,' end quote. Well, Danny, I'll be sure to do a follow up...when you're sober. Next up is the weather. And here's your five day forecast!...Dry...like my humor. That leaves traffic. With the exodus from Wellshire, the trails connecting Tavern Springs and Irongrass to the town have become prime targets for marauders and highwaymen alike. Travelers along these paths are urged to exercise caution. Stay low and stay armed. And that was News Peak—your light in the blinding darkness. Thanks for listening, and as always, may we live in interesting times.* " The sound of the microphone falling to the floor faded quickly. There was a touch of feedback and then lonely static.

Morris switched off the radio. "Yeoman Swain. Always a hoot." Most everyone agreed and Ashur went to get another beer.

"I like your bike," said Keith upon Ashur's return. The motorcycle was parked a short distance away, next to a few other cars. Ashur assumed the battered pickup belonged to the team of scavs, and the lightly armored sedan was Keith's. The few other cars that were there belonged to Sal and his men.

"Thanks. I love the thing to death," Ashur replied. The bike was something special. Aside from the off-road tires and the saddlebags he had attached, the bike stood as it had before the machine that built it: pristine. He had discovered it in what was left of a once great city on the coastline of Lake Michigan, the metallic black paint and chrome workings untouched by the Collapse.

"Harley-Davidson, right?" Keith asked.

He saw a familiar look in the young man's eyes. It was the same one he saw in his own when he looked in the mirror. The boy was a killer. And he was sizing Ashur up.

"No. It's a Triumph," Ashur said over the fire, taking a swig from his cup. The group sunk into a stillness as they watch Ashur and Keith. The vacancy in their voices alone could have silenced a mockingbird.

"How long you had it?"

Ashur placed his right hand on his right knee. "About eight years."

Keith studied the bike. "You wouldn't know a man named Ashur Stanton would you?"

At this, Ashur clenched his right hand, balling up his beige cargo pants, pulling the pant leg up just enough to where he could get at his boot knife. "I've heard his name tossed around but I don't know him personally. Why do you ask?"

"Just 'cause Stanton rides something a lot like your scrambler there. Thought you might have run into him at a bike club or something."

Ashur knew that if anyone had a description of what he rode around on, and then saw that bike, it would be a beautiful giveaway of his identity. "I've never met him. If I do run into him I'll have to ask him where he gets his parts, because that's been the biggest pain with that machine, always a hassle to replace something on it," he said.

The group watched the fire in a pregnant silence, like the space between a lightning strike and its thunderclap. He studied Keith, gauging how long it would take him to make his move. Ashur knew the bountyman was savoring the moment, unaware that Sal had tipped him off. He had another swig of beer and gave Rose the up and down. She looked sick. She could see the way Keith was looking at Ashur. A pause filled only with the sounds of the fire crawled past.

"Hey, Gordon?"

"Hmm?"

"What's your last name?" The boy's face held a perverted grin.

"Whitehead."

The boy dissected the name, trying to match it with anything.

"Why do you use Gordon Whitehead?" he asked finally.

"It's easy to remember…It's the guy that killed Houdini." In a quick motion, Ashur stretched down to grab his boot knife as Keith stood up and fumbled at his waistband. As Ashur flung his knife, a slug from Keith's revolver slammed into his chest, knocking him onto the ground.

"Ashur!" Rose cried out. The guards rushed towards the group, demanding hands and stillness. Jake and Morris cooperated, but Rose sprinted the few feet and fell beside Ashur. He was having a hard time breathing, coughing as if all the air around him had been incinerated. She swept away the flaps of his jacket and pulled up his T-shirt. There underneath, in the flickering light of the flames was black fabric labeled with faded white letters.

"Oh thank God," Rose sighed when she spotted the Kevlar armor.

Ashur got a grip on Rose's arm and pulled her down onto the asphalt next to him. "Be still," he spat out between coughs.

The courtyard gate burst open, and Sal and his guards rushed into the area, all brandishing automatic weapons and barking orders. The goons surrounded the fireside group as Sal moved to the other side of the pit. He found his valued patron's boot knife protruding from the kid's neck.

"Damn it, Ashur. I didn't think we'd've any problems this time!" Sal sounded distraught.

"Is he dead?" he asked, catching his breath.

"Yes! Deader than a Goth party!"

"Then he won't be a problem." Ashur began to laugh until the bald-headed guard rammed the butt of his Tommy Gun into his chest.

Sal raised his hand. "That won't be necessary."

Ashur groaned and rubbed his chest in attempts to dilute the pain. Sal glanced about, eyeing his other guests. Rose was on her back now, propped up on her elbows.

"All right, boys," he said. "Let's clean up the mess." The scavs put their hands down as the guards moved towards the body. Now unrestricted, Rose got up.

"Are you okay!?" she prodded, standing over him.

He found his spilled beer and held it up to the girl. "I spilled my beer. Get me another."

She went from distressed, to amazed, to cold all within the span of a few seconds. Without a word, she took his cup and went to the table where she refilled it from the keg. She came back around the social pit and stood over him, the reflection of the flames in her eyes.

"What?" he asked.

She threw the beer in his face.

***

The night went on. After Keith's body had been dragged off, Sal joined the group around the fire. Rose on the other hand, left. Not physically, but she distanced herself from the men around her, bringing her legs up onto the chair and hugging them. She sat in silence, drinking and watching the fire dance.

"So who gets the boy's things?" one of the scavs asked.

"Well, since it's on my property, I reckon that makes it as mine as my arm, now don't it?" Sal replied. Jake and Morris looked daggers at the innkeeper and then each other. "So, Ashur, what'd Keith want you dead for anyhow?"

He shrugged his shoulders. "You might find this comes as a shocker, but not everybody likes me."

Sal gave one of his toothless smiles.

"But do you have any idea who would put a hit out on you?" Jake asked, apparently more concerned for Ashur's safety than Ashur himself.

"I doubt there was a hit. You heard what the kid said, new to the whole bounty hunter game, wanted to make a name for himself. Assumed killing me would earn him some notoriety."

"Quite right," said Sal. "I'll get y'all some more wood." He stood up and walked off. A moment later Rose went with Morris to refill her cup.

When everyone returned, a long stillness followed and Ashur noticed Jake was studying him, glancing over every so often to watch him. "You know, Ashur, I'm curious. You're an army man, aren't you?" The group's attention shifted to him. Even Rose perked up.

Ashur looked down at his field coat: olive drab green with a matching American flag patch on the left shoulder. "Is it the jacket?"

Jake grinned. "It's just, a man doesn't learn how to handle himself like that overnight, or at the very least without some training."

Ashur met Rose's gaze when he spoke. "No," he said. "I was an accountant. But I did have a bit of an obsession with Clint Eastwood movies. I suppose that's what led me to become a gunslinger."

"Really?" asked Morris.

There was a pause before Ashur broke into laughter. "Nah. I'm just fucking with you. Yeah I was in the Army. But I can't say that made much of a difference. With the world we left, I'm sure all of you had as much experience as I did."

"Yeah," said Jake. "Only we were trained *not* to shoot at unarmed civilians."

Sal grinned. "No wonder not everybody likes you. Was it better on the right hand than under the left foot?"

Ashur let out a chuckle. "At world's end, there's not a fingerbreadth of difference." He polished off his beer. "Here, we're all just people. Right?"

Prior to the Collapse, the air had grown polluted and the streets crowded. The sick, the starved, and the homeless were all a common sight. Countries around the globe launched invasions for resources and living space. Many committed genocide. The United States was quick to follow, removing rights, constructing massive prison camps, taking resources by force, turning the beacon of freedom into a global leader in oppression. This was when the cities were painted. This was when politics was no longer shown on TV. It spilled into the streets. It shattered windows. It bashed in doors. It shot back at anyone in uniform. It was a time Ashur wanted to forget.

The rest of the evening passed without speech. The fire died down as Sal began wailing on his harmonica. He had talent but in time his musical genius began to wane.

Ashur found himself growing tired. "Okay, flowerchild, time for some shuteye."

"I'm not tired," she said vacantly.

He cracked each of his knuckles individually, in a habitual fashion, watching the joints bend. "You want to be out here alone?"

Sal threw another log on the fire. "She's safe with us."

Ashur started to protest but Rose cut him off. "I'll be fine," she said. "Go."

He got up from his seat and stood directly in front of her. "Okay," he said, bringing up his finger to tap on the rim of her cup. Not counting the half-empty beer she had dropped, this was her fourth. "Just pace yourself."

"*All right*," she snapped.

He crouched down in front of the mousey teen so that he was at eye level with her, though she refused to look him in the face. He could feel the group's eyes on his back. "I don't think you understand," he said, dropping his voice to a whisper. "If you're not up and ready to go when I am, I will leave you here. Hold no doubt."

He could tell she was biting her tongue. Without another word, he made for the room. Inside, a lantern was the only source of light. He lit one of the numerous candles on the dresser and pulled off his boots, and then his jacket, shirt, and body armor. A golden ring dangled about his neck on a string. His chest was bruised. The bullet had done a good deal of damage, and the butt of the Thomson submachine gun had not helped. He put his shirt back on, took an extra pillow off the bed, and laid out his bedroll.

Chapter 3

The sunlight glinted off the ocean of white and barbed wire. Ice crystals formed in Ashur's nostrils as he sprinted towards the trench. The snow crunched under his boots and gunfire rang out in the distance. A few bullets impacted the ground around him, kicking up debris as he dove headlong into the foxhole. He hit hard and rolled. When he recovered he found a corporal slouching up against the wall near Garwood, one of his fellow sergeants. Garwood was whittling something, hadn't even looked up.

"You breathing?" he asked

Ashur sat up. "Looks like."

"That's good," the corporal said. "Someone has to fight this war." He scraped some cat food out of a tin with his field knife and shoveled it into his mouth.

Ashur caught his breath before checking the ammo in his rifle's magazine. "Where's Jackson?"

"Stepped on a landmine a few hours back. Blew his ass clean off," said the corporal. "So he's all over the damn place." A mortar shell landed close to the entrenchment, shaking some snow loose. The corporal lost hold of his tuna and it fell into the brownish slush. "Fucking Canucks. That was the good stuff. I hate this war. Why the fuck don't we just leave and come back in the spring?"

"I like it up here," Garwood said as he traded the piece he had whittled for his combat rifle. "The sky's still blue." A

Canadian soldier attempted to rush across the thin wooden bridge that spanned the trench. Garwood knocked him off the scaffolding with two rounds. The hostile had gathered momentum, so his body slammed into the trench wall before coming to rest at the bottom.

"Western flank's open," Ashur informed them. "Lieutenant's given up."

Garwood returned to his whittling knife. "He's fallen back?"

"A tank shell carried him halfway home." An enemy jet flew overhead and was immediately tagged by anti-aircraft flak, creating a lightshow. "We're to join up with the Ninth on the other side of Hay River. Let's move."

It took them three hours to get to the Army's nearest outpost. It was named Audax and it was a mess. People were scrambling for information, running every which way, trying to find out what their orders were. The medical tents were jammed with casualties. Their screams and cries could be heard all throughout the outpost.

He pressed through the crowd and eventually found a staff sergeant who looked like he knew what he was doing. "What's command saying?" Ashur asked.

"We lost contact during last night's snowstorm. Supply's been cut off as well. It may be a while before we hear anything. We'll have to carry on ourselves."

"Who's acting CO then?"

The staff sergeant shrugged. "We had a full lieutenant wandering around a few hours ago. He wasn't much help. No telling where he went. Now I really have to go." He ran off. Garwood and the corporal didn't catch up with Ashur until he was through questioning a second and then a third person. No one knew who was in charge and people were panicked. He overheard a group of men carrying a conversation about going AWOL. In an act that could have had him before a court martial, Ashur fired his rifle into the sky. The camp grew silent. All the scurrying people stopped and the tents emptied out into the sun. A few soldiers had their guns shouldered in response.

He scanned the crowd, searching for an officer. "Who's in command here?"

The camp settled down and even the screams from the medical tents quieted down. The crowd looked amongst itself, whispering in the cold.

From the choir came a single meek voice. "You are, Master Sergeant."

***

Ashur awoke in a black room to the sounds of weeping. He threw off the jacket he was using as a blanket and groped blindly in the dark. He found the electric lantern and after a bit of fumbling with the device, light spilled into the room. Rose was sitting on the bed crying. Her hair had been let down. He rubbed his eyes and forced himself off the floor, cradling his chest. Moving towards the bedside, he half-stumbled over one of her sneakers. She attempted to shield her eyes from the light.

"What's wrong?" He pointed towards the door. "Did any of them touch you?"

She shook her head. "No. They were fine."

"Then what's wrong?"

She looked away and shook her head. He could smell her from where he stood. She was drunk. "You just fucking killed him," she said under her breath. "And you're sleeping like a baby. Unbelievable."

"You knew him?"

"No. I didn't fucking know him."

"Then could you stop crying so I could go back to sleep?"

She slid to the other side of the bed, away from him. "Fuck you, man."

He placed the lantern on the nightstand and sat down towards the foot of the mattress. She was sitting upright against the

32

headboard, cross-legged. "What can I do?" he asked. "What's set—"

"No. Just fuck off." She wiped her face on the sleeve of her hoodie and left the bed. "This was a mistake. I'm just going to go." She rushed to grab her pack.

"Rose, wait. Where are you going to go?"

She put a hand up and braced herself against the wall. "I…I don't…" She then gestured weakly at something and sprinted for the bathroom. He heard a gag followed by the unmistakable sounds of hurling. He sighed and scratched his head, waiting a moment before he shuffled into the bathroom. She was on the floor in front of the toilet. He knelt down behind her as she heaved. Brushing his hands over her head, he gathered her hair into a ponytail and then put his other hand on her back. When she was through being sick, she collapsed onto him, burying her face into his shoulder. She continued to bawl. "I know," he said. "It's no fun."

"I'm really sorry," she said in a slur, talking to his shoulder.

"You don't have to apologize. I know you're grieving." He handed her some toilet paper so she could blow her nose. "Who'd you lose?"

"My nana." She used the tissue and threw it away. "And my brother." She started to cry again. "He died because of me."

He drew her back into his shoulder. "You mean he died saving you. It's different and you know it. Don't do that to yourself. Especially not right now. You're exhausted and right now you need rest." He rubbed her back. "I promise you can cry all you want later, but right now you need to rest." It took a few tries but she calmed herself down. They remained like that for a time, slouched against the bathroom wall. It wasn't long before she started to fall asleep. "We ought to put you to bed." He carried her into the room and set her down on the mattress. He returned to his bedroll and made himself comfortable.

"What are you going to do when you get back to the Springs?" she asked.

"I don't have anything particular in mind. Why?"

"Can I stay with you a while? Till I get everything figured out?"

The old world had been a mess but the new one was not an improvement. The air smelled of cancer, graves were cliché, and long ago kindness had crawled into a corner and starved to death. That thought made Ashur glad he hadn't grown up during this time. "You can, yeah," he said and turned off the lantern. "Now go to sleep."

Rose rolled over and drifted off.

***

The clinking of steel tank treads echoed across the frozen tundra. Ashur and Garwood sat alongside a few others, all of them riding a steel rhinoceros bound for the south.

"What are you going to do when you get home, Stanton?"

Ashur thought for a moment. "First I'm going to hug my daughter," he said. "And then I'm going to have some real food. After that I'm going to take my wife by her hand and lead her into the bedroom. I think I'll start by undoing—"

"I mean," said Garwood, a slim smirk pursed upon his lips. "What are you going to do to keep hot meals on the table?"

"What do you mean? We are the firm and unwavering fist of this nation."

"In case you hadn't noticed, this nation doesn't need us anymore. The war's over. Our tour's up." A fighter jet rocketed past, nearly taking the tops off of the conifers. "You really want to reenlist?"

"Reenlist? I don't know. It's a possibility. I might even go to school and become an officer."

"I've got a better idea that I want to let you in on," said Garwood. "I've heard about this new outfit the feds are setting up. It's called Riot and Urban Control. They pay you in gold. Interested?"

***

Ashur sat up. His chest ached. It was morning but the room was still dark. Their room was one of the ones where the window had been covered up with a board. He turned on the lantern. Rose had slept on top of the covers. He grunted in amusement. Leaving his jacket on the floor, he got up. After setting the lantern down on the nightstand, he shook her by the shoulder. "Up and at 'em."

She groaned and rolled over so she didn't have to face him or the lantern. "Five more minutes."

"Just five." He made his way to the bathroom and lit a candle. Following this, he took his morning piss, washed his face, and sipped some water from the faucet. The hotel didn't have electricity, but there was usually running water on tap.

Written about the restroom were more road messages:

Anarchy is me
> **The forest precedes man,**
> **the desert follows**

> > > **Dead for a long time:**
> > > **an epitaph for the world**

> **For a few easy payments,**
> **you too can learn to steal!**

The "down" in trickle-down economics means we all fall

> **I miss being awake.**

He looked at himself in the mirror: amber eyes prophesizing war, the bags underneath marking the battles. He had been tired for a long while, even in his dreams. There was a crack in his lip that he couldn't stop chewing on, and above his left ear, a thin streak of skin—hair doesn't grow well on scar tissue.

He exited and plopped down at the foot of the bed to lace up his boots. After stumbling over Rose's sneakers for the second time, he tried rousing her once more. But she did not wake. He grabbed what he needed and left the room. In the pale orange sun, it was cold enough to see his breath. The scavs' car was still there, as well as the boy's blood—a dark stain on the shattered asphalt. He found his bike and walked it into the foyer. One of the guards called for his boss.

"Morning," Sal said as he came out of his office. "How'd you sleep?"

He dropped the kickstand. "I've slept better."

"Sorry to hear that." Sal looked around. "Where's the kid?"

He shrugged. "Sleeping in it seems."

Sal shifted his stance nervously a few times. "You're leaving then?"

He nodded.

"Uh…all right. I'll go get the package and have your stuff returned." Sal slunk away into his office while the two foyer guards went to collect weapons from a storage shed. They handed Ashur his vast armory. He began reloading his guns and redoing his holster and knife fittings. Sal came back with a sealed cardboard box, reminding him who the recipient was. It fit snuggly into one of the motorcycle's saddlebags. He finished with his guns, setting his sawed-off into its holster—a routine that was now second nature.

He straddled his motorcycle and set foot on the kick starter. He would have forgotten about the package and started back on his way towards Wellshire had Rose not awoken when she did. He could hear her thumping footsteps echoing across the courtyard.

She skidded to a stop in the threshold between the parking lot and the entrance. "Ashur!" He and her locked eyes. She looked like a startled deer—ridged and panicked, panting hard through the dust she had kicked up. He made no response. She composed herself and then braved a single step towards him, as if inquiring.

He moved his boot off the starting ratchet and waved her over.

She approached, cupping her elbows. "Why would you bother picking me up if you were just going to leave me?" she murmured.

"Half-way's better than no way," he said and got off the bike.

A guard came over with her weapons in a tub. She began collecting them. "I'm sorry about last night," she said without looking at him. She slid a few bullets into one of her revolvers, rushing through the process.

"Don't worry about it."

She finished with her weapons. "I didn't expect for you—I mean I don't really know you, but you don't seem like the kind that would…" She searched for words.

"Understand?"

She looked away and nodded.

"Everyone was your age once. Everyone's lost people, myself notwithstanding. This life sucks. You get used to it."

She put her hair back into a bun while chewing on her top lip. "Thank you for that."

"You ready?" he asked. She held up a finger as if to ask for a moment and then turned away from everybody. He was not alarmed when she braced herself on her knees and threw up for a second time.

"You're a fucking mess, kiddo."

"I know," she groaned.

"You'll feel better tomorrow. Come on."

She gave a coy apology to Sal and the rest of the group and then they departed.

Rose kept quiet at the start of the ride, trying to get more sleep. At least, that is what Ashur presumed. He could feel her head lying on his shoulder. They were riding through the ruins of some moderately sized town when she gave up using him as a pillow. The town ached with disrepair—a charred relic.

"How much farther to Tavern Springs?" she yelled over the wind.

He told her it was another fifteen miles. The bike came up on what may have been a scav rummaging through the scraps of an old Crown Meridian Electronics store. Rose placed her hand on top of Ashur's, which had made its way onto the handle of his sawed-off. As they rode by, she waved at the stranger and after he had found cover, the man returned the awkward gesture.

They passed a sun-faded city limit marker and Ashur slowed down to navigate the narrow streets. "So what's Tavern Springs like?" she asked.

"Never been?"

"No. I've lived in Wellshire since the Collapse."

"Exciting," he remarked.

"You'd be surprised. Like this one time, my brother and I wanted to make fireworks, but all we had was crude-fuel, so we went to the scrapyard and…" She trailed off and thought for a second before speaking up again. "You don't care. Tell me more about the town."

"The Springs is bigger than you're used to. There's better security, decent amount of food and water. Pretty normal town I guess, plenty of creeps, plenty of good folk too. You'll see when we get there."

"You travel a lot right?"

"Me? As an XP? Travel?"

"I wanted to know about Medway."

"It's a hell hole," he said. "They won't let you do anything without the proper paperwork. All the bars are shit. The townies are all jackasses, and no bandits to fight with. Reason being the Medway Trading Company and the Rangers are both based out of Medway, and Rangers won't allow weapons in public."

"You don't like Rangers?"

"Back when they meant something, sure. I still have the hat somewhere. But now they're just the Company's boots on the ground. Aren't worth the gold their badges are minted out of."

The Medway Trading Company was the closest thing to a central government the dead frontier had to offer, and with the Rangers acting as its soldiers, the Company's arms stretched to every corner of the great lakes, and into every man's pocket. The Rangers had originally been established to enforce order in the badlands and foster cooperation amongst the city-states, but with the advent of the Company and bribery, the Rangers remade themselves into paramilitaries—guns for hire. They dedicated themselves to defending the Company's assets and eradicating its competition. When they weren't doing that, they shot at whatever piqued their interest. Justice had never paid so well.

"Huh," Rose remarked. "What about Irongrass?"

"What am I? Your tour guide?"

"I'm curious!"

"Irongrass is another coastal settlement like Medway or the Springs, so it's big. Not a nice place though. It's run by..."

Ashur spotted something on the horizon. Down the road, vehicles approached, not just one, but a whole convoy. Whether they were hostile or not, he couldn't be sure. He readied himself to sprint if they needed to flee. The convoy was comprised of a string of armored military vehicles—an awesome sight. He could make out something written on the lead Humvee's front deflector plate: **KEEP BACK 1000 YARDS**. The logo below the deflector plate was familiar to him: a brass, circular shield with **Aegis Armed Forces** written in the middle.

He laughed quietly to himself. "Aegis."

Aegis Armed Forces was one of the larger private military contractors the scablands had to offer. He had worked with the group before, not as part of their team, but in a coordinated effort. The patron had wanted both Aegis and Ashur on the job, but since Ashur had refused, on more than one occasion, to join the contractor, the customer had been forced to hire them separately.

The two parties met, stopping in the road. A click from every door on every vehicle. A man dressed in aviators and battle armor stepped out of the leading Humvee. He stood before his band carrying with him the smell of gun smoke—the fog of war. Ashur recognized him as Dixon.

The armor Dixon's men wore was retired American Army with a badland twist. It was Celtic-green, made of canvas material, steel plates, and chainmail. The duo was fenced in by roughly forty ironclad men. They brought with them assault carbines, grenades, and an unquestionable tactical superiority.

"On the hunt, Ashur?" Dixon asked. There was a remnant of Gaelic in his voice.

He prompted Rose off the bike and then dismounted. Rose proceeded to stand halfway behind him. "You wish."

"Who's the lass?" Dixon asked.

"Some kid. War orphan." He looked back at her. "It's okay. They're friends…or friendlies at least."

A few of the men chuckled at her apprehension. She slid out into the open. "Hi," she said to the group. Dixon stepped forward and held out a hand. She took it.

"Dixon O'Donnell. Aegis Armed Forces." He turned her hand over and saw the bruises on her face. "Hey if this guy beat you up give me a wink and my boys will take care of him for you."

She smirked. "No," she said, pulling her hand back. "Actually he's helping me out. Right, Ashur?"

He spoke before Ashur had the chance to. "This old wolf? That doesn't sound like him," he said, facing Ashur. He turned back to Rose. "Don't be fooled. I've seen him kill a half dozen people your age. Of course they were armed and shooting at him, so I suppose if you avoid that you might be okay…"

Their conversation was shut down by the rising scream of a tornado siren, a device all settlements kept on hand to warn of an oncoming attack.

A mercenary shouted something and pointed. A car was approaching from an empty plane to the west. They could all see the V-shaped snowplow mounted to the front, painted with a leering smiley face in luminescent white. Ashur made the vehicle out to have once been a Chrysler or perhaps a Buick. He couldn't be sure. The contraption had been cannibalized beyond recognition. The entire car was encased in steel paneling, wheel wells included, and the windshield was slotted with metal sheeting. Affixed to the roof was a set of off-road running lights and the source of the noise—a dismantled civil alert siren, refitted for use as some sick psychological weapon. About the hellish wagon were reddish splotches. At the distance, Ashur couldn't tell if the blemishes were oxidation or blood, or some gruesome combination of the two.

Ashur watched as a mercenary hopped up onto the lead car with a rocket launcher. The platoon dispersed and took up arms, finding cover either off the shoulder of the road or behind the cara-van cars. Ashur grabbed Rose and followed suit. As the bandit grew near, the siren, the gunfire, the shouting soldiers and the growl of all the idling engines, all of it became one noise, one singular rumble.

It grew to a peak and ended in a thunderclap when a rocket made contact with the bandit's car. The fiery wreck tumbled bumper over bumper, bringing with it fast raining shards of fragmented car. The sounds of contorting metal and shattering glass became distinguishable as the civil defense siren faded off. The skeleton came to rest in the dirt, meters away from the road they were on.

"What the bloody hell was that thing?" somebody asked.

"Radio said watch your ass," Ashur told them. He looked at the man with the empty rocket launcher. "Nice shot!"

He gave a thumbs up and skulked off to put the ordinance away.

"My assistance is free of charge," Dixon said. "This time."

"You're running into the big fight?"

Dixon nodded. "Wellshire. People say there's a big uproar out that way."

"So I've been told. This one here says things there are bad."

"You don't say? Hey, since you're here, you wanna lend a hand? I'd be sure you get compensated. More gold than you can spend. More bullets than you can shoot."

Ashur shook his head. "Can't do it, boss."

"You got somewhere to be?"

"I'm running a package at the moment," Ashur explained, knowing their conversation would end with another recruitment attempt.

"The girl?"

"I'm running her too."

"Courier doesn't suit you." Dixon's tone changed. "So much wasted potential. You're bullheaded."

"Career mercenary isn't my type of business."

"You've stacked up a body count that speaks otherwise. Who here would question Ashur Stanton as a merc? You're the same as us, a proper killer."

"I'm not a *dog soldier*. Not anymore."

Dixon nodded. "So you're not. Still the offer stands," he said, knocking his knuckles against his battered chest plate. "We've got plenty of equipment to go around, and you know where to find us. If you've got a ham radio we're on thirty-five-hundred megahertz for about fifteen miles. Let us know you're coming."

Dixon turned to face his men. He gave a simple hand signal and the platoon returned to their armored vehicles. Once they pulled away, Ashur told Rose they were going to scavenge what they could from the cooling wreck. A vehicle that heavily armored was bound to have something worth taking.

In the vehicle, Ashur found a fully loaded .357 revolver. It was not identical to Rose's Smith & Wesson, but near enough for him to give it away. He also found an assault rifle destroyed by the crash—useless, but its half clip of ammo was worth the weight. He also found a locked strong box. The last thing he could pull from the wreck was a short sword with a floral design embossed on the guard and sheath.

He wanted to scrap or sell the blade, but when Rose spotted the flowery design on the weapon, he couldn't help but clip it to her rucksack. Now she wore two guns, handles pointed outward so she could make full use of a cross-body draw, or just as easily, a cavalry draw. But when he made a passing reference to Wild Bill Hickok, she asked who that was.

Ashur and Rose got back on the motorcycle and on their way. It was uneventful hours of wind before sparse spots of shrubbery began unfolding along their path. They were close to Tavern Springs.

After riding into the metropolitan ruins that littered the north bay of Lake Winnebago, they had to dismount so Ashur could roll the bike over the more rickety parts of a bridge

"Why'd you tell Dixon mercenary wasn't your kind of business?" Rose asked.

"Because it's not."

"You were just bound for Wellshire to do the same job," she pointed out.

"I headed out there to work for a week or two. Dixon was asking for something different. And despite what you may have heard, I'm not that kind of crooked."

They saddled up and moments later approached the gate. The entrance to Tavern Springs was made of pieces of a school bus, a shipping crate, and a large garage door. A message had been painted on the door and it was clear that someone had attempted to scrub it off. They had done a poor job:

Up with Slab City. Burn Down the Breakers.

The post had sentries stationed on watch at all points during the day and night, which Ashur thought rather meaningless. Bandits were to be let into town so long as they pretended to be well-mannered. Sentries distinguished themselves as city-ordained by use of an orange band on their right arm. They didn't really have uniforms.

The bike crept up to the road blockade.

"Lemme see the hands!" a voice ordered through an orange, identity-concealing scarf.

Rose did as demanded but Ashur only drew the goggles off his face. "Captain, open this door before I curb-stomp the last bit of your brains out."

"I was just making sure it was you," said the man before he ducked down behind the wall. A cranking noise followed by the sounds of a motor filled the air. The paint-peeled door began to creep upward, allowing them passage.

Chapter 4

The cottage they arrived at was constructed of cinderblocks and sheet metal. It looked more like a utility station than a house. The rustic shelter belonged to Ashur and it suited him well. It was just past noon when they dismounted.

"This is where you live?" Rose asked. The area they had entered was a courtyard, lush with grass, Ashur's bungalow sitting in the center. A corrugated-metal fence ran around the encampment and the gate was watched over by a sentry in a guard post. The only other thing of note in the yard was an old pickup Ashur would use on occasion. "What's wrong with this?"

"I was expecting something a bit more, I don't know, extravagant? Aren't you sort of famous?"

Ashur was well off for the world. In a time when most lived hour to hour, he could afford to live week to week. "I've got grass," he said. "They didn't have grass in Wellshire. And I have a sentry. His name's Scott." He waved at them.

The two of them got off the bike and he unlocked the garage. He rolled the motorcycle into the structure but when Rose attempted to follow him in, he shooed her back into the sun. He set down the kickstand, hung his goggles around the handlebar, and exited. Then he moved to the front door, which was but a few steps away. The first thing he did when they entered the shack was turn on the AC.

"You have air conditioning?" she asked, amazed.

He flipped on the lights. "Extravagant enough for you?"

The house was comprised of three main parts: the garage, the bedroom, and the everything-else room, which they were currently standing in. Before them sat an industrial wire spool turned kitchen table, behind it was a counter with a sink, stove, and a nearby refrigerator. The sink and counter were stuffed with dirty dishes and the floor was strewn with unwashed garments. On the right wall, was a book shelf, fitfully stocked and towering over a burgundy recliner. The last wall on their left housed a wine rack, likewise stocked, but with every drink except wine. It was this wall which connected to the bedroom via a doorway. While the design was limited, the house was fairly roomy. Most of it was empty space.

There was a radio on the kitchen counter. He told her to make herself at home and flipped it on. Only static played. He began removing some of his gear at the table, and Rose set down her things as well. Thereafter, she moved to the bookshelf, silently gazing over the spines of Britannica, almanacs, atlases, dictionaries, anthologies, technical writings—the useful tidbits recovered from the blackened Library of Babel.

"What is all this?" she asked as she reached out and brushed some dust off of a paperback.

"It's what I could find, and I'd greatly appreciate it if you kept your hands *off* them." She retracted her hand as if she had been burned, thereafter turning around to face him. "Some of them are very fragile," he said.

She indicated that she understood and then asked where the bathroom was. He told her it was through the doorway on the left and she disappeared into the bedroom. "What's with the flag?" she asked once across the threshold.

He took off his jacket and walked over to the kitchen sink. "It's a Revo Rose." He splashed some water on his face. "What about it?" The flag was solid black with a white, thorned rose—the standard mark of the revolutionaries. Many of them had slogans underneath. This particular flag had, **We Are the Unfinished Business** stitched along the bottom.

Compared to today, the insurrection of the past seemed quaint. The revolutionist groups were set up as independent cells in every backyard, people helping people. There was no single leader, no head to cut off, and no way to quarantine it. Whenever they were asked who their leader was, they would reply with 'We are all leaders.' That's often where the shooting started. The spectacle was everywhere as they said.

"Long live the Revo," Rose muttered. "Why would you fly the flag of your enemies?"

"I campaigned against them. I never believed they were my enemies. Allowed my men to write slogans on their gear even. Knew a kid that had 'We are all German Jews' painted right on his riot shield. There's poetry in there somewhere."

"There's poetry in the streets," she said, quoting something she had no doubt read on a wall some place. "You had men?"

"I've led many men."

Following this, no further questions came from the room. He finished washing his face and cleaning the dried blood off his jacket. He picked up his equipment and left to place it in the garage. Once back in the main room, he checked the fridge. There wasn't much. He hadn't counted on being home for at least a week.

"Hey, hey, hey, and we're back," the radio spoke as Ashur closed the fridge door. *"Sorry about that. Didn't realize the red light was off. Here's your daily dose of what's choice."* Soft jazz began playing.

"Hey, kid," he called out. There was no response. He turned around and tried again, this time using her actual name but still nothing returned. He made his way into the conjoining room and found her. She looked to be asleep on his bed, face buried in a pil-low.

"You're going to asphyxiate if you sleep like that."

"I don't care." Her voice was severely muffled by the pillow.

"Get up. I've got errands to run."

"Go without me."

"No. I'm not leaving a stranger in my house."

"Can we do them later?" she asked the cushion. "I'm tired and my head hurts." She wasn't much of a drinker. A serene period lingered around the room before he flipped a nearby light switch. The room faded to black. "Thank you," she said sweetly.

He picked up an egg timer he had on the kitchen counter and maxed it out. "Don't steal anything. I'll be in the garage when you wake." He left the quick and dirty alarm on the kitchen table for her.

She exhaled wearily, in a smoky calm. "Okay."

He picked up the radio before finding his way back into the garage. He spent a lot of his time in the garage. The structure sat parallel to the house and was about half the size. It ran deep with exercise equipment at the front, work and ammo benches in the back, and a particular area set aside for his bike. He unloaded much of the contents he had taken as well as acquired on his short lived journey. Once the place was organized he focused on the strong box he had recovered from the bandit's car hours earlier. The only thing inside, however, was an old cassette player that wouldn't turn on. So he tinkered with it. He busied himself, sticking much to his regular routine. It was about an hour later when Rose stood at the entrance to the garage. He was working on his haymaker right then.

Ashur stopped his assault on his punching bag when he spotted her. "Hey," he panted and removed his gloves.

"Hey." She stepped into the garage. "Thanks for doctoring my weapons."

He nodded. In the time she slept, he had cleaned the revolvers—all that was required to tune them. With the short sword, the blade was dull, so he sharpened it and attached a strap so it could be worn over her shoulder. He had left everything on the kitchen table for her retrieval when she woke.

"How was your nap then?"

She smiled at him with squinted eyes, making her way out of the sun. "It was good. Thanks for the bed. Are we going to run those errands?"

He clucked his tongue. "Thought we could have something to eat first."

The offer caught her off guard. "Oh?…okay. That'd be nice." They went inside and she sat at the table while Ashur fixed lunch.

"We're going to do a bit of trading, maybe show you around town, try to find you a job. Then we'll deliver that package," he said and gestured to the weapons she wore. "You don't have to bring your gear if you don't want to. The town's pretty safe."

"I'll bring it."

"I always carry my handgun so you don't have to worry about anything."

But she persisted. A few minutes later, they sat down to a meal of soup and cornbread. When Rose ate, she crowded her food and looped her entire left arm around the outside rim of the plate. He gave her a funny look.

"What?" she said, mouth stuffed with food.

"You definitely had a brother." He nudged her arm off the tabletop. "You don't need to claim your kill. Elbows off the table. Don't talk with your mouth full. And the little fork is for your salad."

"A merc concerned with manners?"

"Don't talk with your mouth full—what did I just say?"

She furrowed her brow and finished chewing. Now that her arms were off the table, she could see that someone had carved a slogan into it: **Fiat money means starving for something that doesn't exist.**

"Did you do that?" she asked.

He shook his head no.

"What's fi-at money?"

"Paper," he said.

She read the etching again, out loud this time. "It doesn't make sense. How is it different from coin or cartridge?"

"No. I mean, it's just paper. Precious metals are useful. Bullets are useful. But fiat money is only worth something when people believe it's worth something. It's only worth something because the people printing it are the ones in charge."

"That's stupid. Why wouldn't they just use metal?"

He finished the piece of bread he was working on. "They did for a long time. The paper used to be backed by gold. But there just wasn't enough of it to go around."

She returned to her meal, content with the explanation. After that, it was silent save for the clinking of utensils. When they were finished, he refitted himself with his knife and handgun. They started off.

The town of Tavern Springs, like most towns, was organized in three zones: uptown, suburbs, and the outlying rangelands. Uptown is where the movers and shakers lived, where Ashur lived, where town hall was—the heart of the city. The suburbs are where everyone else lived, and though not heavily crime ridden, they were largely slums—shanty towns and tent cities. The rangelands existed on the rim of the settlement near the water. This is where a large portion of the town's food came from.

They stopped at the gate and Ashur struck up a conversation with the guard.

"I didn't expect you back so early."

"I didn't expect to *be* back so early," Ashur said. "I want you to meet Rose. If you see her wandering about the enclave, don't shoot at her."

Scott bowed his head at Rose. "Anything else?"

"Yes. Can I get a ride to Vanderbilt's around four thirty? I assume you already tattled on me."

"Yeah I already phoned him to let him know you're back."

"I knew I could count on you."

With that, they strolled out into the blooming city streets. The gates opened directly into town square, the heart of uptown. It was admirable real estate. They rambled past bakeries, delis, tailors, the Medway Trading Company freight office, public baths and theaters, street venders selling fish and haircuts. The buildings were all precarious. In some cases they were so skewed it looked as if a sudden breeze could send them toppling into the street. Some were chocolate, or cinnamon, others toffee, but all were unappetizing to look at—caked in black and powdery ash, patched up with sheet metal, or pallets, or whatever else was on hand. They made the streets look mean.

They pushed past a group of children playing Hopscotch and a small boy tailed them. He tugged on Ashur's jacket. "What do you want, kid?"

The kid thrust his hand forward. "Anything, mister."

"Beat it."

The boy looked at Rose, continuing to hold out his hand. "How 'bout you, miss?"

"I told you to beat it," Ashur said.

The boy did not budge. Rose reached into her pocket and pulled out a copper piece. "Here you go, kid." She placed coin in the child's dirt smeared hands.

"Thanks, lady!" The kid ran off, back towards his friends in the street.

They continued their walk. He had come to notice something odd about Rose, the way she moved now that she was safe from the badlands. She had the gate of a dancer, a gangly stride, as if she were about to do a cartwheel for the sake of the movement. She looked to be free of whatever it was that weighed down the rest of the world.

"Where's your town get electricity?" she asked.

"Solar panels and windmills like the other towns, but we've also got hydroelectricity. About two miles back." He stuck his thumb over his shoulder. "There're a pair of dams that use the current from Winnebago. We sell anything left over to Medway."

"Must be nice. We hardly had lightning back in Wellshire."

"Yeah? Well Tavern Springs stays lit."

"You like it here?" she asked.

"For a town at the end of the world it's not a bad place." When they passed by a fruit stand the curator called out to Ashur and lobbed an apple at him and Rose. They finished them by the time they arrived in front of a two-story building, a store called Lakeside Supply. A sign in its window read, **Fire Sale!**

Ashur was the first one through the chiming door. They took no more than two steps in before a shotgun was shoved in their faces by a rather hairy and disgusting man. Rose's hands went up.

"Hey, Stanton, how's it hanging?"

"A little to the left."

The man cleared his throat and shifted his gaze. "Who's that?" He motioned to Rose with the end of the barrel. The man looked kind of woozy.

"I dunno. She just followed me in here. I think she said something about trying to steal stuff."

The man studied Rose with ugly eyes. "That's a very interesting way you wear your guns, honey." She didn't engage with him but she kept her hands up. The man wet his lips and cleared his throat again, this time in a sickly manner. "Yup. I remember this one guy, they use to talk about him…long time ago. Used to wear his guns—" Ashur gently pushed the muzzle of the shotgun out of their faces. "Well shit, you know it's not loaded right?"

"If it's as loaded as you are we're all in danger."

"Are you terrorizing my guard again, Stanton?" a voice called out from the back of the store. He looked over to the counter and found the store owner, a white-haired gentleman named Curtis. He pushed passed the guard and started towards the back, Rose followed. They passed shelving units stocked with a random assortment of necessities, perishables, and trinkets. The store was well lit with hardwood floors, a basic two story box with a couple of windows at the front, generous floor space for shelves, and one solitary counter towards the back, which blocked entry into a few separate back rooms, as well as some stairs.

"Hello, Curtis, how's the wife?" he asked upon reaching the counter.

"Oh you know…dead."

Rose looked surprised until a shrill voice with no face came from the backroom.

"Quit telling everyone I'm dead! I ain't dead!"

"Well I wish you were!" Curtis called back, sending the woman on a rant. Curtis chucked something breakable into the back room and silence set in. The store owner recomposed himself. "So how can I help you two today?"

"Looking for some trade," he told the proprietor.

"What kind of trade you looking for?"

"Some produce, nuts and berries, dried fruit, any of that?"

"Yeah I got some of that. What do you got for me?"

"I've got half a clip of five-five-six and this." Ashur reached into his pocket and pulled out a portable cassette player and handed it to the vendor.

"I haven't seen one of these for years." The Crown Meridian Electronics logo had worn off long ago but there was still a cassette inside. "But it looks pretty beat up, still work?" The man fumbled with the device before depressing a button. The tape spools began whirling. The earpieces blared. "That's amazing. You find it like this or fix it up afterwards?"

"I tinkered a bit."

Curtis turned the gadget over in his hands, observing the abrasions and the cracked casing. "Looks like more than a bit. You pretty handy with electronics?"

Ashur shrugged. "I'm a jack of all."

"I've always got things that could use fixing, not sure how much I could pay you but if you like we can set up some sort of deal."

"No but..." He looked to his right and found Rose was no longer there. She had made her way back to the front of the store and was aimlessly wandering through the aisles of sales items. "Flower girl?"

"Uh-huh?"

"They string you up for sticky fingers around here," he told her. The shy disposition she had picked up since their encounter with the guard only progressed. He turned his attention back to Curtis. "No I'm not looking for a job but do you have anything on the lighter side?"

"For her?"

"Yeah. Nice kid."

Curtis shook his head and put the headphones up to his ears. "No. Sorry, I really don't need anyone else in the shop." He held up the music player. "Can I assume the creator of this mix tape is no longer with us?"

"Oh yeah. He's real dead," Ashur remarked. Rose returned to his side and said nothing.

"Then the world's a better place. Pick out what you think's fair and bring it up here."

A few minutes later the deal was made and they exited the shop. He placed Rose in charge of carrying everything, which was not but two bags.

"Were you serious about the stringing people up thing?" she asked as they stepped onto the sidewalk outside the storefront.

He moved her slightly and pointed up the market street. Above a faded store sign, some distance away, was a flagpole mount, on which hung a man, a potato sack over his head. His coat was red but the blood was dry and his shoes had long since been stolen. The bags put over thief's heads were what struck chords with most people. It made them into proper scarecrows.

"You didn't lift anything, did you?" he asked.

"No. But that's a little harsh, don't you think?"

"People protect what's theirs here like they would in the scabland. Someone steals something from you, you go get it back. There's nothing the sentries can do unless they saw it. There are no courts here. No real ones anyways."

When they got back to the house Ashur unloaded the bags. He left the weapon related ordinance in the garage and then followed Rose into the house, stowing the food in the kitchen. When he was done, Rose hovered around and wondered when they were to deliver the package.

"I've got to wash and change before we go," he said, cleaning some morning sand out of his eyes. "You should too. Do you have anything nicer to wear? Like a dress? Or anything not covered in snot and tears? Vanderbilt keeps only the most dignified company."

"Who is this guy anyways?"

"Vanderbilt? Is that whole village living under a rock or are you an oddity?"

"It was a small place," she said.

"He's the mayor."

Ashur showered and cleaned up, collecting his dress shoes and suit. When he reentered the main room, the radio was singing on the counter and Rose was muddling through his cassette collection. He picked up his shoulder holster and started putting it on.

"Find anything you like?"

"Huh? Oh," she said, now noticing him. "I'm sorry. I didn't think you'd mind."

"You even know what those are?"

She shook her head. "They hold music right?"

"Yeah," he said, grinning. "They're called cassettes."

She reexamined one. "Who's Bruce Springsteen?"

"Nothing but a memory."

She put the tape down and studied Ashur. "You look nice," she said. "If I didn't know better I'd assume you were mannerly."

"Says the feral child who can't eat in public."

Chapter 5

The ride was a short one, ending when they pulled up in front of the urban château that had once been city hall. The massive golden-domed structure was fenced in all around with an armed sentry stationed near the gate. The original gold had run off of the dome during the Collapse and painted the tower below it. Because of this, Vanderbilt had the dome re-gilded just a few years ago.

Ashur had the package seated in his lap. He was dressed in brown suede with a red tie. Rose on the other hand wore black jeans and a long sleeve white tee—she didn't own anything formal. They stepped out of the old Appleton police cruiser that had brought them to the mansion.

"Here to see the mayor," Ashur said to the sentry once their ride pulled away from the curb. Rose stood at his side.

"Business?" the man asked.

"Package to deliver."

"What about her?"

"She's a new resident. Brought her along to meet the mayor. You know how Vanderbilt loves meeting everyone."

The sentry nodded. "Weapons?"

Ashur unbuttoned his jacket and flashed the .45 in his underarm holster. When the sentry looked at Rose, she admitted to carrying a butterfly knife. Ashur had made her leave her guns and sword at his house.

"You can leave your equipment with me and then head on in," the sentry said.

Ashur forced a smile and looked down the road. "You must be new here."

"Excuse me?"

"Call up to the house. Tell them Stanton's here to see the mayor."

The sentinel eyed Ashur fiercely before he grabbed the radio off his belt. "Ms. Hall, there's a Mr. Stanton here to see the mayor. He's refusing to give up his weaponry."

In a moment the radio spat out an indistinct reply. The sentry apologized and stepped out of their path. They passed through the gate and started up the walkway. This was the Breakers of the New Gilded Age. It was riddled with bullet holes and scorch marks. Before the final set of steps sat a fountain. The centerpiece was one of the Roman captain Horatius brandishing a sword.

"What calls for the VIP treatment?"

"I work for Vanderbilt," Ashur said. He rang the doorbell.

"What kind of work do you do for him?"

"Whatever he pays me to do. Expeditions mostly: scouting, scavenging, training new recruits, stuff like that."

The door opened and they were confronted by a good-looking blonde wearing a large pair of silver aviators. "Hey, asshole." She saw Rose. "What's with the streetwalker?"

"Rose, you'll have to excuse Stacey. She doesn't play well with the other children. When she was little, all the other play-ground kids would take turns pinning her to the ground and stuffing worms in her pants."

Stacey was not a sentry like the man that watched the gate. She was a Mayor Vanderbilt's personal bodyguard, though she also took up the job as the town's Master-at-Arms for Vanderbilt's sentry force. While Ashur held no official title, the sentries also recognized Ashur as their superior.

"I'll show you how well I play with—"

"Ms. Hall, who's at the door?" an angelic voice called from somewhere inside the house.

"No one important, sir," she said while stepping back to let them in. They entered the building and Stacey closed the door behind them, thereafter disappearing into one of the luxurious mansion's many catacombs. The mayor entered from another.

"Good afternoon, Mr. Stanton."

Eugene Vanderbilt was a blue-blooded man of substance, roughly fifty years of age. He signed his name like Juan Ponce De León and walked with his chin held an inch too high, as if he were constantly on the verge of sneezing. And though he differed on etiquette and dress, he was ordinary in most other respects. He was of only moderate size and average build. He had a simple complexion and a proper haircut. He had no intelligence above anyone else's, no genetic trait that made him superior. He was not a god nor a devil. He was but a man. Yet he was obeyed.

"Was Ms. Hall stirring you up again?"

"No, sir."

"Par for the course I guess," he said, knowing she had been. "So what can I help you with today and who is this that you have brought to me?"

"I have a package for you and this is your newest resident."

"What a treat," Vanderbilt said with a funereal smile. "I am Mayor Vanderbilt. I must ask your name, my dear."

"I'm named Rose."

It was quiet for a moment.

"Last name," Ashur prompted lightly.

"Oh, I'm sorry, sir. Rose Waters."

Vanderbilt and Rose shared a dainty handshake. Anytime Vanderbilt offered a handshake, which was rather often with the work he did, a small portion of a prison tattoo would jut out from underneath his sleeve's cuff. "It's nice to meet you, Ms. Waters.

Welcome to Tavern Springs. I hope you fall in love with this town as much as I have." He studied her closely as they ended their formality. His icy blue eyes flickered in the same fashion Ashur's did, though they burned not half as intensely. They had dimmed, his belligerence obscured by something—years of work, money, authority, and a unique pretense of courtesy. "So what is this package you have for me?" he asked.

Ashur handed him the box and he opened it. Vanderbilt laughed with elation. "I wondered when these would show up. You know it is quite difficult to find dependable couriers these days, present company excluded of course." He turned to Rose. "This man is sturdier than an oak. Never fails me."

Rose smiled with something that was not necessarily fake, but determinably polite. "He can handle himself," she said.

Vanderbilt's gaze fell on Ashur like an axe. "If I remember correctly you were out of town for the time being. Why are you running a package for me?"

"I arrived back in town only this morning. The package was payment for a stay at Emerson's."

"Ah yes, Emerson. That man has quite the vocabulary, does he not?" He reached into the box and pulled out a pack of Little Trees. Vanderbilt turned them over in his hands and hefted them.

"Why would you order air fresheners?" Rose asked. "If you don't mind my asking."

Vanderbilt looked up in surprise, glancing between Rose and Ashur. He noticed that they were still standing in the main rotunda.

"Oh how rude of me," he said. "I am being a terrible host. Please come in, come in. Would either of you like a drink?"

"That's all right. We don't want to be any trouble," Ashur said.

"Nonsense, my friend. Come along and relax. The both of you look so tired. Are you sure there is nothing I can get you?"

"If you insist, a scotch on the rocks would be nice."

"Very well. And for you, my dear?"

"Just a water please."

Vanderbilt called forth a servant and placed the orders to the kitchen, adding a brandy for himself. "There's actually an item I've been wanting to show you," he said to Ashur. "And I just know you will love it."

As they followed Vanderbilt down a hallway decorated with masterful paintings and elegant tapestries, classical music lightly filtered through the air.

"It's *beautiful*," Rose remarked, astounded by the magnitude of it all.

"What is, my dear?"

"Everything."

"Yes, it is, isn't it?" Vanderbilt stated in his own breed of marvel. "But I'm quite partial to the music myself."

"Wagner. Very nice," Rose commented.

Vanderbilt commended her ear for music and then asked how she was familiar with the Victorian musician. She admitted that her nana had had a thing for classical music. Vanderbilt and Rose had just started a conversation about Mozart when they were interrupted by a servant with drinks. Thereafter the group found its way into a newly built addition to the house—a massive garage filled with a number of classic cars.

"Please pardon me for so rudely disregarding your question earlier, my dear, but I thought it best to save the explanation."

They strode past and assortment of classic Austin-Healeys, Chevys, and Fords, passing into a separate room, which was the mechanic's shop. There in the center of the room sat a single car, which appeared to have been designed solely for the purpose of horsepower and sex appeal.

"This is what the air fresheners are for," Vanderbilt said.

"What a machine," Ashur uttered upon seeing the vehicle.

"You're free to take a look if you wish."

The group approached the vehicle. The car was a flawless 1967 Mercury Cougar. The pony car glowed florescent black with tinted windows and polished chrome accents. But there was something else on the car that added to its head turning ability. Mounted on either side of the hood was a six-barreled minigun.

Mayor Vanderbilt opened the driver-side door and hung one of the Little Trees around the rear view, afterwards letting Rose and Ashur examine the interior as he moved away. Vanderbilt soon began going over the vehicle and weapons with Ashur. He did this for a long while, giving Ashur access under the hood and anywhere else he wished.

"So what's the Cougar for? An addition to the standing army of sentries?" Ashur asked.

"No. It is more of a trophy than anything else, a luxury I have wanted for a while now."

Just then, Stacey entered the garage. "Dinner will be started soon sir," she informed her boss.

"Very well," he said before turning to Ashur and Rose. "Won't you two join me?"

They stood there, both wanting to decline but saying nothing.

"My apologies. Do you have somewhere else to be?"

"No, sir. Dinner would be great," Ashur agreed.

"Superb. Two more for dinner Stacey."

"Yes, sir," she said and turned to leave.

"Stacey, before you go, may I borrow you handgun for just a moment?"

His bodyguard made what was most likely a perplexed face underneath her trooper shades before obliging to his request. Ashur and Rose watched as Stacey drew her M9 and placed it in her boss's hand.

"Now everyone, you may want to move behind the Plexiglas I have set up just over there." He gestured to the far end of the shop and everyone aside from Vanderbilt himself did as he suggested. Stacey ended up standing right behind Ashur with Rose on his left.

"Now, Mr. Stanton, I know you had to think this car was for no more than a cruise around the block, right?"

"It's very clean and I see no armor, but you've also had off road tires put on and mounted a set of miniguns and on the hood."

"Precisely what I wanted you to notice. Why guns but no armor?"

"Right," Ashur agreed.

Vanderbilt raised the gun and fired at the car. The sound of a ricochet was heard and when the resonation receded, Vanderbilt approached the classic, pointing out how the door was scratched but the bullet had crumpled up and fallen on the floor. "Likewise, the windows are a specialized polycarbonate which utilizes aluminum oxynitride," he said. "ALON glass for short."

"Come look for yourselves," Vanderbilt invited.

The group did as he instructed. There was a chip in the black paint from the glanced bullet but nothing more.

"Does it have run-flat tires too?"

"It does, Mr. Stanton. Very shrewd."

"But now you've chipped your nice paint," Rose commented, scrutinizing the mark.

"Not to worry, my dear, I'll have that fixed up by tomorrow," Vanderbilt said as he handed the gun back to Stacey. She holstered the weapon and then left the room. Vanderbilt walked over to the car, as if being drawn to it, and rubbed the hood.

"So, Mr. Stanton, what do you think of her?"

"I love her, sir."

"How about you, Ms. Waters?"

His question broke her out of the boredom induced trance she had lapsed into. "Huh? Oh, I think it's pretty," she spoke with a smile that was not returned.

"Quite. Now if you'll excuse me, I'll go make sure they start dinner properly. We will be having steak. Is that all right?"

Rose hesitated so Ashur answered for her. "Yes, sir. That sounds excellent."

"Feel free to browse around while I'm gone," Vanderbilt said and exited the room.

She spoke up the instant the door closed. "I don't like him," she said. "He's well-mannered but…he's just wrong."

"He acts polite because he is not a polite man, tries to hide it in the way he carries himself though. He was never elected mayor. I highly doubt he's a real Vanderbilt. That being said, he keeps this town running. It evens out."

An unwanted silence passed through the room and Ashur left the workshop to look at the other cars. She followed close behind. They stopped in front of an old Bel Air convertible. Ashur circled around and studied it. The turquoise throwback gleamed with fresh wax. He opened the driver-side door and got in, making himself comfortable on the leather seat. Curious as to where Vanderbilt kept the keys, he checked the visor and a number of other spots around the car's cab: nothing. Rose walked around and got in the passenger side, pulling her legs up and crossing them on the seat.

"So how did you end up working for the mayor?" she asked.

"When I first rolled into the Springs, the town was young and wayward, Vanderbilt hadn't yet reined it in—this was years ago, just after I'd left the Rangers. I got into a brawl. No one was killed, but it had taken place uptown and that irked Vanderbilt. He had me bound and brought into his office. He had a little glint in his eyes back then. I read him and he read me, not a word between us. He uncuffed me and sat me down to a meal alongside himself and Stacey. He smiled, took a sip of wine, and then he said, 'How would you enjoy working for me?' I played nice and that was that."

Just as Vanderbilt showed Ashur a pretense of courtesy, Ashur showed Vanderbilt a pretense of subordinacy. He kept Ashur on a chain, a chain forged of flawed steel by a careless smith.

"What kind of work did you do for him? General expeditionary stuff like you do now?"

"If you exclude Stacey, I'm Vanderbilt's right-hand man," he said. "I gave the town its doctor. I organized the sentry force, ran caravans, put down the local gangs."

"That sounds like you did a lot for this town."

"I washed a broken window."

She made no further comments on the subject and they soon sat in silence. This was quickly filled by Rose who began to whistle a tawdry tune. The melody flowing from her pursed lips filled the garage with something childlike, a certain playfulness. And amidst its happy notes, Ashur was reminded of something— elusive lyrics from days gone by.

She stopped. "Sociopath withstanding, I like the house. It's so…"

"Excessive?"

"In a whimsical kind of way, yeah. It's like a monument."

"Whimsical? I see this excess. And I see people trying to breathe in dust filled shanties, huddled together at night to keep warm."

"Dinner bell!" a voice called. The voice was Stacey's. She was no longer wearing her sunglasses. She had somewhat more severe facial features, not ugly, just sharp.

Ashur and Rose left the car and followed her down the corridors littered with relics and fluttering music. When they reached the dining hall, Vanderbilt was waiting at the head of the table for them, their meals already laid on their jade plates.

"I hope you all enjoy. My chef can work miracles," Vanderbilt said as everyone took a chair. The meal consisted of steak, corn, and mashed potatoes. They dug in, enjoying every bite of it, knowing they were truly lucky. A meal like this anywhere else would have cost a fortune but they were being fed here for free.

At the outset of the meal, Stacey reached across the table for the salt. Seeing that it was barely beyond the reach of her fingertips, Rose set down her fork and handed it to the woman. "I could've gotten it myself," she said.

Rose's eyes flickered away. She held her tongue and picked up her fork.

"So, Ms. Waters," Vanderbilt broke in. "Am I right to presume you hail from a township?"

"Yes, sir."

"I thought so. You seem far too well-mannered to be from the Interior or the South." This was the first and only natural sounding statement Vanderbilt made their whole visit.

"Thank you. I'm from Wellshire."

Vanderbilt nodded and took a sip from his wine glass. "Yes. I have heard things are getting bad there, aggressive raids," he said.

"They are," Rose confirmed. "Thanks for letting me into your town."

"But of course. We love new denizens." He took another sip of red wine and about twenty minutes later, people dressed in white, kitchen outfits came in and cleared the table of dirty dishes. "I hope you all have room for desert. We'll be having crème brûlée." Everyone at the table agreed that it was a good choice. Another flash of white outfits and their dessert was served.

"May I be excused for a moment?" Rose said. "I need to use the rest room."

"Of course, my dear. The bathroom is out that door and then the third on the left."

"Thank you." She got up and walked out. The door closed quietly behind her.

"So, Mr. Stanton. How have you been as of late?"

"The same as ever, I suppose. Yourself?"

"Quite all right, thank you for asking. Now tell me, what is the story with the girl?"

"Found her on the roads outside Wellshire the day before yesterday. Gave her a lift into town. Guess I'm stuck with her till she figures out whatever she's doing. She's between homes at the moment."

Vanderbilt raised an eyebrow. "That is awfully gracious of you. Not quite what I had come to expect from yourself."

Ashur finished another drink and started on his crème brûlée. "I tried to get rid of her. She wouldn't have any of it."

"It is only reasonable that she would want to stay at your side. You do come across as a capable man."

"Maybe she knows she wouldn't do well if I threw her to the wolves."

"She *is* only a kid. If she sticks around, perhaps you will teach her the trade?"

"Her?" he scoffed. "No. Doesn't have the stomach for my line of work."

"You of all people know tougher skin can be learned. You ought to think twice before setting her loose."

"I'll take it into consideration."

"Good," said Vanderbilt as he too started his dessert. "I'm surprised I don't have you over for dinner more often. You have worked for me for—what is it now—five years?"

"Just about."

"In that time I have gathered that you are more of a brazen, up-front sort of fellow. Am I wrong?"

"No, sir."

"Then I hope can enlighten me on something—that is—why is it that some people seem highly hesitant around me? Do I conduct myself in an awkward manner or am—"

"You're a liar," Ashur said. Stacey, who had been largely indifferent to the table talk, tensed up in her seat and began looking back and forth between the two.

The corners of Vanderbilt's mouth tightened, revealing a bleached set of perfectly straight teeth—a smile for the straightjacket. "Excuse me, Mr. Stanton? Perhaps you have had a tad too much scotch."

"You asked why people are uneasy around you. It's because you're a liar."

"And just what exactly is it that I have lied about?"

"It's not what you lie about it how you lie about it. You walk around here pretending to be personable, proper, and right-minded. But some of us—the more observant one's at least—know something's off." He leaned forward slightly. "Some of us can see through the split stiches of that poorly tailored suit you're wearing."

Vanderbilt let out a cackle that engulfed the whole dining hall. It bounced off the walls and it filled in all the cracks—it cut to the bone.

"Sir," Stacey said. "If you want me to—"

"Please, Ms. Hall. We are having a perfectly civil conversation. No need to grow uneasy." His steely eyes fixated on Ashur. "Do you understand why I dress myself up as I do?"

"Showmanship."

"I'm not sure I follow."

"Take a militia, for instance, train them day in and day out, wipe your enemies off the map, take what there is to be taken, and people will fear you. Now take those same men, give them rules, uniforms, assign them ranks, cut their hair—only then will you have an army. Fear becomes respect. And respect…is a much more powerful faculty."

"Well said, Mr. Stanton, well said. I have kept close tabs on you, as I do with all whom I employ. You are a career soldier with honors. The company you keep is next to none. You are arrogant, belligerent, and crude." Vanderbilt took a sip from his wine glass. "But you are careful. And you are *very* clever. A lot more than you let on. It is quite the curiosity really."

"How so?"

"I work to keep the townspeople, my employees, the outsiders, all under the impression that I am—*we* rather, are building something nice here, which in most respects we are."

"You eliminate any reason for your authority to be questioned," Ashur said.

"Precisely. You on the other hand, it seems, work to make sure people see nothing more than a man with a gun and a flask. You could be sitting on this side of this table if you desired to. I'm certain of it."

"And that's the part you find a curiosity," he stated. Stacey, who had been watching him with the eyes of an eagle since the start of the conversation, kept a hand on the pistol in her holster. The large mahogany table obscured the matter but regardless, Ashur knew this was the case. He gave her a wink.

"Correct," said Vanderbilt. "Would you be so kind as to explain that to me?"

"It goes like this, sir: if I fail, you fail. But if you fail, no one is going to so much as bat a lash in my direction. And there is a difference between conducting a mission and running a town. You've got something biting at your ankles every day, a whole town just waiting to put your head on a pike the moment you fail them. Obviously, for all that risk, you get a nice car, a nice house, jade plates—"

"You really think being a politician is more dangerous than working in the scablands?"

"Civic leadership is why the scablands exist in the first place." Ashur stared at a painting on the wall. It was a Renoir—a reproduction of course. "I don't see any point to sitting on a throne.

The world's on its way out, didn't you hear? Good riddance I say. There never was anything great about it." They could hear Rose coming down the hallway.

"I am afraid I have to disagree with you. I believe we, as a people, will grow and adapt to our new world. We will rebuild. We will evolve." Rose walked in and quietly returned to her seat.

"Fortunately," said Ashur. "Or unfortunately, however you want to look at it, evolution begins at inception and invariably ends in extinction. There is no coming back from this."

"We will have to agree to disagree then."

The group finished their dessert with a few idle comments about the town's history and this year's racing season. Stacey calmed down and when the duo were finished thanking Vanderbilt for the wonderful evening, she saw them out.

Chapter 6

At any given time, Whiskey Breeze was dimly lit and slightly smelly. A surround sound system funneled music into the bar, a card table at the back was alive with gamblers, a number of dartboards hung along the walls, and tonight the booths were mostly vacant. The main floor, with its tables scattered about, had the usual crowd: two notorious pickpockets were loudly accusing each other of stealing, a couple were mingling lips, and an old man had passed out in his chair, a hand nicked his half-finished drink and fed the man it was attached to.

"That was track fourteen by artist unknown," said the radio. *"Cheers to you, pirates. Here's track fifteen."*

When Ashur and Rose had gotten back to the house to change out of their formal ware, he told her that he was going out to a bar and that a bar was no place for children. She maintained that she was not a child and so came with.

He took a seat at the counter, greeting the lone guard on duty in the process. Rose sat nearby. She left a stool open in between them. Without delay, the bartender, a dark skinned woman in an apron, approached the two of them.

"Good evening, Ashur," she greeted. He returned the greeting and then introduced her to Rose. They got on well.

"Lulu's about the closest thing I have to a friend in this town," he said.

A grin arose on Lulu's face. "I'm just nice to you 'cause you tip well. Now what'll it be?"

"What's on the menu this week?"

"We have Company moonshine, Company vodka, Company mead, Company whiskey, or Company beer."

He ordered a whiskey on the rocks and Rose got a water.

"Coming right up." Lulu walked away.

Rose asked him if he came here a lot. He told her he was here maybe twice a week. Lulu returned with their drinks and he paid her with a few bronze pieces. They chatted for a bit, the bartender included, a little about the bar and a little more about the Springs. When Wellshire was brought up, Rose shied away. He told her she should not be worried, that Dixon could get the town under control. She told him even if he did, there would be no point in going back there. Lulu placed Ashur's second drink in front of him. He paid her.

"What'd you do back in Wellshire?"

"Helped out around my nana's farm with my brother," she said.

"So you would be useful on a farm then."

"He used to call me Rose-uh-Sharon, 'cause I never did my chores. I was always off exploring the scrap yard or the fringes of town, listening to the fire stories. So really, I'd be more useful in the badlands."

Ashur scoffed. "Would you now?" he said. "How'd you come to that conclusion?"

"People let their guard down around me. I'm quick and agile. I would make a badass sidekick," she said, setting his wallet down in front of him.

He put it back in his pocket. "Sidekicks are for superheroes."

"And?"

"And this *isn't* a comic book."

"Come on, you're an adventurer and I'm…I'm a troubled youth with nowhere to go. We'd make a good team."

"You're missing a mean streak," he said. "You're not a fighter."

"But you'll teach me. Won't you?"

"Why would you want me to teach you?"

"Like I said, I listen to the fire stories."

A woman's hand landed on Ashur's shoulder. "Hey there, Ashur." She placed herself in between Rose and him. "She's a little young for you, ain't she?" She wore a skimpy outfit that she had surely put together herself in an effort to broadcast as much cleavage and leg as possible.

"And how."

"In that case, I'm free right now."

"Maybe another night, Marla."

His statement did not deter her. She let her hand loll carelessly around in his lap. "Oh come now," she puppy-dogged him. "How about half price? You're a wonderful lay."

He lightly grasped the woman's wrist and moved her clumsy fingers away from his crotch, dropping her hand as if it were a dead rodent. "Flattery will only get you so far."

Someone entered the bar and Ashur's every muscle tightened involuntarily, setting upon him a rigid look, as if he were an animal ready to pounce. The music shut off, a glass fell onto the floor, and the hooker cleared out. The bar went silent as everyone studied their new guest—a Ranger. Ashur recognized him as Bill Slugger.

"I heard this was a fine place to get a drink," the Ranger announced. From somewhere in dimly lit the tavern flew a knife. It planted itself into the threshold behind the Ranger. He didn't flinch.

"Ya heard wrong!" said the card player in a Packer's Jersey. Ashur had gotten drunk with him a number of times but couldn't recall his name.

"Did I now?" Slugger asked. "How's about we take a looksee what kind of folk we have in here tonight." Slugger spotted Ashur almost immediately. Heavy-healed footsteps came their way. Rangers felt they were, in the classical sense, cowboys. They usually dressed in dusters, bandanas, cowboy boots, and always the signature Ranger hat—a Stetson. "Fairytale Grimm, how you been, partner?" When anyone entered the Rangers, they were expected to earn a new name. Fairytale Grimm had been Ashur's. Slugger planted himself in the stool between Ashur and Rose.

"I've been all right, boss," Ashur said.

"Can I get you anything, sir?" Lulu asked.

Slugger shot her a gaze. "Can't you see I'm talking to my friend, you knuckle dragger? How about you leave us be?"

Lulu stepped away.

"Damn pushers," Slugger said. "Am I right?"

Ashur took a sip of Whiskey and said nothing. Slugger was the epitome of a sellout, and an idiot. With the help of the mirror behind the bar's shelf, he examined the star badge Slugger had pinned to his duster. Flowing across the middle of the gold star was the word, **RANGER**. Curved, running around the top of the badge was the phrase: ***Salus Populi***, and around the bottom, curved upwards in the same fashion was the second part of their motto: ***Iustitia Omnibus***. It was not the Latin that confused Ashur. It was its placement. The language of justice had no place on a Ranger.

Slugger cleared his throat and glanced down at the hunting knife clipped to Ashur's belt, and then spotted the .45 he had in his shoulder holster. His jacket did not do the best job at concealing it. "You know it's illegal to carry in a bar, don't you, Grimm?"

"Not in Tavern Springs, boss. The whole bar is packing."

"Well according the Rangers' statutes, as declared in—hell, you know this one. Go on and tell the good folks here."

Ashur unwillingly abided. "As declared in the nineteenth act of the Ranger Syndicate, it is illegal to bring any firearm, knife, club or other bludgeoning or cutting weapon, carried openly or concealed, of any length or nature, into any establishment that sells alcohol." He was trying his best to play nice. Rose, on the other hand, was trying to fall through a crack in the floor. And Slugger took notice of this. He examined the weapons she wore and the worried look on her face.

"Don't worry, honey," he said. "You just sit there and look pretty. You're fine." He turned his attention back to Ashur. "So you know it's illegal and you do it anyways? You think you're above the law 'cause you used to run with the Rangers?"

He looked at the gun in Slugger's holster. "Tell me, Billy kid, are you inbred, or just plain stupid?"

Slugger narrowed his eyes at Ashur. He ripped the XP from his seat and pinned him against the counter. Most of the bar spoke out in defiance but no one did a thing, not even the guard. "You think you can say whatever you want to a Ranger?"

"There are no statutes against it the last time I checked," said Ashur.

Slugger noticed Rose watching their skirmish intently, along with the rest of the bar. He mouthed off to her. "What are you looking at?" She returned to staring at the floor. "Wait a second," the Ranger said and eased up. "Is this one yours, Grimm?"

"No," he said through clenched teeth.

"If she's not with you then why's she sittin' so close?"

"I don't know. Maybe she thinks I'm cute," he offered before Slugger pulled him off the wall and knocked out his footing, landing him on the floor.

The card table at the back came alive with objection. "You best leave that man alone, son," Packer Jersey called out.

"Or what?" Slugger asked while he made himself cozy next to Rose. "Hey there, honey. How's about we ditch ol' Grimm here and ride off into the sunset together. What do you say?"

"No thanks," Rose said, watching Ashur get up off the floor. The guard stood on the boarder of the altercation.

"I so graciously invited you somewhere. It's rude to say no."

"Please, leave me alone," she said, refusing to make eye contact with him. "You should leave."

"Listen here, you chicken shit." Slugger reached out and grabbed Rose by the upper arm, pulling her off the stool. She yelped. "When I ask some—"

Ashur broke his wrist.

Slugger reeled back in pain while attempting to retrieve, with his left hand, his service revolver. Ashur and Rose and the guard and the rest of the bar had a gun on him in an instant. Slugger stopped and put his hands up, his wrist flapping about in a fashion that wrists do not ordinarily flap about in.

He looked to Ashur like a caged beast. "You'll regret this," he said and made his exit from the saloon.

***

Later on that night, after the bar emptied out, Rose asked Lulu if she would allow her to play darts. Lulu took a glance at the empty area containing the dartboards.

"Sure, sweetie. I don't see anyone else playing."

"Want to play Shanghai Sharps with me, Ashur?"

By now, Ashur had stopped drinking and was caught between day dreaming, and chatting up Lulu. "Maybe in a minute. Why don't you go warm up."

"K," Rose said and left the bar stool. He watched her walk over to the area set aside for darts and unstick a set of throwing knives from a table.

"So what's with the girl?" Lulu asked as she cleaned a glass in a fashion that would suggest she wanted it to sparkle.

"Went to Wellshire to make some money. Found her instead."

"And now you're babysitting her?"

"Looks like it."

"And you're helping her because you have a heart of gold, is that it?"

"Does that not seem like something I would do?"

Lulu furrowed her brow. "You come into my bar, sometimes three nights a week—"

"That's because I'm so madly in love with you," he confessed.

"You just don't strike me as the charitable type."

"You just got through telling me I tip well," he countered.

Lulu put down the glass she had been cleaning and picked up a new one. "So how long are you going to babysit her for?" There was sparse applause in the background.

"I don't know," he said as he cradled his head. "Try to find her a job, decent place to stay. So until then, I guess."

"You ought to just adopt her," Lulu said, playfully.

"Well she's mostly grown up already. But it looks like she could use a hand, at least for a while. I don't know. We'll see how it pans out."

When the world before crumbled, it left in its wake many children without parents, and many parents without children. Naturally, the two groups found their way to each other and people, at large, had come to accept jury-rigged families as a normal occurrence.

"You really think that's something you'd want?" Lulu asked. Another wave of applause clouded the background, more organized this time.

"Kids don't scare me."

A man at the other end of the bar called for Lulu. "Just be good to her, Ashur," she said and then wandered away. There was another round of applause, this time with some cheering. He finally acknowledged the row and turned around to see what was going on. There, stuck to Rose's dartboard, were two throwing knives within the bull, and one on the bull's eye. Rose caught his gaze and smiled. She was standing at least ten paces away.

"You're shitting me," he said. He walked over to the dartboards. "Where'd you learn to throw knives like that?"

"My brother and I used to do this most every night. There wasn't much else to do in Wellshire. Now let's play," she said while prying the knives from the board.

"Sure." Ashur plucked another three knives from a nearby table.

"Throw to go," Rose said.

"I haven't played in forever."

"I'm sure you'll do fine. You're no stranger to chucking knives."

"And I've had a few."

"Just throw," she said, smiling.

Ashur drew back his hand and let loose the knife. It lodged itself into the outer rim of the board—out of the play area. Rose tried to conceal a laugh. She didn't do a very good job. Once recomposed, she sent one of her knives at the board, nailing the bull's eye and solidifying her as first turn.

"Jesus, girl," Ashur remarked as they retrieved their knives.

They moved back to the throwing line and Rose started. She hit a single, double, and triple space—in that order. "Shanghai. I win." The card table near the back roared up with a mixture of laughter and applause. Discovering he hadn't a snowball's chance, Ashur put his knives back on the table and turned to walk away.

Rose grabbed his wrist. "Oh come on, don't be a bum," she said. They played again, and continued to play for nearly half an hour—Rose going easier on him, but still winning every game. After about his eighth loss, Ashur set his knives down.

"I think I'm done," he said, feeling defeated. Rose smiled and did not stop him when he left her for the card table. She continued to practice her through before she came over to the poker table.

"Ashur, I'm tired. Can we go back to your house now?"

"We can go back to *my* house, sweetie pie," one of the men at the card table told her.

Ashur told him to hold his tongue. "Give me twenty minutes and then we'll go."

"Please, Ashur. Let's just go," she urged. "I'm tired." A few of the men also urged him to go, wanting him to default on his hand. But Ashur wouldn't let that happen.

"You know the way," he said while digging into his pocket. "Go if you want to." He handed her a set of keys. She took the keys and wandered away after wishing Lulu a good night.

"Cute kid," Packer Jersey said. Ashur had learned his name to be Colfax.

"Thanks," he said and picked up his cards—a pair of aces and a pair of eights, all black. He was on a hot streak tonight, having won enough miscellaneous cartridges and coin to feed himself for the week. Generally, when Ashur played, he sat facing the saloon doors. Tonight however, that was not the case, as there had only been one seat open at the table.

Because of this, he didn't notice when Bill Slugger stumbled in to take his life. "Damn you, Grimm!" he said and drew his gun. "Take this!"

There was a crack and a muffled thud, like wet leather on concrete. Then the bar got very quiet. Lulu cupped a hand over her mouth while onlookers stared at the assailant in disbelief.

Ashur spun around just in time to see her drop the gun. Rose, drenched in blood and grey matter, stood over the crumpled heap that had been a Ranger, quivering as if she had been struck by lightning. "I...he was going to shoot you."

Ashur went to her.

Minutes later, a Crown Vic pulled up outside and two sentries entered the tavern. They saw the dead Ranger and then they saw Ashur. Then they dragged the body away.

***

Back at the house, Ashur cleaned her up. She had fallen into a trancelike state of shock. Since the bar, she hadn't said a word, hadn't looked at him or anything with the most remote of interests. Her eyes were stuck to something a thousand yards away and she never blinked, not once.

He gently removed her bloodstained hoodie and cleaned the remainder of the blood off her face. She had received a small cut on her cheek, perhaps as a result of a flying skull fragment. Afterwards, he took her hoodie and went into his room, placing it in his washing machine. When he came back, she was sitting there like an alabaster sculpture. He debated about whether or not he should let her be and hope that this would be over in the morning, or if he should push her over the edge.

"Rose." He crouched down in front of her. "I'm not going to insult you by asking if you're okay, but I'm not sure what to do. So you do what you have to. Whatever it is. Scream. Shout. Cry. Break what you want. Just do…something."

She wet her lips. "I think I'd like to be alone."

Ashur nodded in an understanding manner. "That's too bad," he said. "I'm not leaving you alone."

Tears squeezed into her eyes and ran down her cheeks in rivulets. "I feel sick."

"That's okay. Do you need to throw up again?"

"Not like that," she said and rubbed her eyes. She was shaking. "I just…everything is so fucked up. My family, my home—I've never killed anyone before."

"You've made all the right calls. You know that."

She shook her head in confusion. "No."

80

"Then you tell me what you think you should have done."

She did not reply.

"Your nerves will be shot for a few days. You're going to relive it. For a while. You may be angry, or numb, or—"

"Numb," she said, nodding.

He put his hand on her knee. "It'll pass. I promise. It always passes."

"I don't know what to do."

He opened his arms to her and she collapsed into them. "Can you sleep?" he asked.

"I can try." Her voice was scratchy and unreliable. He brought her into the bedroom and put her down on the bed. "You'll wait until I'm asleep right?" she asked. "You'll let me fall asleep first?"

He crawled in alongside her. "I'll be right here."

She was asleep in seconds it seemed. Ashur was not far behind. It was a solid sleep. He did not even dream. When the sun rose, she was in his arms, her head laid on his chest.

"Good morning." She sounded rested.

He reached out and began running his fingers through her hair. It had been let down last night, when he was cleaning it of blood and brains. He picked out a piece he had missed and flicked it across the room. "Morning, flowerchild. Did you dream?"

"No."

"Lucky you."

His sleep had been a black one. He had no idea how long he had been out, but when he woke his muscles were stiff and unresponsive. As a result, he was not eager to move.

Rose inhaled sharply and tensed up as if she had been jabbed in the ribs.

"Thought about it?"

She tried to relax. "Yeah."

"It'll happen for a few weeks."

"You've got a lot experience with this stuff."

"Me?" Ashur yawned. "This whole damned world's shell-shocked."

"Did you ever go to a baseball game," she said, trying to change topics. "You know, before everything?"

"I went to a few Reds' games."

"Reds?"

"The Cincinnati Reds. I grew up there—well there and St. Louis."

"What were baseball games like?" she asked.

"They were…hard to describe, really."

"Try."

He shrugged. "Peanut shells on the floor, organ music, little kids in the stands with baseball mitts waiting to catch a foul ball. It always looked like something out of a postcard."

"I bet it was something to see. I see pictures of things sometimes and I…I'm lost for hours. I go mad if I don't find someone over thirty to ask about it." She looked up and took note of the wedding band on his necklace. She played at it. "So what's this?" she asked.

He took the ring from her and tucked it into his shirt. "Nothing." A silence grew between the two of them.

"That's okay," she said finally. "What now?"

He rolled her over and got up. "Breakfast?"

Part 2
Run, comrade, the old world is behind you!

Ashur crept through the house as silently as he could. This was at the dawn of the New Age, when new skills were being forced upon anyone who wished to survive—how to find food, how to handle a gun, how to live a life undetected. Luckily for Ashur, the end of the last age had prepared him for the beginning of the next, and many of those same skills had been long ago mastered. Unlike the masses around him, he had lived into an age that he could understand. This was his advantage.

The rotten hardwood underneath his feet cried out in pain and a man stepped out of the bathroom. But it was dark and the figure struggled to see anything. Ashur calmly shouldered the pump action shotgun he had found while scouring the basement of the house. It had but two shells.

"Stevenson?" the man said in a hushed tone. "Stevenson, is that you?"

"Nope." Ashur sent a shell into the man's stomach. He collapsed onto the floor and did not move. Ashur pumped the gun and switched on his helmet-mounted headlamp, illuminating most of the house's upper floor. In a swift yet rigid manner, he turned a corner and moved through the joining hallway. A second man came sprinting out of the room at the end of the hall to investigate, nearly impaling himself on the business end of the scattergun.

Ashur put him down and kept moving. He entered the room and found a woman. She was blinded by the headlamp.

Her hands went up. "I surrender," she said in a hoarse voice. "Don't shoot!"

Ashur checked to make sure no one else was in the room. It was clear. In a single motion, he moved towards the woman, tossed the empty shotgun away, pushed her onto the floor, and reached for her hip, relieving her of the sidearm she had neglected to draw. She was quivering against the wall, trying to speak and breathe and panic all at the same time. He twisted the headlamp so it pointed at the ceiling, allowing the woman to see him. She wore an American Army uniform, just as the two men had.

"How many of you are there?" Ashur asked. She couldn't speak. He knelt in front of her, keeping the gun trained on its target. "Look at me," he said, voice slow and even. "Breathe…if you cooperate you will live."

She made a few visible attempts to slow her heart rate.

"How many are you?" he asked again.

"Three…in-including myself."

Ashur transitioned from kneeling in front of her to sitting. His lungs shuffled a breath out and then in, and then again. Afterwards, his breathing returned to normal and his muscles slackened. "Now you're one," he said while wiping blood off his face. He was covered in the stuff. He checked the handgun's magazine and reinserted it. "You were smart to surrender."

She said nothing in return so he continued.

"Whose command?"

She hesitated. "W-We're rouge. No command—not for over a year."

"Army?"

"Yes."

"I was in the Army once. Fought in the big one at Yellowknife."

A pause.

"I-I'm just a medic," she said.

"I applaud your bravery," he said. "Anyways, this is how it's going to go. It's very streamline. You're going to show me where you keep your guns, ammo, meds, and food. I will take half…and then I will leave. Are we at an understanding?"

She went to speak but stopped herself. And then tried again with the same result. Finally she gave up on speech and nodded.

***

Ashur wandered through another one of the scabland's grey evenings. Only last week he'd passed through the haunted city that had once been Cincinnati, up to this point he'd avoided going into cities but winter was setting in and food was scarce. It was only this morning that he'd killed a family for their supplies. He'd offered to only take a third but no amount of compromise would convince them to part with their lifeblood. And so they had to die.

He found a secluded area fenced in by rubble and sat down to make himself a meal. Beans were on the menu. He started a fire and unpacked for the night, setting the supper over the flames. There was then a noise from the ruins. She had been following him since their encounter three weeks ago. He had known about it the whole time and left the occasional scrap to string her along. She reminded him of someone he missed dearly.

"Come on out," Ashur called. "I know you've been following me." There was no response, so he got up and quickly pulled her out of the rubble.

"I-I'm sorry," she said. "I don't want any more trouble."

"No trouble. I'm not going to hurt you."

"No?"

"No. What's your name?"

"I'm April."

"April, I'm Ashur. Thought I'd come tell you that if you're going to continue following me you may as well travel with me."

He pointed to his bloody forearm. "I got shot this morning. I'd like to make use of your talents. There's a hot meal in it for you."

She didn't know what else to do, so she agreed. He led her back to his camp site and she tended to the wound he had received. He counted himself lucky. Infection on the road spells disaster, but he had the luxury of being tended to by a medical professional.

"You didn't have to kill the child," she said as she finished with his bandages.

"You saw," he said flatly.

"Yes. It was atrocious."

"It was sickly. I couldn't have cared for it."

"You still shouldn't have done that."

"You're suggesting that I should have let it alone and wait for exposure to take it? Or wait for someone desperate enough to come along and make a meal out of it?"

"I mean…I didn't ever—"

"No, I don't think you did. You watched. If you think I'm so atrocious then kill me. You can take my life from me—you have that right. But you have no right to judge me."

She moved back a little. "Are…are you drunk?"

"No. Don't be stupid," he said. "I found some tranqs."

She looked away. "Maybe I should go."

"You're welcome to go as you please, but you've been watching me. You know you're safer in my line of sight." She was reluctant to agree. "And I kind of need you here right now," he admitted, pushing his wounded arm towards her. "You wouldn't let me die, would you?"

Shortly thereafter, the meal was served and they ate dinner, sparing speech. "Where are we going anyways?" she asked as they finished.

"St. Louis. I had a few relatives there. And after that, the Great Lakes. I need to get back to Chicago. I abandoned my men there. I need to see what's become of them."

"What were you doing this far east?"

"Looking for my family."

"I assume you didn't find them."

"No," he said, voice slow and soft. "I found them."

Chapter 8

The evening moved in. It was getting cooler now. Ashur and Rose were trekking along the coast of Winnebago, heading south. He had told her they were going backpacking again. In the past couple of weeks, he had begun teaching her the basics: survival skills, scavenging, and physical conditioning.

"I'm hungry." She had carried twenty pounds of gear ten miles before bringing it up.

"Look around you," he said, gesturing to the shrubbery that blanketed the coastline. "Find something to eat." He and Rose dropped their gear in a clearing and began foraging. The first thing Rose went for were some dandelions. She piled them on and shoved a bushel into her mouth.

"And what are those?" he asked.

"Tarax-acum office-inale?" she pieced together. He nodded at her, after which she proceeded to attack a nearby cluster of the flowers. When she had cleared the area, Rose noticed he was eating the greens of another plant, and storing some of them in a bag. But when she attempted to eat the leaves, he grabbed her wrist.

"What are these?" he asked.

"I dunno."

He took them from her and put them in the bag with the others. "What's the first rule of foraging?"

She sighed. "If you don't know what it is, don't eat it."

"Exactly."

"But you're eating it!"

"Because I know what it is."

"But I'm hungry."

"Hungry is better than dead. Go get your botanicals book."

She wandered off and came back with her book, riffling through the pages.

"Notice how the leaves grow out and close to the ground," he said. "That's called a basal rosette. Leaf patterns are integral to identifying a plant."

It took her about two minutes to find the plant. By then Ashur had finished collect the leaves and returned to eating them. "It's a broadleaf plantain: plantago major," she said. "Is that right?"

He nodded. "Its leaves are edible when young. As it gets older they become stringy and you have to boil them. It tastes earthy, a bit like a mushroom but there's a bitter aftertaste." He gave her a handful of younger leaves.

She wolfed them down. "Why are you keeping some?"

"Read up on their uses."

Her eyes flickered over the text. "'Plantain is found worldwide, and is an abundant and accessible medicinal herb, containing many bioactive compounds, including ursolic acid, fl...'" She trailed off for a moment as she read over the names of the compounds, most of which had no meaning to her or anyone else outside of a lab. " 'For thousands of years, plantain leaves have been applied to wounds, sores, and stings to promote healing.' Cool." She picked a few handfuls more of the younger leaves and ate them. "Can we eat the food we brought now?"

"Weeds have supported humans for thousands of years. And they will continue to support us until we make camp. Just be thankful there aren't any more wild animals to hunt. You'll never have to learn how to skin something."

"I am thankful for that."

Ashur pulled a blue flower off of a bush. "This is Chicory."

She went to her book. "Uh 'Chicory: Cichorium Intybus. Also known as Blue Daisy, Coffeeweed, or Succory. Not to be confused with its cousin Cichorium Endivia…leaves are edible as a salad green, roots can be used as a coffee substitute.' Coffee's a hot drink right?"

"You don't know what coffee is?"

She shrugged. "I know what it is, I just haven't had any."

"Yeah they can't grow it any more. It's caffeinated like tea, only stronger. It's made out of a bean." He handed her a few Succory leaves. "You can eat these."

Her face turned to disgust when she popped a few in her mouth. "It's bitter."

"I said, 'You can,' I didn't say you'd want to. It's toxic to intestinal parasites though, the roots especially."

She spit it out. "I don't think I'll ever be hungry enough to eat it. Can we make camp soon?"

Ashur stood up and grabbed his pack. "You're supposed to be running this, remember? So if you think we should make camp, pick a site."

She picked up her rucksack and they continued on their merry. They had about thirty minutes of sunlight left when they came to a larger clearing. "How's this?" she asked.

"You tell me."

"Not too far from the water, high ground, decent amount of shrubbery to keep us hidden. I think it's good."

"Then here is where we make camp."

"Is it good?" she pried.

"It's good."

With that, they set up camp. Rose pitched the tent and found the cooking supplies while Ashur started the fire and journeyed to the lakeside to get a pail of water. She began cooking when he returned. In addition to some jerky, they were having a vegetable medley: snap beans, sweet corn, green peas, and some vegetation they had foraged along the way.

"So how'd you learn to do all this?"

"Reading, a little bit of formal learning, but largely trial and error," he said. "I've lived most of my life with a compass in my back pocket."

"What made you do it?"

"It was one of only a few options for my younger self. And a few years down the road, it became the only option for everyone. Now I can't do anything else. This is where I belong. In there I…I just wait to be called back out here. You live a life like that and at some point you realize you can't have a pedestrian living. If this is what you want to do, that's something you need to understand."

"I understand."

"I'm not sure you do. When I go out in the field, you don't know if I'm alive or not until I roll up to the gate. How hard is that for you?" She did not reply. "The only reason this right here works, is because I can bring you with me on occasion. If I couldn't, you wouldn't see me for days at a time. Weeks sometimes." He held eye contact. "You can't have kids. You can't have a husband."

"I could leave it after a while. Start a family then."

"The girl who ditched farm duty to go exploring? You're going to stick around and what? Plant seed? Watch the gate?"

"Yes. I could," she defended.

"I'm not trying to scold you. I just want you to know what it takes from you. This profession is lonely, dirty. This profession is consuming." Their conversation died down after that. Ashur stopped eating his meal about halfway through. As soon as Rose finished hers, he offered it to her.

"You're sure?"

He nodded. "You're getting a little thin."

She took it from him and started in on it, halting after a few spoonfuls. "Thank you."

***

The next morning was damp. Their breath had condensed on the inside of the tent. Ashur rolled over in his sleeping bag and nudged Rose. "Wake up," he said, his eyes still closed.

She curled up to find warmth. "Mmm why?"

"You need to start the fire."

"Why?"

"Because you need practice."

"I know how to start a fire," she said. "I'm not a halfwit."

"Prove it."

She crawled out of her sleeping bag and found the slam rod fire starter. Halfway through unzipping the door, he reminded her to take her gun. She took it and exited. It must have been nearing eight o' clock, still cold enough for Rose to see her breath. There were no birds, no chittering insects, just a bone-dry wind.

The familiar sound of a gun hammer being drawn back broke the calm. "Ashur."

He swiped his .45 and stormed out of the tent. Rose was standing there, staring out towards the lake.

A man meandered about through the bushes, a large basket upon his back. He noticed them. "Sir," he said.

Ashur flipped the safety on and tucked his gun in his waistband. "You're not a sentry," he told him. "Don't call me sir." Ashur recognized the man from town. He was in his thirties, scrawny with a ponytail.

"Mr. Stanton then. Good morning. I didn't mean to disturb you."

"It's all right. You find anything interesting out there?"

"I did. There are some Nannyberry trees growing about five miles south of here. Would you and your friend like some berries?"

Ashur looked at Rose. "Sure."

The man approached. He took his basket off and rummaged through it. The nannyberries were in a tin. Ashur took a handful and gave them to Rose, then took some for himself. The forager had a few as well.

"What are you doing out here?" Rose asked, tasting one of the berries. It tasted similar to a blueberry.

"Gathering. I sell produce to townsfolk, seed to farmers and gardeners."

"You're not carrying a gun," she said, continuing on the berries. "Isn't it dangerous out here?"

The man shrugged. "The only people I meet on the coast are travelers looking for some water or others like myself. I've never had any trouble."

"We were going to have breakfast in a bit, if you'd like to join," Ashur said.

"I wish I could, but I've got to get back to the Springs. Commute, work, commute, sleep, and all that." On that note, the man swung his basket onto his back and wished them well.

Chapter 9

A slender gypsy and his dog wandered through the wreckage of Milwaukee's aerodrome. They were winding down for the day. Currently, they were scavenging. The first place they checked was a convenience shop near an Areomexico gate—just some old magazines. The man walked back to the gate and up to the window. A number of planes lay on the tarmac, most of them with drooping wings and melted wheels. He kicked out the glass and attached a grappling hook to the ledge.

"Moonraker," he addressed his dog. "Post up."

The dog sat, after which the man repelled two stories to the ground. From there he moved towards the nearest plane, climbing up onto the wing. He found he was unable to gain access through the door. It may have melted shut. However, from where he was, he was able to see an alternative—a sizably larger plane, its doors had all been opened. The plastic slides, however, were long gone. He climbed up. Once inside, he scoured the service area. It was untouched. Nearly all of the food had gone bad, the mini bottles of booze, however, would fetch a good price.

With his pack full, he left the plane and returned to the rope. About halfway up, he could hear Moonraker growling. He prepared for a fight. Rolling up onto the ledge, he sprung up, drawing a long-barreled revolver. The scene was as such: Moonraker stood ready to pounce, eyeing an armed, mangy man and a young boy. The gypsy steadied his gun on the man. Nobody moved.

"That thing even loaded?" asked the gypsy. "They rarely are." The man did not reply, but it was easy to see he was frightened. The boy equally so. He was no more than ten. "Moonraker, at ease." The dog stopped growling and sat. The gypsy lowered the hammer on his revolver. "Hey," he greeted the boy. "I'm Jackstraw. Is this your dad?"

"Don't talk to him," said the father. "You got something to say you say it to me."

"I wasn't sure who was running the show," Jackstraw said, his attempt at a joke falling by the wayside. The man was silent, still terrified. "Do I have something to say? Yeah I got something to say." Jackstraw holstered his revolver and walked right up to him, nose to nose. "Boo," he said, and then slunk off into the growing darkness. Along the way, he picked up a piece of rubble and chucked it at a glass display stand, shattering it. "Either of you hungry?" he called back down the terminal. "I know a great little hole in the wall just up here."

They ended up making camp together, Jackstraw giving them food. They sat around a fire while the boy finished his meal. Moonraker stayed alert regardless of how many times his owner relieved him. Jackstraw's portable radio was playing some bubblegum pop. It faded into the background as the DJ came about. *"Early reports of Wellshire's sacking have been confirmed. The town is now under criminal control. When posthumously used as a puppet by one of the marauders, Mayor Anderson had this to say*: I'm dead. Free stuff for all the bandits. *One of my liaisons attempted to get the Rangers' opinion on the matter, but when she pressed a representative of the Rangers for an interview, he shot the recorder out of her hand, claiming, his finger slipped."*

"Why are you guys out here? The road's no place for someone his age."

"There was a sickness in our village," said the father. "I decided we'd take our chances on the road. We're headed up north. Maybe find work in Medway, or Irongrass. Why are you out here?"

"I'm a tracker," was all he really had to say, but he carried on. "From New St. Lou. Got a brother up north. Heading up there to pay him a visit."

"He's got a bounty set on him?"

Jackstraw nodded. "I've wanted to get out of town for a while now. The opportunity finally came down the pipe."

Chapter 10

It was a dreary Tuesday afternoon. Ashur and Rose were catching a movie at the local cinema, an old Charlie Chaplin film. They were just about the only people in the theater.

"Is the whole thing in black and white?" she asked, munching on some popcorn.

He looked at her funny. "Yeah. That's how they were back in the day. I like them better in black and white anyways."

"Why?"

"I don't know. It reminds me of a simpler time I guess."

"These are simple times," she said.

"I suppose that's true."

The movie opened with World War I trench warfare—barbed wire, mortar shells, Maxim machine guns, and the rest.

"Is that what war was like?" she asked as the camera panned over to the artillery firebases behind the lines.

"The war with Canada was awfully similar, trench-laden, but in general no. War was much more open than this."

"What was the war with Canada like?"

"No one wanted to be there. We dragged our feet. And no one expected the Canucks to resist like they did. They picked up a tip from their arctic buddies: the scorched-earth policy, burned their oil fields, their lumber. Drew us all way up to Yellowknife."

The scene on screen became one of slapstick comedy. An artillery shell had misfired and fallen to the ground. The commander sent Charlie Chaplin to check the fuse. However, as he walked around the shell to get to the fuse, the shell would rotate, matching his speed, even changing directions as he did. Charlie stopped walking in order to contemplate how he was to get to the fuse. When he did this, the shell ignited like a sparkler and spun wildly, startling the mustachioed hero. He fled the scene and dove for cover.

Rose found this utterly hilarious, laughing until she cried. "I thought this was going to be lame but this is great."

***

Rose whimpered as Ashur eased the knife out of her thigh. She grabbed at his arm.

"I know, sweetie, I know," he whispered. A man lay nearby, bloodied and quivering. Ashur had beaten him half to death with nothing more than his fists and the shop counter they were currently hiding behind. The knife came out.

"*Fu-u-ck*," she sobbed, burying her face into his shoulder to keep quiet.

"Good girl." He let the wound run for a moment to see how bad it was, then went for his med kit. "We got lucky. He missed your femoral." He had already cut away her pant leg. He wrapped the gash in gauze and cloth and began applying pressure. "I think we should clean and stitch it here, as soon as we can."

"Just don't cauterize it," she begged.

"No. I shouldn't have to."

They were on a scavenging run, checking out old Oshkosh city, about twenty miles down the coast of Winnebago. They had scouted it out a week ago and found it vacant. Specifically, Vanderbilt had sent them in search of a part for their water purification system. The one in Tavern Springs had failed, so they were going to fix it. A pair of engineers and an expeditionary force had been sent out with them, but they had gotten separated during an ambush. Right now, the bandits were searching for them, sweeping from building to building.

Ashur could hear another one of them growing close. He took Rose's hand and placed it on the bandage. "Keep pressure on it," he mouthed.

"No, no, no. Don't leave me here," she said.

He held a finger in front of his lips and disappeared into the arena of overturned shelves and waterlogged merchandize.

A lone thief entered the store. "I know you're around here," he called, starting inward. "I'm gonna find you. And then you wanna know what I'm gonna do?" Ashur found an old-world coin on the ground and tossed it across the shop. It pinged off of a shelf, drawing the man's attention. "What? Quit fucking around and show yourself." He carried on. The soles of his boots clicked on the linoleum floor as he moved through the first few isles. He wound up moving to search the main the counter. He saw Rose slouched up against the back wall, revolver in hand, and his comrade nearby, his brains on the counter. "What the fuck?" the man breathed. Ashur got behind him and swiped the bandit's pipe out from underneath him. He clubbed him in the back of the head with it. The pipe bent and the man fell to a kneel, his arm braced against the counter. Ashur dropped the pipe and put him in a chokehold before he could call out to his friends. Near passing out, the outlaw attempted to gouge at Ashur's eyes, so Ashur smashed his head against the counter. He went limp.

He held the chokehold for a few more seconds just to be safe. "And that is why you always bring your battle buddy," he said, dropping the man.

"Holy shit, Ashur. Is he…?"

"No. He's just passed out." He brought out a zip tie and closed it around the man's throat in order to finish the job.

"Don't…" Rose said.

He watched her. "He won't feel a thing. He won't even know."

"Please," she said. "I'm asking you, please cut it off."

He swallowed hard and then did as she asked. He zip tied the man's hands together and gagged him instead. Afterwards, he moved back to her. The bleeding had slowed enough to allow him to work on it. He brought out a bottle of pure grain alcohol. "This is going to hurt." He poured it over the wound. She flinched and suffocated her whining. Next he brought out sutures and began stitching her up. The wound was just over an inch long. "This was supposed to be milk run. You're not ready for this."

"Clearly," she said and sniffled. She held on to his shoulder the entire process. Once it was sutured, he poured some more alcohol on it and wrapped it up. "We need to find the rest of the team."

"What if we just wait them out? These guys aren't well armed. It's only a matter of time before the expeditionary group cleans house. Right?"

They had heard a number of skirmishes take place since everyone was scattered. When they were jumped, there were more arrows coming at them than bullets.

"They've got the numbers. But you're right. Sitting tight would be the best course of action. Sitting it out's just not my style."

"Well, at the moment, it's mine."

He nodded. "We should still move to a better hiding spot." From the front of the shop, he could see an old drainage pipe. It ran underneath a small bridge. The road was clear of any highwaymen. He brought her up onto his shoulders in a fireman's carry and started for the alcove.

"Ashur, wait." They hadn't even left the store.

"What is it?"

"There is a postcard over there."

"Really?"

"Yeah, it's right there in the stand." She pointed to it.

"No. I mean, that's what you're concerned about?"

"Just grab it," she said. "It'll take like two seconds." He took the post card and proceeded to the pipe. Whatever river had once run through it was now long dried up, nothing but red dust.

Rose sat across from him in the tube, studying the postcard. **Greetings From Sunny Winnebago!** it read.

"You live on Lake Winnebago. Why do you need a postcard?" he asked. They kept their voices low the entire stay in the pipe.

"I like to see what it was like. So people still went fishing back then? But for sport?"

"Yeah. People did it as a hobby. It wasn't like the rickety buckets they have floating out there now, scraping up whatever they can. And at night, people used to go out on big party boats and get drunk, dance all night."

"That sounds like fun. Did you fish?"

"Me? No."

"What about hunting?" she asked.

"No, not really."

"You hunt bandits."

"The most dangerous game," he said. "They're almost as smart as deer."

She cracked a smile. "So, this is fun."

"Fun. Yeah. How's your leg?"

"It hurts," she said and put on a smile. "A lot."

"It shouldn't be too much longer." They had been listening to the sporadic gunfire in the distance. It was gradually growing closer. Ashur went outside and checked the surroundings. All was calm. Someone had been posted up in the pipe long ago. They had taken to doodling nearby:

I am a Marxist of the Groucho variety

And I declare a permanent state of happiness

We will not disarm

**We are neither political demonstrators nor vicious thugs.
We are people filled with rage.**

He lit a road flare and tossed it out into the street, far enough away that it would not give away his location. He returned to the pipe. Rose had some grime on her face—wet ash. He licked his thumb and cleaned it off. "What's up with your parents anyways?"

She fussed at his hand. "Dead."

"Food riot?"

"Some kind of riot," she said, fascinated with the postcard. "I don't really remember."

"I lost mine in a riot too. Is that why you and your brother were living with your grandma?"

"Yup."

He checked his handgun to make sure it was ready to go. "You're handling this really well. I'm proud of you."

"Does that mean I'll get paid for this?"

"You need money for something?" He gave her money when she needed it, which was rarely. Occasionally she would need sundries or gear.

"Not really, but it would be nice to have something of my own."

He ran his tongue across his back teeth. They were bleeding from an earlier hit. "I can understand that. How's ten percent of anything you join me on?"

"Is that a lot?"

"It's gas money," he said. "Enough to go out with that boy you've been hanging around with. What's the story with him anyhow? The miller's son?"

"There's no story. We're just friends."

"Uh-huh. And if elephants could fly you'd make a fortune selling umbrellas."

"What's that supposed to mean?"

"Boys his age don't have girls who are just friends."

"Well he does," she said, shifting her sitting position to take pressure off her leg. "I'm not into him. He's kind of an ass."

He spit some blood into the dirt. "Tell him that and watch him disappear."

"I don't know. He seems like the persistent type."

"Then you come tell me and I'll send some men."

"Oh my God, Ashur." She finally looked at something other than the picture of Winnebago. "You don't need to beat him up."

"Oh don't be dramatic. They wouldn't lay a finger on him, just scare him."

She shook her head. "I think I can handle it. And what about you?"

"What about me?"

"You should take Lulu out."

"You don't date your bartenders, kid."

"Well why not?"

"Because then you can't drink to forget them."

Just then, a voice filtered in from outside. It belonged to a highwayman. "We know you're out here somewhere!"

"Oh really?" Ashur said under his breath. "What gave it away?" He drew his rifle off of his back but before he could do anything else, a torrent of gunshots rang out. He looked to Rose. "And that's what happens when no one teaches you basic tactics." He stepped out of the pipe to wave his men down. There were three of them. "On me."

They approached and took a knee, watching out for more bandits. "We're holed up in a book store three streets over. Both the engineers and the vehicles are secure. Two fatalities and a casualty, but we're ready to move on the pump station."

"Rose is in there. She's been injured. She's okay but she can't walk." He sent a man to retrieve her.

"Hey, Corporal," she greeted. They could all hear the conversation from outside the tube.

"How do you want to do this?"

"Over the shoulders?"

A moment later, the man stepped out of the drainage pipe carrying the girl. Ashur put a man on point and they left the scene.

Chapter 11

"Breaking news bulletin: Aliens have landed on Earth. More on that later. For now, here's what's choice." Something from a Rat Pack member started playing.

It was getting later in the evening and above the horizon, what was left of the light had turned to a hodgepodge of saffron and violet. Rose carried on cleaning the gun she was working with, just as Ashur had taught her. Once she was finished, she stripped and clean a few other weapons he had lying around the garage. Then she sharpened her butterfly knife.

Once she was done that, she exercised shortly and then went inside to cook herself dinner: eggs and toast. She finished eating and then cleaned up her mess in the kitchen, as well as the one Ashur had left from the morning. Then she showered and redressed, double-knotting the laces on her boots. Ashur had taught her much in the past months. It was a mutual relationship. He kept her fed and housed and warm. He taught her what he knew, and in return, she tried to keep him from himself.

Rose walked outside and caught Scott as he was packing up for the night. "Howdy, Scott."

"Evening, Rose. The night guy will be here shortly."

"I know. I just wanted to see if you wanted to...you know. I don't have enough muscle to do it on my own. I'll buy you a drink?"

"Don't worry about it, kid. Come on."

They began walking through the streets of Tavern Springs. As they did Rose whistled a tune. Once she was bored with that she asked Scott how long he had been working for Ashur. It was a couple of years he told her. He had not always been Ashur's guard. People pushed by in twos and in threes. The uptown was generally lively on a Friday night. In the dust of what had once been a city, there were theaters and bars and street hustling youths. They moved past a clinic and a water-well. There was a show going on right outside the jail. All the buildings were lit up like Tin-Pan Alley. The streets, however, were dark from place to place. When they passed into the one of these dark intersections, the lights from all the buildings would contrast with the sheer darkness, stacked blocks of light, people behind each pane going about their days. She glanced through the grimy window of a cheap bistro, imagining what everything looked like from the outskirts of town—like a big boat sailing through the water.

It all felt permanent.

They reached Whiskey Breeze and entered. Ashur's face was firmly planted on the bar, his hand still clutching a drink. Rose and Scott walked up to the counter and took a seat on either side of him. "You sure you don't want a drink?" Rose asked.

"The day I let a teenager buy my booze is gonna be a sad day."

"How about water then?"

"That'll be fine," said Scott. "I could use one."

Lulu came out of the kitchen with a pair of meals for two men in a booth at the back of the establishment. Then she returned to the counter. "Hi, Scott," she said. "How's the family?"

"The wife is happy as ever. But the kids are good."

"I'm glad to hear," she said with a warm smile. "You guys just here to pick up Ashur or would you like something to drink?"

"We can stay for a little I think," Rose said.

"All right then. What'll it be?"

"A water for Scott and I'll have some warm cider please."

She poured their drinks and Rose paid her.

"How's your night been?"

"Pretty quiet for a Friday," Lulu said.

Rose gestured at Ashur. "And his night?"

Lulu pulled the unfinished drink from his unconscious hand. "He was more tired than drunk. This was only his third."

"We won't have to carry him home then," Scott said.

Lulu had a sip of Ashur's drink and then poured the rest out. "I haven't made near as much money off of him since you moved into town," she said. "I think you're good for him."

Rose smiled one of her sudden, shy smiles at the drowsy XP. They had their drinks and then attempted to rouse Ashur. At first he made only unintelligible bubbles in the pool of his own drool that had formed on the counter, so Rose batted him across the back of the head. He perked right up, on high alert. The first thing he did was dismiss Scott. Then he and Rose began homeward. He would sway every so often, so Rose grabbed him by the upper arm. They returned to the cottage, after which, she plopped him down on his bed and untied his boots.

"Hey there, flower girl," he said.

"Hullo," she hummed while removing the boots from his feet. They were still covered in ash. He had gone out today—a job from the mayor. "How was work?"

He cleared his throat. "Not good."

She put his boots by the front door and returned to him, sitting at the foot of his bed while he sprawled out. "Would you like to talk about it?"

"Why would you want to hear this?"

"Just so you don't have to deal with it alone."

"That's not really your job. I'm the adult, remember?"

"But I'm the one that brought you home. And I'll do it again when you need me to."

He wet his lips. "We lost a guy today. We were scavenging and the roof collapsed. We couldn't get to him in time."

"And you feel like it's your fault?"

"It is my fault. He was my guy. I sent him in there. And he died. He was twenty-three. A fucking kid."

"You didn't know the roof would come down."

"No, but you still have to inform the next of kin: the widow, the parents, God forbid the children. You can actually *see* their hearts break. And they look at you like…" He shook his head. "You just know it's your fault."

"Ashur…"

"I'm going to sleep now."

She picked at her cuticles. "Do you want me to stay with you?"

There was a shared pause. "No," he answered.

"All right then," she said. She left to bring him a glass of water. He was asleep by the time she returned.

***

Ashur stood over a table, a wide, tactical map of the city laid out before him, corridors, bottlenecks, barricades, his men—the docility of war on paper. Violence hummed in the background. Garwood entered the tent clad in RAUC armor, as Ashur was. Government issued, it was onyx-black with metal plates over the chest, crotch, thighs, shins, back, shoulders and forearms. Only joints were left exposed, to allow for movement. The only color on equipment was the white stenciled letters on the back plate, overtop of the shoulder blades: **Riot and Urban Control**.

Garwood removed his helmet, which had an attached ballistic mask to protect the life as well as the identity. "Commander," he said. "We've lost another two men. The Guard has broken ranks and some have even joined the Revolutionaries.

Something needs to be done now! Three days is long enough. Give the order."

Ashur looked up from the table and stared through his officer. Then he left the tent. Ashur's command was situated on a tall platform in the middle of a Chicago street. Below him was a wall of his men, armed with riot shields and clubs. He looked out at the streets: smashed windows, broken doors, rioters scattering about like ants, painting everything in sight.

We The Corporations of The Untied Sectors of America…

By stopping our machines together, we will demonstrate their weakness

> **Paint the Grass Greener? No we'll make it Red**
>> **There will be no return to normal**

The police are joining in: the beautiful blue turncoats.

Some of the buildings had been, as it seemed, smashed in by a massive fist. Ashur identified a fire crew attempting to suppress a blaze and sent a few men to protect them from the chaos. His men—he had lost half a score of them to this city. Garwood strode out onto the platform and stood by his commander.

"The people are demanding a bucket and we're forcing the cup," Ashur said, a clever smirk planted on his face. "But here's the genius of it. They're both empty."

"Sir?"

"Do you know why they pay us in gold, Garwood?"

"Because we do the heavy lifting?"

"Just the contrary. Our generation has taken part in the single greatest power struggle in the history of mankind. As a result, we sit here, watching the empire tear out its own entrails as the civilizations before us have done. The US Government is no longer a legitimate entity to many. They're just another tribe in this melee. Our superiors pay us in gold because they know that we have the skillset and the mindset to maintain control. But moreover, they know how many sectors would fall if the people who make up the RAUC joined the revolutionist ranks. Aristocrats scrape the bottom of the well and beg us to take what's left so that they can maintain some semblance of authority. We are not foot soldiers. We're the appointed warlords. We are the coming law."

"And when the gold runs out?"

"Then we fight for the people. When we bring down the titans, the country will thank us. We'll be all—" There was then, in a frozen second, two gunshots, one incoming, one outgoing. After which, the shouts of the rioters reclaimed the streets. Ashur had made the decision to leave his helmet inside the tent, giving the sharpshooter a target. The counter snipers Ashur had posted dealt with him quickly, but not before their commander had been struck—a graze above the left ear. It bled profusely as head wounds generally do. Garwood called for a medic and knelt next to Ashur.

He sat up and took another look at the rioters in the streets and the burning junkyard of Chicago. "Give the order," he said, blood streaming over his eye. "Switch to live ammo. Kill 'em all."

Garwood nodded before pulling the radio off his belt and relaying the command. It was an instant. The officers on the line dropped their shields and clubs, trading them for the machine guns they carried on their backs. Like roaches when light is introduced, the protesters scurried for the shadows. And as bullets were let loose, for the first time in thirty years, a beam of light broke through the pollution over Chicago. The effect was magnificent.

The city fell into bloodshed as the first ray descend. The air, first orange and then red, turned into a shimmering gold as the inferno spread. And where the first beam struck the asphalt, the earth shattered. Like a coal town collapsing into the mine it's built upon, entire streets and city boroughs disappeared overnight. Some people were struck by bullets, some were run down by speeding vehicles, many were crushed by the collapsing cityscape, but almost all were caught in the light and boiled away until they were nothing but bones.

This moment would become the creation myth of a new world.

***

"Ashur," she said, standing over him. "Ashur wake up."

He awoke, drenched in sweat. "Who says that folktales aren't true?" he asked the darkness.

"You're dreaming again."

He sat up. "Sorry for waking you."

"Are you going back to sleep? It's still a few hours before sunup."

"No," he said. "No I don't think so." He stood up and grabbed the water off the nightstand, quickly emptying the glass. Rose took his bed and curled up with his pillows. It's what she normally did when she had to wake him. Her cot was not the most comfortable.

"Won't you tell me what you dream about?"

Ashur refilled his glass in the kitchen and then finished that one, after which he leaned on the threshold of the connecting doorway. "I have these…" He paused to catch his breath. "Attacks of the past. They don't only come in dreams. But they're a bit like drowning."

Chapter 12

Ashur and Rose lounged in a booth at Whiskey Breeze, grabbing lunch after training. Colfax sat at the back, dealing Stud to his buddies. Other than them, the staff, and a daytime-drunk who had passed out on the floor, the bar was empty, and no one, it seemed, was carrying on much of any conversation.

"This next song goes out those adorable little snuggle-bunnies currently trying to break in and eat my vital organs." "Just What I Needed" by the Cars began playing.

"Can we go bowling tonight?" she asked.

"Bowling?"

"Yeah. Does Tavern Springs have a bowling alley?"

"I think so," he said. "It used to at least. Why on earth would you want to go bowling?"

"Because it looks like fun."

"We could go bowling. *Or* you could work on your knots."

"*Or*," she said. "We could just go bowling."

Just then, a lantern-jawed man armored in cookware entered the saloon. "I'm looking for a man named Stanton!" he shouted. Ashur didn't move.

Colfax took note of this. "Why are you looking for a man named Stanton?" he asked after the tavern had returned to silence.

The man drew a gun. "You know where he is?"

"I may have some semblance of an idea about where he could possibly be."

"Don't play games with me," the man said and cocked his pistol. Ashur didn't let the situation escalate any further.

"I'm right here, boss. What do you need?"

"Looks like I've blown into town with the bad news," he said and pointed his gun. "Your head's got a pretty penny on it."

Ashur took a bite of his cornbread. "And this is dead I'm assuming."

"Er…you're worth more alive, but your rep says that's not likely to happen."

"You never know. I could be a pretty agreeable guy." A few of the poker players snickered at this proposal.

"You're not going to come quietly," said the bounty hunter.

"You know that for a fact? You shoot me now and you're losing money."

The look on the man's face was remarkable as was the one on Rose's.

"Uh…well, no. *Will* you go quietly so I can collect my bounty?"

"Sure," said Ashur.

"Really?"

"Uh-huh. But until then, you want to join us for lunch? I'll buy you a drink."

"Um…" the man lowered his gun in confusion. "Okay? Okay. But no funny business. Or I'll shoot you dead."

"I wouldn't think of it." The man sat down across from Ashur and next to Rose. She looked nervous, being boxed into a corner in a tense situation. He asked the man what he wanted to drink and then ordered it: a pint of mead. "So I'm Ashur, and this is Rose—say hello Rose."

"Hi."

"Uh…" the man said. "I'm Ted."

Ashur took another bite of his meal. "So how big is this bounty?" he asked, mouth still full of food.

"One-hundred platinum dead. A hundred-fifty if you're alive."

Ashur almost choked. That was Rockefeller kind of money. Ashur had enough saved up to pay him off if need be, but it would be all of his savings. "That's a good deal of money. Why am I wanted?"

"I didn't ask. I don't really care. I just want my money."

"I see. And how long have you been in the business?"

"I guess it's going on just over two weeks," Ted said. "I never gave a thought to the tracker's trade, but when I heard about the price on your head I figured I'd give it a shot. Turns out I'm pretty good at these dangerous games."

Lulu came out of the kitchen with the man's drink.

"You ever play Five Finger Fillet?" Ashur asked as she set it on the table. "Now there's a dangerous game."

"In my younger days sure," Ted said, reaching for his drink. "Why?"

"I've never been any good, thought maybe you could help me practice." Ashur stuck his hunting knife through the man's hand, pinning it to the table. The glass of mead was knocked onto the floor, making an awful mess. The man screamed in pain and went for his gun. But Rose pulled it first and put it to his head.

"*Oh God*," he screamed. "*Oh God it hurts!*"

The bar's guard sat not far from the altercation, going about his merry. He was on his lunch break. "You're an idiot," he said to the tracker and then continued with his grits.

"Now tell me," Ashur said. "Who was it that put the bounty on me?"

"*I-I can't tell you*," the man cried. "*He'd have me crucified.*"

Ashur twisted the knife.

"*Okay! Okay. Just stop for a second.*"

"Tell me and I'll stop."

"*Aaaagh!*" the man screamed. "They…they call him the Cadre. That's all I know. I swear on my mother's life!"

He twisted the knife again. "You must really hate your mother."

"*Aaahgh! He's…he's some hotshot at New Valley, r-runs the place. Now please stop.*"

Ashur eased up and the man dropped his head onto the table. He began to sob. "Now, bountyman, if I let you live am I ever going to see you again?" He cried for a time and Ashur had to restate the question before the proper answer was given. He removed his knife from the tracker's hand. He was gone in seconds. Thereafter, Ashur fell into thought.

"The Cadre," Rose said after noticing this. "That name means something to you."

"No," he said. "Not a thing. That's the part that worries me."

Chapter 13

Ashur knocked Rose onto the ground once more. He threw the butterfly knife into the grass next to her.

"Again!"

She picked up the knife and rushed him. When she made a swing, he caught her wrist and stepped around to pin her arm to her back. He forcefully relieved her grip on the blade and then shoved her forward, over his boot. She grunted when she hit the ground, barely stopping a face-plant by breaking the fall with her forearms. Ashur let the knife land close to one of her hands. He was going to break her legs and teach her how to walk again. And it was danger that he used—the greatest educator of them all.

"Stop fucking around!" he shouted. "Get up and fight!"

She started at him again, aggressively swinging the blade in complete disorder.

"If you can't learn to fight properly I'll put you out on the street," he said while he dodged her swings. After a close one, he knocked her onto the ground again. "I mean that, kiddo. Two weeks out there'll harden you the fuck up."

She remained on the ground this time, and Ashur saw her wipe a tear away, trying to hide it from him. It's what he had been waiting for.

He dropped to his knees. "Rose, look at me."

She did so. Rivulets trickled from her eyes. A second later, she tried to slap him across the face but Ashur caught her hand before it made contact. She started to bawl.

"You feel that? All the hurt, the confusion, the rage? You take it, all of it, and you put it away. *Shut it down.* If you let your emotions seep out in a fight, they will cripple you. So you bury them. Switch them off." He helped her up and cleaned some dirt off of her face, giving her a moment to recompose. "You're doing great," he said. "You can do this."

Once she was ready, he took a step back and they started again. This time, when she assaulted Ashur, she was more focused, more precise. In a few seconds, she nicked him with the end of the blade and that's when he put her in a half-nelson. He got hold of the knife and let her go, neglecting to put her in the dirt. "Much better," he said, holding up his arm to show her the blood.

She made a face. "Can we be done yet?"

"Yeah, I think we can take a break if—" It was then. There was a grave explosion to the west. A civil alert siren began howling and in an instant the streets were an ocean of chaos, waves of panicked people rushing every which way. "Scott!" shouted Ashur. "Call the depot!"

"I'm on it," he replied before getting on the landline inside his guard booth.

"Rose, get in the house."

"What's going on? I want to come with you!"

"That's not an option. Get inside and lock the door. Anyone comes in that's not me or Scott, you shoot them."

Ashur hurried into his garage and put on his set of heavy body armor. After which he grabbed his handgun and made sure Rose had locked the door from the inside. There were screams in the streets, all bleached out with sirens and a few more distant explosions. Scott came out of his booth dressed in his own set of body armor and carrying an assault rifle.

"Cruiser's in route," he said.

"Keep her safe."

"You can count on it."

Not a second later, an old patrol car skidded to a stop in front of the enclave, blue lights flaring. A duce and a half truck followed close behind, carrying a squad of specialized soldiers. Ashur had handpicked and vetted each one long ago. They wore black ski masks, combat helmets, and full suits of steel-plate armor. And when the sirens sounded, they belonged to him. A legionnaire hopped out of the cruiser and tossed Ashur a Kalashnikov rifle. He primed it.

And then they were gone.

***

Ashur sat in a plush leather chair directly opposite of Vanderbilt, Stacey likewise. The battle was done.

"What is our status?" Vanderbilt asked.

Stacey started to speak but Ashur shut her down. "Raid was repelled. They went for the dams. There were seven civilian fatalities—workers at the facility. Of the sentries, twenty-six casualties, one of my own legionnaires included, and nine fatalities. I'd expect it to climb to another six or seven by tonight."

"Quite unfortunate. And how did the dams fair?" At that moment someone up the river flipped a switch and the power returned.

"Damage was mostly superficial," Stacey jumped in, trying to assert her position as Master-at-Arms. While she officially held the title, she handled nothing more than the day-to-day, it was Ashur who the sentries and Vanderbilt turned to when shit went sideways—that's assuming he was in town and clear-minded. Since Ashur's establishment as a pillar of the sentry force, he had missed only one raid, and on that occasion Stacey acted in his place.

"Any leads into the faction responsible?" Vanderbilt asked.

Ashur retook the conversation and Stacey took the liberty of leaving the room, seeing it was pointless to try to play with the big kids.

"None. They didn't identify with any gang. But they were far more organized than they should have been. Had it been on a level playing field, they would've been on par with the sentry force."

"I would say. What was it? Twenty-six?"

"And nine dead."

"That is terrible," said Vanderbilt. "Do you expect a follow up attack?"

"It's hard to say. We dealt them a good deal of damage, took out more than fifty of them. But it was a targeted attack. They wanted the power out. I'd put the town on alert and mass sentries at the dams and wind-farms as well as the springs. We're not dealing with a normal road gang."

***

Ashur unlocked his front door and went inside. Rose came out of the bedroom and met him. Her hair was a mess. She'd attempted to use Ashur's old Ranger hat to hide it. She rushed over and gave him a hug, asking him if he was okay.

"I'm fine," he said. The speckles of blood on his clothing had already dried and went unnoticed.

"What happened?"

"Dam got raided by some badland gang—nice Stetson by the way. It's what that scrubby red head of yours always needed."

"It's not scrubby," she defended. "So is everything okay?"

"For now. But we did lose a number of men."

"Yeah, who were those guys that pulled up in the big truck?"

"In the black? Those are the Axehandle Hounds."

"Sounds like a sports team," Rose remarked.

"Yeah? Well they play for me. They're my company of sentries."

"You have your own company of sentries?"

"I handpicked and vetted each one on that force. They're all ex-military or police. Since their creation, I've taken to leading them whenever the siren sounds."

"Why haven't you brought them out on expeditions?" she asked.

"I have. They're always my first choice for an expeditionary force. You've even met a few. They just don't get geared up like that unless there's a raid or something of the nature. But here, check out what I got," he said before pulling out a laminated slip of paper. "A skybox pass to next week's Grand-Prix."

"No way!" She nearly tackled him for the luxury pass. "How did you get this!?"

"Vanderbilt is going to be busy with the town next week so he gave it to me as a little thank you present."

Her radiance dimmed. "But I can't go to Medway. I killed a Ranger."

"I don't think anyone's aware of that. Even if the Rangers knew, they wouldn't care. He didn't have a partner. Bill was a blackguard, even by their standards."

Chapter 14

They rode by a forest. Hill upon hill as far of the eye could see of toothpicks stuck in the dirt. It looked like a dark wood out of a German fairy tale. The naked sky, pale as an oyster shell, contrasted with the blackland dirt. The effect was sickening.

They rode under a freeway bridge. A new sign had been posted on the top of it listing points of interest and their respective distances. Something named **Looking Glass Point** was only two miles out.

"Rose, pay attention. You don't want to miss this."

"What is it?"

"A contra-spectacle. The first wonder of the new world."

When they came upon it, the sun of high-noon made it shimmer like an ocean of gold. It ran on for miles, engulfing a centerpiece: a lighthouse upon a jutting rock, faded from red to a muddy brown by the Collapse.

"Is that Lake Michigan?" she asked.

"Just watch."

As they drew close it became clear. It was not Lake Michigan. It was not even a lake. Not anymore. What had been the hope for a sight of beauty fluttered away, being replaced by a scene of the Sun's power.

"Oh," she said softly, taken aback.

Looking Glass Point was the single largest plain of glass in all the five lakes, thick enough to drive across. It was as Ashur described it, a contra-spectacle. Forged by nature's backlash, the glassed countryside was seen anew one night a week when the Looking Glass Point Society turned on the lighthouse to reap the grain of the Elysian Field.

Just off of the plain, in the distance, a tower of thick, black smoke rose, the likes of which reminded Ashur of the darker days when the sun was scarce and every city had a funeral pyre.

"What happened there?" she asked.

A mile later, they came upon a caravan. It had been decimated moments ago. The plume of black smoke rose from the cargo, all of it set in a pile and torched till it crackled. Around the site lay a number of dead Rangers and a number of others. Ashur couldn't tell which ones were bandits and which ones were the Company's hired help. They all looked clean. In the moments thereafter, a second convoy appeared on the horizon. Ashur pulled an injured, delirious man from the ash and into the road. When the Ranger squadron crept up, he was waiting. Three cars, each carrying two to three Rangers, stopped opposite of them and the wounded survivor. He was hemorrhaging blood, and unless someone stopped it, he wouldn't be around much longer. The Rangers left the vehicles and stood in a herd, just within earshot. One officer stood before all the others. Pinned to his especially clean, and pressed, black duster, was a badge like all the rest—yet more glorified.

"Howdy, Deputy," Ashur said in a put-on southern drawl. "Impressive response time."

"What happened here?"

"I believe the technical term for it is, y'all got fucked."

"Is this your doing, Grimm?"

"You think I'd be standing here if it was?" He hoisted the wounded man up on to his knees. "This one might be able to shed some light on it. He one of yours?"

"I don't recognize him," said Deputy Sloan. "Doesn't look like a Company man either."

Ashur knocked him around a bit and he perked up. "Hey, bandit boy, suns up."

The kid looked around, his eyes dilating sporadically. "Grimm? Grimm. Gri…" He saw the squadron of Rangers, then the man towering over him, and a girl a few paces back near a the motorcycle. He began to laugh an incessant, dry, wheezing laugh. "Fairytale Grimm? How'd he get a name like that?" he said mockingly. "Have you heard of his handiwork? What else would they call him?"

"Ask him who he belongs to," Sloan called. None of the Rangers seemed eager to advance.

"He's coming for you, Stanton. Gonna skin you. Your pretty girl too…crucify your town. Make throws…out of the lot of you," he said faintly, blood streaming out of his mouth. He was getting heavier. The man went limp and Ashur released his grasp. The corpse settled in the dirt.

"What do you make of that?" Sloan asked.

Ashur looked at the burning cargo, all the dead bodies. They had taken nothing. "This was done to make a point," he said beginning towards the deputy.

"I'd appreciate any insight you have," the deputy said, likewise walking to meet him.

If there was anyone in the Rangers Ashur thought highly of, it was Deputy Sloan. Even if he did work for the Company, his actions continued to embody the old Ranger principles. As long as his heroics didn't interfere with business, the boss gave him no heat.

"You're looking at a man who calls himself the Cadre. He's got some heavy influence over the dregs of New Valley as I understand it."

"How do you know this?"

"I've had to dispatch no more than a couple of his bountymen. He wants me gone, whoever he is."

Sloan smirked. "How big's the bounty on your head."

Ashur returned the smirked, like it was a thing to be proud of. "That's a stupid question to answer."

"Well, it's not much to go on but thanks," Sloan said while looking over the dead bodies and the pile of burning merchandise. "It's something." They shook hands and parted ways. Ashur collected Rose and they continue onward. The duo passed a number of travelers and caravans as they neared Medway. These routes were safe. Or so they had been up until late.

The next structure they came upon was colossal: Grand Citadel Dakota, the heart of the Rangers. A work of masonic engineering, it had taken years to complete. Laid out as a six point star, the fort looked as uncompromising as it was self-righteous—a monument to old world values. On one of the outlying buffers to the structure was Medway's town motto, **Ex Pompeii Romam Surgit**, with their English transformation below, **From the Ash Rises a New Kingdom**.

Medway's front gate was grand, as was the line that formed outside it. The grand prix was a cause for travel, and therefore, traffic. They crept to a stop behind a blue sedan and Ashur set his feet on the ground to stabilize the bike.

"How long is this going to take?" Rose said as she squinted to see the end of the motorized river. Ashur didn't respond. Instead he picked up his feet and blasted down alongside the line of cars, provoking horns and foul language from the other tourists. The checkpoint was tall and produced from stone, as the Citadel was. The masonic extravagance braced a massive, iron bell as well as a neon sign with the town's name. A few cars were poised underneath the enclave, presently being searched and their drivers' paperwork checked.

The entire lineup was honking now, flashing high beams in protest. One of the Rangers notice Ashur sitting at the front and came towards the bike. "Back of the line," he said, shotgun in his hands.

"You don't understand—"

"I understand fine. Go to the back of the line."

"Do you *know* who I am?" he asked.

The Ranger studied them for a moment. "I know who you are," he said finally. "And I don't care. Back of the line."

"It's a matter of urgency. Deputy Sloan sent me to report—"

"Deputy Sloan did no such thing. I talked to him myself just a few minutes ago. Now," the officer said as he cocked his shotgun. "*Back of the line*."

"Is there anyone else around I could talk to? Someone I know perhaps?"

"Is that how this is going to go?"

Ashur was about to turn away and head for the back when a tall, shoe-string man in a varsity jacket walked up. "Ashur?" he said. "Ashur Stanton is that you?"

It was Top-Driver Danny "The Dirty" Danworth. Ashur had met him back in his law enforcement days while on auxiliary duty at the track. A dreadful mix of frat-brother and redneck, Danworth was well known to most as a card-carrying member of the debaucherous party.

"Danworth," Ashur said. "How's it hanging?"

"A little to the right," he said. "Just getting done with all the travel formalities. Y'all coming to the race this afternoon?"

"Wouldn't miss it for the world. We've got a skybox."

"No shit? I'll have to stop by before—"

The Ranger with the shotgun cut them off. "Sir, you need to move on so we can process the next in line." The group of Rangers that had been huddled around Danworth's battle-ready Barracuda were now talking to the next driver in line.

"You think you could squeeze us in there, Danworth?" Ashur asked. "The line's terrible."

"They're making you wait?"

"Yes," the Ranger jumped in. "We are. They have to wait like everyone else."

Danworth smiled. "Not anymore they don't."

"I don't think you have that kind authority, sir."

"Do you *know* who I am?" Danworth asked.

"Everyone here is aware of who you are. But that doesn't change anything."

Danworth pulled another smile on the man. There was something hopelessly deranged about it. "You two don't go anywhere," he said before starting over for his car. He came back with an official-looking piece of paper and threw it in the Ranger's face. "They're my plus two," he said. "They're in my group."

The Ranger read over the gilded document and then eyed them all with the spite of a bested bureaucrat. "Very well," he said quickly. "Grimm, pull your bike on through next to his car."

Ashur did as instructed and they got off. Both Ashur and Rose were in awe standing next to the Barracuda. Danworth's car was glorious: neon green paint, with a single stamped-metal piece for the engine hood and rear trunk. The rear window had steel louvers and the wheels had contact guards as well as jutting tire shredders for death-racing. On the stainless-steel hood, above the hood pins and below the bloodstain was painted in a stylized font, **The Dirty Danworth**. The number twenty-nine was likewise, painted on the roof.

"I can't believe you actually, personally know the Dirty Danworth," Rose shrieked.

"He's an old acquaintance of mine."

"Acquaintance?" Danworth broke in, catching up with them. "I've let you ride in my car. I don't do that for just anybody."

"All right then," Ashur said. "We're old friends. So would you like a ride in the Barracuda?"

"Oh my God. Can I?" she asked Danworth.

"Wish you could, darling, but I replaced the passenger seat *long* ago," he said, sounding mournful.

"With what?" Ashur asked.

"Why a mini-bar of course!"

The Ranger came over with a plastic tub to collect the duo's weapons. Rose unloaded her guns and handed them over, then her sword and throwing knives. But the Ranger continued waiting. Ashur nudged her. Then she added her butterfly knife to the tub. The official got a second box for Ashur. He unloaded his rifle, handgun, and shotgun and gave them up, followed by his hunting knife. The Ranger waited. Then Rose nudged him. Only then did Ashur add his boot knife and brass knuckles. But the Ranger stayed, shaking the box at him. He rolled his eyes and then spit a razorblade into the bin.

"Holy shit, son," said Danworth. "You're a dangerous motherfucker."

Ashur smirked. "You ever need anything taken care of, just give me a shout."

"You'll be the first I call."

The Ranger took their things inside and came back out to search the bike for prohibited items. He found none. "Your weapons will be stored under Danworth's name. I assume you're all familiar with our laws. If you have any questions, there's an information building right over there." He pointed to a portable office. "Enjoy the race."

With that, the group prepared to leave the checkpoint.

"I'll see y'all at the race," Danworth said, unnecessarily sliding into his car through the window. "Come see me after my victory lap. I'll pose for pictures. I'll even let the lady touch the gold." He drove off, a ferocious sound following the Barracuda. The duo followed his path.

Medway proved to be an unreal city. Its pretentious Latin motto had some ground to stand on. Its paths were cobblestone and polished, its streetlamps tall and crafted. Its temples of business were concrete and steel and plate-glass. No graffiti here. It looked less like a new Rome and more like an old English commons. A crowd flowed over a bridge as they rode through the city streets, each man's eyes fixed before his feet. Ashur could pick out the occasional exception: a robber baron crowned with a silk hat, chin held uncomfortably high to compensate for the others.

Rose remained thunderstruck at the sight of it all, mouth left agape. "I finally get to see the great city."

"Is that what they call it?"

"How can you not love this place?" she asked as they stopped at a red light. "Look," she said, pointing at a man in a suit reading a newspaper. "There's a man in a suit reading a newspaper." The man gave her an odd look and then scampered away to find somewhere else to read.

"Don't point, Rose. It's rude to point."

"Sorry."

The Medway Amphitheater dwarfed any contemporary structure Ashur had seen, excluding Grand Citadel Dakota. Set in drab concrete and capable of seating thousands with ease, it was oblong, and laden with beautiful stone work, sculpted iconic columns, and statues of heroes, amongst them, the Roman captain Horatius and his faithful companions.

Chapter 15

The track for the grand prix was the classic figure-eight. Heavy trucks lumbered around it, wetting it down with vast tanks of water. This was done for two reasons, first, to keep the dust from kicking up during the race, and second, to ensure the track was slippery enough for a good show. Groundlings were already starting to find their places on the edges of the tracks. No one much worried about the possibility of a car spinning off adding some more color to the race. Those seats were, after all, the cheapest.

Ashur and Rose moved along through the crowds in the concessions area before eventually finding the elevator to the sixth floor—the corporate suites. They followed the bending corridor until they got to their door. Ashur pushed the buzzer and a staff member came to the window: a twenty-something Aryan girl scattered with freckles and hair like a river. She wore a tight tank top and a short skirt. They fit well.

"May I see your suite pass?" she asked.

He pressed it up against the glass and she opened the door.

"So pleased you could join us again this year, Mr. Stanton, and…guest." She paused for Rose to insert her name and then looked her over. "Mayor Vanderbilt was too busy this time around as well, I take it?"

"Yes," Ashur said. "That man's going to work himself to death someday soon."

"That's a shame. But I'm happy you two were able to make it here to enjoy the show. First things first, let's get the formalities out of the way shall we? The reservation pass and coats and drinks and such," she said with a practiced smile. Ashur gave her the pass and then his field coat, Rose decided to keep her hoodie as the luxury suite was well air conditioned. Ashur ordered a brandy, he had been craving one since he smelt it on Danworth, and Rose ordered a cider.

"I'm sorry but I'm going to have to ask you for some form of ID. Medway has a strict drinking age of eighteen."

"I'm afraid this is her first time to Medway," Ashur answered for her. "She doesn't have any papers."

"Then I'm afraid I'll have to offer you something else to drink. We have a wide assortment of other refreshments."

"Are you sure you couldn't overlook the bit about ID?" he asked.

"I'm sorry, Ashur. I can't do that. So what would you like, honey?"

Rose ordered a cola and the attendant disappeared. There were probably twenty seats in the box, almost all of them destine to lay empty in a sold-out amphitheater. The room was complete with its own bathroom, bar, buffet table, and viewing area, which included a row of seats at the top with a counter. Up in each corner of the room were swiveling flat-screen TVs so that no matter which way one faced, they could see the violence in Technicolor. The two went to find a chair at the viewing counter.

"What was all that about?" Rose asked.

"What do you mean?"

"She gave me the up and down when I got in here, and then she wouldn't give me a drink. And she called you Ashur."

"It's probably because she thinks you're…" Ashur trailed off and pretended to be interested in something else.

"She thinks I'm what?"

"Huh? Oh I forgot what I was going to say."

That moment, the bright-eyed attendant came back with their drinks. "The pre-race destruction derby will begin in about an hour. Food will be available at the buffet soon after that. Is there anything else I can help either of you with?"

"No," Ashur said. "Thank you." He watched her as she walked away. When he was finished, he found Rose had been staring at him.

"You know her. That's it isn't it?"

"No. That's not it at all."

"Then what is it?"

"I knew her," Ashur said.

"What?" It took Rose a couple seconds to get it to click right. "Ew!" she exclaimed. "I didn't want to know that."

"Then you shouldn't have been so nosy."

"But I don't even…like, *how?* You were here alone before—"

"She asked me if there was anything she could do to make my stay more enjoyable."

"Oh God!" she said, covering her ears. "That just made it so much worse."

Ashur laughed till he snorted. "That was rich," he said afterwards, as he wiped his eyes. They watched the stadium fill up with patrons while sipping on their drinks. The water trucks finished slicking the dust and soon cars were brought out for preparation of the derby. Ashur stood up calmly. "I'm going to head to the bathroom," he said. Rose barely noticed. When he got there, he was first delighted to see they had added TVs to the bathrooms since last year. Then he made a beeline for the first stall and threw up. Blood churned in the toilet bowl with whatever was left from his breakfast.

"Stomach's so raw it's kicking back brandy," he said to himself. He wiped his mouth and then washed his face. The derby would be starting soon, a six car free-for-all. Nothing extraordinarily exciting happened in pre-race derbies, but they were fun to watch nonetheless. He returned to the counter and settled in next to Rose.

"Do you have any siblings, Ashur?"

He looked over at her and the gaze he caught confused him. "I was an only child. Though I did live with my aunt and uncle the latter half of my childhood. My cousin and I grew pretty close. He considered me a brother, liked to address me as such."

"Yeah?"

"Yeah. He made it through the end of it all. Became a renowned tracker—still is one if he's living. Why the sudden interest?"

"Because your brother's at the door," she said.

"What?" He turned around and saw a familiar face in the window. It smiled at him. He always hated that stupid smile. Wanted to drive a fist right into it.

"Are you going to let him in?"

"I don't know. He could be working for the Cadre. Johnny is a bountyman after all."

"But we're safe here," she said. "No one has any weapons."

"That's exactly why we're not safe." He started towards the security door and depressed the button for the speaker. "Hello, Johnny."

"I go by Jackstraw now."

"You'll always be Johnny to me. What are you here for?"

"You don't sound excited to see me. I can't drop by to say hello?" Jackstraw pushed his face up against the glass so that he looked like a thing deflated. "Why won't you love me?"

"You never drop by to say hello."

Jackstraw pulled his face back. "You're right, little brother. I'm afraid I've brought some bad news, but I'd rather deliver it in person."

"We are in person."

"You know what I mean. Open the door."

Ashur stepped back and opened the door, allowing Jackstraw to slither in. He stood near the same height as cousin. He was gaunt and slick with the bone structure of a gypsy and the eyes of a marksman—metallic grey. Draped over a semi-completed set of riot armor was a navy-blue fireman's jacket, and clipped to his belt was a smoke jumper's nickel-plated badge. Had there been any doubt that he was kin to Ashur, the name STANTON across the back of the jacket eliminated it.

"What's the news?"

Jackstraw put his hand on Ashur's shoulder. "My mom passed away."

He frowned. "I'm sorry to hear. I assume the funeral has already been held."

Jackstraw nodded.

"I'm sorry I wasn't there."

"It's not like I could have phoned you up and said, 'Hey, run on down to New St. Lou for a little.' Now could I? You guys never got along anyways."

"Regardless," he said as they returned to the countertop. "She took care of me. I owed her that much at least."

Rose stood up to greet them. "I'm sorry about your aunt," she said to Ashur and then hugged him.

"Thank you," he said. "Johnny, this is—"

"Rose Marianne Waters, of Wellshire," he stated. "Your…" He broke off to find a word, inspecting her as he did. "Ward."

"My ward?"

"I believe that term works. Yes." Jackstraw reached out for a handshake, taking her in. "You are quite the looker, aren't you," he said and then got around to her face. "I like your freckles."

"Nice to meet you too," she muttered, dropping his hand. "How do you know me?"

"It's my job to know things about people. I get paid to know things like how to get an audience with Ashur Stanton." He turned to Ashur and said, "Can I get something to drink? I'm parched."

Without hesitation, he grabbed the glass his brandy had been served in and began towards the bar, Jackstraw in lockstep.

"You still drink like it's the end of the world?" Jackstraw asked.

"I just quit actually."

"You picked a hell of a time."

"Is there any other time?" Ashur asked, thereafter ordering a ginger ale. Jackstraw got a mineral water, as well as a gin and tonic. Ashur dropped a bronze piece on the counter as tip.

"Thank you," she said as she scraped the coin into her hand and then pocketed it. "Food will be here shortly. Will there be anything else?"

"No. Thank you."

They returned to Rose, drinks in hand, and sat down at the counter to watch the destruction derby. It had only just begun and none of the cars had been knocked out yet.

"So how's the tracker's trade been?" asked Ashur. "How's the Southland?"

"Both are pretty bad. I've had a hard time finding work ever since the Pope took power in New St. Lou. That whole city is a nut-case. And with mom gone I don't see a reason to go back."

"If you decide to stay, I don't think you'll have trouble finding work up here."

"That's good to know," Jackstraw said. "The XP life treating you well then?"

"No shortage of coin on my end. I've been sitting pretty for years since I started contracting for Vanderbilt. Of course I still have plenty of independents."

"No shit? Well if you're interested I heard about one here in Medway. Basic scavenging run but the client's on the Company's board, so the payout's something like twenty-gold."

"I might take you up on that."

"I hope you do."

They took a moment to watch the instant replay of the first knockout. His coach had thrown up a red card so the players were now returning to their starting positions while it was under review. Eventually the officials concluded that the aggressor had purposefully slammed into the opponent's driver-side door with excessive force. He was given a black flag, but because of the nature of the game, both drivers were out of the fight. The crowd booed, some at the driver, some at the officials. But all of them quickly forgot about it when the derby continued.

Jackstraw leaned forward so he could make eye contact with the girl on the other side of Ashur. "Now what's the story with this one?" he asked.

"Don't you know already?" she mocked.

"Just your name and what you look like and where you're from. And your grandma's farm, and your brother, and—"

"I'm Ashur's protégé. Been running with him near eight months. Not much of a story."

Jackstraw sounded surprised. "He's training you?"

"He is."

"So you live with him?"

"What's it to you?"

Jackstraw grinned. "She's got some fight in her, Ashur."

"Stop treating me like that," she said. "I'm sick of people treating me like that."

"Like what?"

She eyed at the attendant across the room, catching her gaze. "Like I'm fucking him," she said. The blonde glanced away and then wandered off to find a chore more productive than eavesdropping. Luckily for her, the door buzzed. "That will be the food," she said and answered it. The derby was down to two by the time the buffet table was set up. The group got up and made themselves plates. There were platters of wings, sandwiches, and hotdogs. Back at the counter, the group began on their food as the winner of the derby emerged: a beat up Chevy Blazer with a German flag painted on the roof. He made half a victory lap before his transmission spontaneously gave out, allowing the track keepers to come on and prepare the dirt patch for the race.

Ashur took a bite of a hotdog, and keeping his eyes on the track asked, "Are you here to kill me, Johnny?"

Jackstraw went on unfazed by the question, picking up his drink to wash down a chunk of sandwich. Rose on the other hand was glued to the conversation like a kid past curfew to a bad horror flick. "To be honest," he said. "When I got to the door I was still undecided. But now you're treating me to a hot meal, free drinks, and the show of the year." He looked at Rose. Contempt sparkled in her eyes.

Ashur continued working on his food, talking with his mouth full. "If Rose wasn't here would you axe me?"

"You know, times are tough and life's a cutthroat business," Jackstraw said and wiped his greasy hands on Ashur's shirt, pretending to pat his shoulder in a brotherly manner. "But at the end of the day you're still family." He took a moment to light a cigarette. "And without family, what do you really got?"

Chapter 16

The grand prix was prefaced as it had been every year since the foundation of the Blackland Racing League seven years ago. The eight contestants stood in a lineup in the center of the arena while a camera displayed their faces on a jumbotron.

"Thank you, ladies and gentlemen, for joining us the afternoon for what is the Blackland Racing League's seventh annual grand prix," the speakers boomed. "I'm your host GL, here to start everything off, and sticking it out with you through those long and tiresome Medway Trading Company adverts. Speaking of which, this year's grand prix is sponsored, solely and wholly, by the Medway Trading Company, your friendly, mom and pop mega-corporation. If a holocaust didn't destroy big business, I don't know what will."

While this went on, the MTC's logo flashed on the jumbotron and all the smaller TVs in the suites. The entire arena in fact was plastered in Company ads. These were soon replaced with a close up of the pin on Danworth's varsity jacket, which designated him as last year's champion. In fact, he had been the champion for the past two years, and before that he had been a member of the League since its founding. Everybody loved him because no matter how bad the wreck was, he always walked away. During interviews, he claimed it had something to do with his special brandy.

"Let's get this year's Exordium underway. Starting us off, and with no need for an introduction, we have Top-Driver Danny 'The Dirty' Danworth." A montage of clips of his carnage began playing on the screen. There were a number of takedowns, a pileup he had induced, a beheading with a tire-spoke, and then two check- ered flags. *"He will be driving his famous green-machine, the Barracuda, under the flag of the number twenty-nine. Two years our champion, and seven years the senior most racer, Danworth hails from that untamed wilderness we call the Southland."*

His image faded away, being replaced by one of a large Spaniard with a dragon tattoo on his face. *"In the second seat we have Solrac Fernandez, driving the Trans AM under the number twenty-one. In the third placement, it's Red Julius in his cherry-red Thunderbird under the number five-and-a-half...one moment please."* He broke off and whispered to an aid before then continu- ing with, *"Apparently that's correct. Moving on. In the fourth bracket we have number four-twenty-seven, Sivart Marsh in the Charger. Next is Smitty in his Ford Mustang, number forty-two. After that is The Wizard, number eighty-eight in the Buick Grand National. Jordi Mcknot takes the seventh bracket in his blacked out Camaro under the number thirteen. And lastly, playing the part of the underdog, we have El Bobador, number ninety-nine, in what looks to be a very pedestrian Mercedes Benz."* The image on the screen transitioned from El Bobador—a pale, blonde-haired man with a gruesome scar across his eye—to the image of his car. It was clean and unarmored with a broad band of black tape across the backend which denoted a novice racer.

After that, the camera panned out to encompass all of the sacrifices. In one unified voice they spoke the traditional opening to the game. *"We who are about to die, salute you. Avete vos."*

A fire was lit at the head of the figure eight and the racers proceeded to their cars. Danworth once again, unnecessarily, got in through the window of his car and then poured himself a drink.

Over the loudspeakers, from the Racing League's sergeant-at-arms, came, *"Gentlemen, start your engines."* The line came alive with the combined growl of eight ferocious vehicles—a roar that told the crowd that the racers held little intention of showing mercy to their engines, their rivals, or themselves. *"This race will conclude at either one hundred laps, or the disabling of five of the eight vehicles. Any spectators in fear for their life should leave the track immediately. This will be your only warning. There will be no black flags."*

Some of the groundlings scurried off of the edges of the dirt track, while others simply moved towards the back, so that they were behind a barricade of people. When they settled, more spectators had stayed than left. And then the flag dropped.

All the cars came around the first lap with no drama, and the second, but after that contact was made. The first hit was delivered from the Wizard to Danworth—a love tap. El Bobador placed towards the last position but kept close enough to be out of harm's way when it came to the center intersection. The Dirty Danworth, Fernandez, and the Wizard all competed for the top spot, with Smitty not far behind.

The seventh lap was where things got hectic. On the straight, the Wizard overtook Danworth and at the turn spun out on the wet mud, stopping just before the crowd. It left only the left side of the track open. Red Julius was boxed in on his left by McKnot and from behind by Marsh. As a result, Julius dealt the stalled Wizard a glancing blow, which deflected him into McKnot, causing an obstacle Marsh couldn't avoid. By the time they had untangled themselves, sending mud all over the groundlings in the process, they were a near half lap behind, which made for exciting crossroads. Danworth maintained the lead, followed closely by Smitty and then Fernandez.

At the second crossover since the wreck, Smitty and Danworth were neck and neck, careening towards a collision with the Wizard. No one braked.

Smitty plowed headlong into the Wizard, killing them both on impact, while Danworth had his backend clipped, sending him spinning down the straight. He leveled out and then drove in reverse for the length of the straight. When he slid around the bend, he flipped a J-turn, keeping his spot at first. Smitty and the Wizard, their momentums combined, skidded through the plywood wall set up to denote the figure 8 and came to rest in the expanse, inside one of the loops. The Wizard's Grand National started on fire thereafter.

The racers didn't have to go so fast that they would wreck. They didn't have to kill each other. But they chose to. They did it for the money, and the fame, and the bloodlust. This was the fun and these were games—racing as it ought to be. No one, not the racers nor the spectators, cared if anyone bought it. With a life in this world, there really was nothing to lose. Anything was better than dying of old age as far as they were concerned.

The race calmed down after that, a few bumps and scraps, a spinout or two, but nothing serious. At lap sixty, Fernandez pulled into first, followed by Julius, pushing Danworth into third. They rounded a bend in succession. What occurred next was very, very quick. Fernandez lost traction and began fishtailing as he came onto the straight. Seeing this, Red Julius sped up to give him a helping hand, but it backfired. Julius was swept away, downriver by Marsh as they met at high speeds in the intersection. Marsh's Charger tumbled bumper over bumper into the crowd, crushing a number of people. Red Julius's Thunderbird followed soon after. It was an hour before anyone came to right the vehicles and clean up the mess.

Fernandez, having lost total control of his car, rolled and was ejected out of the driver-side window into the path of Danworth.

He pulled the handbrake and tugged the wheel, attempting to slide into Fernandez mid-flight with the broadside of his car, but he had braked too early. Fernandez simply rolled over the roof of Danworth's car and landed in the mud. When Fernandez found his bearings and stood up—it was clear that his arm was broken—he was cropped off at the shins by McKnot and became a gory hood ornament. His head smashed through the Camaro's windshield. They replayed that one in slow motion a number of times. As for Fernandez's Trans AM, it lay abandoned in the last quarter of the second straight.

That was the end of the game. As the checkered flag fell, Danworth came out as reigning champion, Jordi Mcknot took the runner-up, and El Bobador, who had done his best to avoid any and all conflict in the race, took home the bronze.

Chapter 17

Ashur stepped over the skeletal remains of someone from long ago. Having left their vehicles a ways back, he, Jackstraw, and Rose trekked through the pathless country, over fallen structures and cracked infrastructure. They were working the job Jackstraw had mentioned before the race. They were going to a sugar themed amusement park to look for a teddy bear. Now out in the blackland, Jackstraw kept a long-barreled revolver strapped to his hip and slung over his shoulder bounced his prized Stratofield anti-tank rifle.

"We call them brothers so long as we have what we want. You don't see the milk of human kindness in the bellies of the starving. What's that say about us as a species?"

"Man isn't inherently good or evil, Johnny. He's violent when oppressed. He's gentle when free, as is most every creature." Ashur laced his fingers together and helped Jackstraw and then Rose vault over a toppled truck trailer. It had the amusement park's logo painted on the side.

"Uplifting," said Jackstraw as he pulled Ashur up. "Not what I would expect from you."

They chuckled at each other.

"I don't get it," Rose said. The sound of a car missing a muffler was audible some distance away.

"You didn't miss anything important. Why don't you hold up here? Jack and I'll do a bit of scouting. We'll call for you when we're ready."

Rose set herself down against the skeleton of a sedan and brought out a canteen. "Just don't leave me out here long. It's creepy out here." He nodded and then left to catch up with Jackstraw, whom had hopped a chain-link fence into the unpaved parking lot. When he caught up, they were standing atop a hill, overlooking a small portion of Candy Mountain's entrance. A Ferris wheel, rollercoasters, tilt-a-whirls, all lay lifeless under a sky of mixed greys and browns. Signs of an approaching storm were present. This was considered scenic in the New Age.

"Behold, the first society to live amongst the ruins of its own creation," said Jackstraw as he pulled something out of his pocket and handed it to Ashur. It was small earpiece. Ashur inserted it into his ear, afterwards, waltzing towards the edge of the hill and peering over what was left of a cinderblock wall. At the base of the embankment, a pair of Rangers moved about near their truck. One was placing some scrap iron in the bed while the other watched.

"Check it out, Socrates," said Ashur. "Lollipop Rangers."

"I got five silver says one round."

Ashur agreed. They shook hands and Jackstraw starting humming while he set up his rifle on the dilapidated wall. He finished adjusting the scope and, keeping tune loud enough for the Rangers to make out, sang, "*More than this, you may behold, the fountains flow with brandy, the rocks are like re-fined gold, the hills are sugar candy.*" When the cowboys turned to draw their guns in response, their heads lined up perfectly. He fired. Both Rangers fell dead and the truck's back-left tire deflated. "I'll be expecting that five silver."

"It's yours."

Jackstraw unsheathed a knife and carved two more tally marks onto the receiver of his Stratofield.

"You keep tallies?"

"Just head shots." The sniper finished with his gun and stood up. "You don't?"

"I think it's tasteless." Ashur stuck his fingers in his mouth and let out a high-pitched whistle to call for Rose. "Defacing a beautiful piece of equipment like that." They started down the hill and got to where the Rangers were.

Rose reached the congregation in a quiet and timely fashion. "Why'd you kill them?" she asked upon seeing the corpses.

"I bet Ashur five silver that I could get them both in one shot."

She glanced between the two XPs. "You two are definitely related. Aren't the Rangers going to come after us or something?"

"Nah," said Jackstraw. "Things happen to Rangers in the badlands all the time. It's a—what's the phrase?" he asked, snapping his fingers in thought.

"An occupational hazard," Ashur finished for him.

"Yeah, that."

"Did you have a partner while you were in the Rangers?" she asked Ashur, opening the door of the truck to search for anything useful. She found a can of red spray paint.

"Every Ranger is supposed to have a partner."

"But you didn't. Slugger didn't. Why not?"

"Because he was a cowboy."

"I meant you," she said. "You know I meant you."

He checked one of the Ranger's duster chest pockets. He found a photo of a young boy and mother. It was recent. "Because after the world ended I had a hard time relying on anyone. Is that what you want to hear?"

She stowed the paint can in her pack. "You mean trusting them?"

He returned the photo to the duster before anyone else could see it. "I didn't want to be responsible for anyone. I just wanted to go lone-wolf for a while."

"I guess that's changed, huh?"

He kicked a bit of dust up onto her boots. "Keep looting, flower girl."

Jackstraw came over to relieve the dead Rangers of their sidearms and badges. As he did this, he started up singing his broadside ballad again. He sang of a land not far from here, where the pigs called out to be eaten. The people there wore silks and velvet and the pudding couldn't be beaten. He finished with the Rangers and walked over to the hood of the truck. "*Rose water is the rain they have, which comes in pleasant showers. All places are adorned brave, with sweet and fragrant flowers.*" Rose made eye contact with him. "Hey, Red. Do me a solid and pop the hood." She hopped in and found the release latch. An audible pop. Jackstraw went straight for the wiring loom, slicing it.

She left the pickup. "You think there's actually a place out there like that, Ashur?" He brought himself up from whatever he was doing, looked at her deadpan, and then return to looting. "Well I like to think there is," she said. "Somewhere."

"That's the adventurer's spirit in you," Jackstraw said. "Never stop looking, kid."

They pushed on into Candy Mountain. The place was coated in pink and yellow, the mixture faded to a fawn by the sun. The ticket booth was just as desolate—cracked wood under brittle paint, a number of flyers roaming about the ground. Rose was the only one to actually go through the metal turnstile. It was locked up so she had to give it a good shove and ended up a few steps behind the others. "I wonder what became of the carnies," she said.

"You mean…you haven't heard?" Ashur said.

"Heard what?"

He let his voice fall into an eerie groan. "Late at night, killer cannibal clowns prowl this fairground, searching for their stash of stolen tickets and eating random teenagers."

"*Stop*," Rose griped. "I *hate* clowns."

"Say, I've heard that," Jackstraw joined in. "And they have stale candy corn for teeth and an unnatural ability to avoid the dunk tank balls, causing the thrower untold amounts of harassment." Even Rose laughed at this.

The group wandered into a corridor with concession stands and picnic tables. There was a comment about funnel cakes before Rose asked where they were supposed to find a teddy bear. Ashur halted and the others did the same. The rusted creaking of the fair reminded him of something he had heard on the northern front during the war—the rumbling of troops and transports behind enemy lines on quiet nights. He felt an internal spring winding tighter and tighter. In a moment, he would once more be thrust into the world of violence and bloodshed.

He drew his lever-action rifle and methodically moved to cover behind an overturned hotdog stand. Rose followed his example, noticing that Jackstraw was no longer with them. The next noise they heard was the shriek emitted when a needle first touches vinyl. Throughout the air fluttered the tune of "Abdul Abulbul Amir." Bulbs flickered as Candy Mountain came to life. Bells rang and merry-go-rounds picked up where they had last left off. An electronic fortune teller bayed their attention, promising to reveal what life had long kept concealed. Jackstraw saw them first, flipping through the air from roof top to roof top, quickly and without faltering.

"*Lissome Clan,*" he told Ashur over the earpiece. "*What the fuck are they doing out this way?*"

"It's a travelling show," Ashur said and then to Rose: "I've dealt with these guys. They're agile and fast, carry melee weapons. Keep your distance."

The acrobats quickly boxed them in on all sides, running along the tops of the concession stands and rides. The most of them were painted white and carried war clubs. Their movement settled as the last verse of the song came to a close. Jackstraw sang along with it. After this there was undisturbed stillness.

A solitary man, dressed in a dapper coat and top hat stepped out of a tent at the far end of the corridor. He carried with him a cane clutched in white, gloved hands. He spun it fervently. "Come one! Come all!" he cried. "Come see the circus at the end of the Earth! Open this fall, an utter rebirth. I'll invite you but once, impart it to you. You'll play the dunce and the games shall ensue. 'What games?' you may ask. Why they're the bloodiest kind. One task to complete, all rules left behind. If you should succeed— unlikely this day—please cart up our things, and haul them away. Keep what you will, but if you should fail, well, my friends that's the end of your tale."

A second stillness set it. Jackstraw broke it. *"How do you kill a circus?"* he asked.

"Go for the juggler."

"What juggler?" Rose asked. In what the tribals might have taken to be bolt of lightning from God, their circus crier was cut down before them. With that first gunshot, the cotton-candy coated violence began. They closed in. Ashur dropped two at the far end of the corridor before turning his attention elsewhere. Rose flung a few throwing knives before pulling her revolvers. One of the knives caught a native in the throat as he jumped down from a pizza booth. Another of the clan leapt up, coming down on top of Ashur, swinging his club. He held up his rifle to block the blow, but the hit knocked the gun out of his grasp.

Ashur stunned the wastelander with a quick fist between the eyes and then grabbed his shotgun, tucking it in underneath the combatant's chin. He pulled the trigger and a barrel of double-aught buck blew out of the top of tribesman's head. He dispatched the second barrel into another savage and dropped the gun, before drawing his pistol and turning to find Rose. She, having run out of bullets, displayed her own agility as she kicked one in the side of the face, afterwards running him through with her short sword.

The final three bandits fled the corridor out of fear. Following this, two gunshots separated by the space of a few seconds rang out from the Ferris wheel, with a third following a period after that. Jackstraw had cut them down. *"Three for three,"* he said. *"I guess I win a prize."*

Ashur smirked as he collected his sawed off and rifle. "Yeah. Come on down here and pick it out."

"Wilco."

"Are you talking to Jack?" Rose asked, likewise collecting her guns.

"Yeah. I've got an earpiece in." He removed it and turned it off, showing her. Keeping his pistol out, he moved on, into the large striped tent the crier had come out of. It kept company to half-eaten meals and a game of joker poker that would never be finished. The place smelt poor, despite the crier's proposal that they take what they wanted should they win the game. A radio sat preforming on the same table as the cards. "Baby Elephant Walk" danced through the air, an odd choice, even for the eccentric DJ. While they searched the tent, the tune abruptly cut out and was replaced by Yeoman Swain's voice.

"Ashur Stanton," the stereo stated and then paused. They stopped what they were doing and looked at the radio, then back at each other, and then back at the radio. It could not possibly be talking to him. *"Yeah, you. I'm talking to you."*

"Yeoman?"

A moment later, the DJ burst out with laughter. *"Nah, I'm just fucking with you. I really hope you were listening to that 'cause I don't think any of my other listeners found that entertaining. Anyways, I wanted to tell you that you should lay low for a time because the big bad Ranger Syn—"* Yeoman Swain got slapped. He muttered something to his antagonists and then started over. *"I normally don't do bounty announcements on my show, because I—being of sound mind and body—would never condone such violent acts of barbarism, but this time if I don't—"* He laughed nervously. *"They're gonna kill me. So here it goes, boys and girls: The Rangers are offering a blackland shattering five-hundred platinum for the expeditionist known as Ashur Stanton. But hold on a second, folks. Before you sharpen your hatchets and go out clubbing anything that resembles our scabland's own Whiskey Warrior, pay attention to this key caveat: The bounty is only claimable, if he is brought in alive. Another point I would like to add, it being of my own judgment is that even if you somehow could bring Stanton in alive, the Rang—"* Ashur heard Jackstraw coming and rushed to unplug the radio.

He entered, sweeping aside the tent flap. "Find anything?"

"Cold meals and a deck of cards," said Ashur.

"No giant teddy bears?"

"No giant teddy bears."

"You'd figure even one of the Lissome Clan would need a cuddle every once in a while."

"Who's paying twenty gold for a giant teddy bear anyways?" Rose asked.

"That would be a very lonely Company robber baron who doesn't know the value of a gold piece," said Ashur.

"Let's carry on then," said Jackstraw, leaving the tent. They began searching for the carnival games area, finding it as their best chance. Even the fairgrounds hadn't been immune to revolutionary graffiti:

Boredom is counterrevolutionary

   The Gov't runs on a license.

   Revoke it.

The economy is wounded.
Let's finish it off!

      Commute, work, commute, sleep…
   Without law there can
   be no lawyers' fees
"The Sun was in my eyes," said Apollo.

"I like that one," said Jackstraw.

"Hold up," Rose said. She brought out a can of spray paint and began tagging a ticket booth. The two of them watched.

I Too Wish To Write Poetry

They soon came across a homeless gentlemen and asked for directions. "The gamin' area used to be just yonder," he said, pointing. He smelt of burnt popcorn and wore a tattered striped shirt. He began to wander off.

"Wait," said Ashur. "Did you used to be a carnie?"

"Of course not. I was a carnie."

"Oh," he said, a tad confused. They continued on in the direction the man had pointed them in. They found nothing but a few baseballs, which in their day had no doubt dunked more than a few mouthy clowns. Then Jackstraw spotted a booth on the edge of the area. While the rest were fallen to pieces and bedraggled, this one seemed to be fully intact, as if the apocalypse had passed over it. What's more, there was still a carnie behind the counter offering prizes. And there were a number of giant teddy bears hanging from the ceiling.

"Hello again," he said when they approached. "Here to play a game?"

Rose looked back at the brothers Stanton and they shrugged. "How much?" she asked.

"A bronze piece for three throws."

She placed a bronze piece on the counter and the carnie gave her three plastic rings. The objective was simple. Get the rings over necks of the bottles that had been lined up. For every ring, the size of the prize increased, with the highest being the giant teddy bear. Rose missed all three. She played again, with the same end result.

"Are these games rigged?" she asked the carnie.

"A carnie rig his games? Why I've never heard of such a thing."

Jackstraw stepped forward, searching his pockets. "Of course they're rigged. But there's still a way to win. Carnival games aren't about playing. They're about beating the system." He came up with an empty pocket and turned to Ashur. "Can I borrow some money?"

"You're always 'borrowing' everything of mine." He handed him a coin.

"Just think of it as an investment," said Jackstraw, trading the coin for plastic rings. "See how the bottles are slanted away at an angle, and placed so close together?" he said to Rose. "It makes it nearly impossible to land a ring on it when throwing from the front."

"Then how do you win?"

"You have to play outside the box." Jackstraw tossed the first ring, not at the bottles, but at the carnie. He ducked and the ring ricocheted off the back wall. With the bottles at such a slant, it landed around the neck of one. "Like that." He did the same with the other two.

"Three for three. Very nice," said the carnie. "Well played. Pick any prize you see."

Jackstraw glanced back at his companions. "Should I get the magical unicorn? Or the moldy Bart Simpson stuffy?"

"Just get the teddy bear, John."

Jackstraw asked for the giant teddy bear and the carnie used a long pole with a hook at the end to bring it down and deliver it to the man. Jackstraw gave it to Rose, telling her she could carry it back for them.

"This thing is actually pretty awesome," she said.

Ashur looked it over as well. "It's clean and intact. Should get the reward no problem."

The group turned to thank the strange carnie for the experience. But the booth lay empty. Not even Jackstraw could track him down.

"Jeepers," Rose said. "Let's get the fuck out of here. This place is eerie."

With that, they travelled back to where they had left their vehicles. Jackstraw drove something he had built himself. It resembled a sandrail or bush buggy. It had a metal chassis cover and a roof rack loaded down with gear. A fire axe was mounted horizontally along on the back, the way one would mount a gun on a gun rack. It was still dirty with the death of some poor bastard. He took the overstuffed teddy and placed it in the passenger seat.

"You have a two-seater," Rose stated.

"For my dog Moonraker. He's back at my place."

"Where you living now?" Ashur asked.

"Oh not too far from here actually. Got myself a little camp. It's just temporary of course, till I get back on my feet."

"I'm sure the twenty gold will help out with that," Ashur said while handing over the five silver he promised earlier.

"You act like I'm taking the whole reward."

"You are. Rose and I are going to head home from here. No point to returning to Medway."

"Except for the fact that there's gold to be got," Jackstraw offered, confused.

"We didn't come for the coin. We came for the fun."

"You guys have a fucked up sense of fun."

"We're Stantons. Comes with the name."

Jackstraw nodded. "Can't argue with that."

"Before you go," said Ashur. "I want to know what you know about the Cadre."

"I thought you would. He's a shadowy figure, runs New Valley, strolled in a few months ago and took the place. He doesn't have much in the way of history, just showed up one day, best as I can figure. From what I've gathered, he doesn't like to show his face. Apparently he's only got half of one. He's united all of the tribes and gangs. I was surprised that we ran into a Lissome cell. I figured he would have absorbed them already."

"So he wants a brass hat then."

"No. He's already got a brass hat. He's shooting for a crown. He took Wellshire. And I've heard he raided the Springs not long ago."

"He did. Tried to cut the power."

"He's going to from city to city, working his way towards the Rangers and the Company. He hasn't touched the baron of Irongrass yet, but I don't know how long that will last. You better be careful. He wants you dead and gone." Jackstraw gave Rose the up and down, but not in a sexual way as he had done at the amphitheater. "Your girl too."

"What does he want *me* dead for?" she asked.

"Probably for your association. He's clearly got a bone to pick with Ashur." To Ashur he said, "You've pissed him off, that's all I can tell you." He moved towards his buggy and got out a set of keys.

"One last thing," Ashur said. "Take off that jacket. Don't wear it inside Medway."

"Why's that?"

"The name Stanton isn't as popular as it used to be."

Jackstraw nodded and sighed, beholding the ruins around him. "What happened to us, brother? We used to run this little world."

"You ran your company into the ground and mine tossed me out when they were done with me. We just haven't dusted ourselves off yet. We'll be making headlines on News Peak sooner than you think. Have faith."

Chapter 18

Ashur rolled around in bed, not wanting to leave its envelopment, but the sounds of heavy wind and clanging metal gave him no peace. He left his mattress. Rose was awake in the recliner, reading *The Anarchist Cookbook*. At the table sat an Axehandle Hound, dressed in black combat gear from head to toe.

The radio sat on the counter: *"...Can you believe he actually said that? Well he didn't. It was a bad joke. Anyways we're on to the weather. And it looks like it's going to be a nasty one out there today, folks. The greater Great Lakes area is going to be blanketed in black rollers from now until—hell I don't know, I'm not a weather person. Just stay inside and hunker down, board up the windows if you can. To those who don't have anywhere to take shelter, why the hell are you listening to the radio in the middle of a sandstorm? In sports, it's been declared open season—by me— all bandits are fair game..."*

"Good morning, Ashur," Rose said.

He rubbed his face and yawned. "Morning."

"Looks like we're stuck inside today. Black blizzards."

"So I hear," he said as he began the process of making an Irish coffee, or Irish tea as it were. "I also see that you're reading the cookbook. How do you like it?"

"I didn't even know they had books like this until I met you. No stories, just information. It's so cool."

"You're a curious sort."

She smiled at him.

"And by that I mean you're weird," he said. She frowned at him and returned to her book. He sat down at the wire-spool table with his tea and looked at the Axehandle Hound. "Why are you in my house, Sergeant? You're supposed to be an outdoor dog."

"She brought me in because of the storm," he said through his balaclava. "I ordered everyone else to the depot. I figured it was my duty to stay behind and guard you."

Ever since the bounty issued by the Rangers a couple of weeks ago, at least one of the three squads of Axehandle Hounds had been stationed alongside Ashur's usual sentry, by order of the city. A few Rangers had shown up initially to collect, but when they saw the military presence, they turned tail. Despite that, a number of attempts had been made at capturing Ashur. Though only one of the aggressors had been a denizen of Tavern Springs. The rest were outlanders in poorly ordered mobs. A number of people had died on the enclave lawn lately, and while it was good for the soil, Ashur did not enjoy spending all day, every day, stuck inside.

"Go be with your comrades," Ashur said. "Or your family if you've got one. I don't think we're going to have any takers today."

"Aye, sir." The sergeant got up to leave. "What the hell did you do to get the Rangers so irked?"

Ashur raised his brow. "I wish I could say. I mean I have been involved in the recent disappearances of three of them but they shouldn't have any way of knowing that. I don't know and I'm not going to risk walking into a gallows to find out. That'll be all for today."

When the Axehandle Hound opened the door, he stepped outside as quickly as possible, to avoid letting the dust storm inside.

Rose turned the page and broke study. "You didn't have to send him out into that," she said. "You could have let him wait until it calmed down a bit."

"He's got goggles on. He'll be fine."

"Why do you dress them up like that? All blacked out with no faces. They look so…alien."

"That's the whole point."

"Oh," she said. "So what are you going to do today?"

He grabbed a bottle of Company whiskey from the wine rack and dropped a dab into his tea, waited a moment, and then added another. "You're looking at it."

"Breaking your dry spell? I thought you were lightening up on your liquor."

"Accidents can be atoned for."

Her expression became one of sincerity. "You shouldn't drink so much."

"Why, did you want some?" he asked, shaking the bottle at her.

A thin smile broke through. "You know what I mean."

"Yeah, but it's a special occasion. Come on, kid. Get drunk with me."

"Why? What day is it?"

Ashur raised his brow. "It's *to*-day, sweetheart."

"Anniversary?"

He didn't respond. She made a somber face and went back to her book. She had come across an article on how to turn a shotgun into a grenade launcher and was deeply enthralled, spending much of her day reading. He took up a book beside her for a time. After lunch, when he tired of reading, he listened to old cassette tapes and worked on his bottle. She tried to relieve him of it once but he wasn't having it. It was that night that Ashur made himself sick. Rose spent the evening caring for him the same way he had taken care of her when they first met. She left a bucket and glass after glass of water on his nightstand.

She spent that night up and down, waking when he woke, sleeping when he slept. By dawn, the storm hadn't broken. When he regained consciousness, he could smell food being prepared. She brought him breakfast and compelled him to stay in bed until the following day. The storm hadn't let up much so there wasn't much he could do anyways. On the third day his hangover subsided and the winds of the storm died down. A few hours later and a calm set in. Ashur said they should go help the town with the damages done by the storm. Rose agreed that they could go assess the state of the town.

Ashur's bungalow hadn't taken much of any damage but the same could not be said of the rest of Tavern Springs. Though reconstruction periods after black rollers were a common occurrence in all towns, things looked grim: power lines severed, toppled wind turbines, shattered windows, children coughing up bloody wads of dirt. It hadn't even stopped ashing yet.

Ashur started up the old truck he had in the yard and they started by helping a group clear a road not far from Ashur's neigh-borhood. An old building had given way during the storm, littering the street with bricks and plaster. Work went on for a few hours, evacuating loads of debris. There was one man who was going at it with a broom, trying to push the dust from the street, back where it belonged.

Ashur and Rose returned to the house just before noon for some lunch: beans over rice. They were both covered in dust and very hungry. They ate quickly. Towards the end of their meal, there was a knock at the door. It was Scott. He directed Ashur to the mayor's office. It was urgent and he hadn't time to dress.

As always, Stacey was the one to answer the door. "You know," she said. "When someone leaves a bag of shit on your doorstep, they usually have the courtesy to light it on fire first."

Ashur stared into the silver lenses of her shades and said nothing. "What's the matter, genius, can't think of—"

He stepped forward and strong-armed her out of his path. He moved down a few corridors and found the mayor's office on his right. He entered. "Vanderbilt."

"Hello, Mr. Stanton. Please, sit down."

In times of crisis even the mayor slackened his dress code. He wore khakis and an untucked button up without a tie. Another prison tattoo poked out of the undone collar. There was dirt under his fingernails and grime on his face. It was clear that he had been helping out in the clean-up.

Ashur placed himself in the chair in front of Vanderbilt's desk. "What do you need done?"

"I like that about you. When the going gets tough, you get going. You take pride in your work, and this town." Vanderbilt cleared his throat. "Yes, well, with the raid last month and the sandstorm, the town is running low on medical supplies, but I am afraid with reconstruction I won't be able to spare many men or vehicles for the expedition. So use your best judgment when picking your men and resources."

"I'll take care of it," he said and stood up. "Is there anything else, sir?"

"How is your little flower fairing?"

"She's very well, thank you. Learning quickly."

"Good to hear." Vanderbilt had an odd expression of conflict on his face, Ashur chalked it up to the issues of reconstruction. "That will be all, Mr. Stanton. God speed your return."

When he returned to Rose, she was consoling a child who had lost their parents in the storm. She'd found him crying on a street corner and now he clung to her leg.

"What'd the mayor want?" she asked.

"The town needs medical supplies. I'm setting out today."

"I'm coming with you?"

He nodded and then had a passing local woman he knew take the child from Rose. They returned home to gear up. He went to the book shelf and pulled out a large road map, the kind one might find at a gas station or convenient store. He unfolded the map and laid it on the table. Rose came over to the wire spool. The map had a large diamond shape drawn on it, which marked the main trails. Each vertex of the diamond labeled with the name of a city-state, and the map also held the names of dead lakes and rivers, a few landmarks, Interior paths, as well as the Southland cities and the eastern Great Lake settlements, all the way out to New York.

"You've mapped out the badlands?"

"There's a mapmaker I run expeditions with every few years. He gives me copies," Ashur said and placed his finger on a landmark. "There, Desiato General, in the Interior. That's where we'll go."

Chapter 19

They rode along in silence. He had handpicked a route with the scrutiny of a king, and so far it had proven effective—no disturbances. But that was not the case for their whole journey. They were about ten miles out from Desiato General when they passed through the remnants of a suburb. The houses were identical, a Levittown, and were the only organized semi-structures the duo had seen for the past five minutes. While riding through the neighborhood, a man stepped out into the middle of the street and blocked their path. Ashur stopped a generous distance away.

"Please, can you help me?" the man called over to them as he shuffled towards them. "I need some help."

"Are we going to help him?" Rose asked.

"Get off the bike." They dismounted and he killed the engine.

The man continued to gain ground in their direction. "My boy's sick and I need some help," he hollered.

Ashur could hear birds chirping. "What's wrong with the boy?" he called back.

The mange ridden and filthy man continued his trek towards them. He was maybe thirty meters out now. "He's got a bad fever," the man informed him.

"I think we can help," Ashur told him. Thereafter, he turned to Rose. "Kill him," he said.

"What?" she breathed. She stood wide-eyed. She did not budge.

"Do you hear the birds?" He pulled the Winchester off his shoulder and the man whom had been approaching turned to run. Ashur sent a slug into his back and he fell to the ground. At the sound of the gunshot, another five men sprang from the wreckage of the houses on either side of the bike. They rushed towards Ashur and Rose, all wielding weapons of pathetic proportions. Clubs mostly, one had a rusty machete, another was utilizing nothing more than a brick.

Rose drew her revolvers and Ashur shouldered his rifle. Together they quickly dispatched the shoddy gang in a volley of flashes. Once they were all dead, Ashur collected his thirty-thirty casings, as they could be reused or traded elsewhere. Rose likewise took this time to reload her revolvers. She had managed to take down two of the bandits.

"Hijackers?" she asked. He only nodded. The agonizing groans of the bait were heard. "We're not going to leave him like that, are we?"

"Of course not," Ashur said. He slung his lever action over his shoulder and started down the street. The man was still crying in pain as Ashur hovered over him. He had lost a good amount of blood but the stream had yet to slow down. Ashur unsheathed his knife, rolled the man over, and slit his throat. The raider choked for a while before finally bleeding out. He cleaned the blade on the dead man's shirt, after which he put the knife away.

"Should we bother searching them?" she asked upon Ashur's returning to her.

He looked at the impoverished bodies. "I don't think they're going to have much, but go ahead if you want." She searched them and found nothing of interest. Before she got back on, Ashur grabbed her arm and halted her. "You going to keep your lunch?" he asked.

She took a breath. "Yeah. Yeah, I'm good."

They continued their trip. A short ride and they passed out of the suburbia and into a rural desert. The roads were quiet for the rest of the trip and soon, they stopped atop a hill, where they could take in the view. On a barn nearby: **See Dead City**.

It was a scrapheap city—a long abandoned jungle gym ravaged by junkyard tornados. It was as if the invisible hand of Death had reached down and snatched away all the world's color. Even silence was forbidden here, kept at bay by the sounds of dry thunder. No life was visible.

Road signs were planted, as if a Burma shave campaign:

Cowboys and Indians
    Roman games
        Such odd things to survive the flames

The medical complex towered over the structures it surrounded. The main building may have been six or seven stories prior to the Collapse but had now been reduced to three. Ashur found a space in the parking lot, which was comically, a very difficult task. The parking lot was jam packed with the skeletons of hundreds of cars. The ER would have been inundated with burn victims during the global collapse. Ashur laid out the kickstand and removed his goggles.

"It's very important you listen to everything I tell you," he said once they were off the bike. Rose nodded. "A hospital is a pretty big attraction, so it's likely to be home to some bad guys. It's important that we do this quickly and quietly. So stay close, stay low. Understand?"

She nodded again. He drew his handgun and started towards the compound, keeping low against the remains of cars. She followed suit. They crept towards the front door unobstructed by any enemies. When Ashur pried open the dead, automatic doors, the natives gave no response. He and Rose started in slowly.

Ashur crept to a standstill. Because of this, Rose got a step ahead of him. The second she did, he grabbed a wad of her hoodie and yanked her back. She grunted at this and then he hushed her. She gave him a look, as if it ask why he had handled her as such. He guided her gaze downward. There, strung across the floor, was a tripwire. The wire was connected to the pin of a hand-grenade, which was set up against a small wooden brace to make sure the grenade did not come along with the string when pulled.

"An easy way to get rid of the nosey and blind," he whispered.

"You saved my life."

"I guess that makes us even. Now go back outside."

Rose moved back through the doorway and down a small flight of concrete steps that graced the entrance. When Ashur saw she was at the bottom of them and back on the sidewalk, he punted the grenade off the tiny wooden pike, sending it down the extending hallway that was the main foyer. The instant the thing went sailing through the air Ashur turned and sprinted towards Rose. He jumped to the bottom of the steps, pulling Rose to the ground.

The grenade went off.

"I thought we were supposed to be quiet," Rose said.

"Just knuckle up and stay hidden. Trouble's on the move."

Sure enough, the hall soon buzzed with the barbarous sort, curious to whether or not their hazardous snare had captured any grub. Ashur and Rose kept themselves tucked down right outside the building, below the stairs.

"What the fuck," a male's voice said. "Where's the kill?"

"You have the mental capacity of a God damn peanut. It's obvious that your trap malfunctioned," a female voice retorted.

"Then explain to me how in high hell the grenade got to this end of the hallway," the male countered.

Ashur looked at Rose, both her revolvers were drawn. He re-adjusted his grip on his .45 before nodding at Rose. They both stood up. He counted a band of six bandits in the hallway. They opened fire into the group. Three of them fell instantly and a fourth only a split second afterward. The rest took cover in the rooms on either side of the hall. Ashur and Rose advanced into the foyer, taking cover behind the receptionist's desk. They sat idle. A fog-like silence set in.

In the past few months, Rose had learned the basics of squad tactics—the importance of stealth, communication, lines of fire. He began signing to her, telling her to cover him while he checked his ammo levels. He had only a few bullets left in his magazine, but when a voice left the hallway, he reinserted it.

"W-Who's out there?" one of the cutthroats called.

"Me?" Ashur asked. "I am but a lowly bible salesman. I go by the name of No-Faced Jehovah's. I'm known to some as the best bible slinger in the all the five lakes."

"What are you doing?" Rose asked.

"Figuring out where they are," he whispered. "Now give me all your spent cartridges."

She opened the cylinder on each of her two guns and gave Ashur a total of six .357 casings—three from each revolver. She also took this opportunity to reload.

"Who sent you? What do you want?" the bandit shouted out.

"Jesus sent me. And I just want a moment of your time." Ashur made the man out to be in either one of two rooms. He stood up and trained his barrel on the nearer of them. "I've got a special deal on a trip to the fiery place." He tossed the spent cartridges onto the dingy, tile floor, causing resonations to echo throughout the foyer. He swore loudly after this to complete the stage act. When the bandit poked his head out to evaluate, Ashur took his life away. In the same breath, a woman with an M16 assault rifle step out into the corridor, screaming a spirited cry. He dropped to the floor, but when he heard the rifle misfire, sprung out from behind the counter. He missed his first shot and by the time he had hit her she was down the hall.

He started off in a full sprint after her, hopping over the dead bodies in his way. He swung around the same corner the bandit had taken, finding it a dead end. She was standing there, fumbling with the gun. When she saw Ashur was waiting in front of her, she panicked and the rifle clip she was working with fell from her grasp. She dropped the rifle and took a step back—nowhere to run.

Her shoulder bled profusely. He had clipped her wing. She protected her ribs, palms outward, as though she were trying to spare herself from an oncoming blow. With her immobilized, and Ashur's gun now being empty, he began to change magazines, reloading as he had done a hundred times before. The movement was not instinctual. It was mechanical, not like an animal, but like clockwork. The woman watched, quivering. The slide on his pistol slid forward, locking into the proper position. What came out of her mouth would best be described as terror in its purest form. This is when Rose arrived at Ashur's side. She saw the cowering woman and turned away just in time.

"Please—" the woman forced out.

He pulled the trigger and she slumped to the ground, a lifeless shell. When he turned around, he found Rose propped up against the wall with her mouth buried in her sleeve.

"Keep it together. We're almost done here."

She said not a word and started off down the hall, fingernails dinging into her palms.

"Rose?"

She didn't respond. He caught up to her and grabbed her.

"Let me go!" she yelled. "Stop *manhandling* me!"

He eased up but did not let go. "If you're mad at me, yell at me, slap me if it'll make you feel better. But you *cannot* walk off. Not out here."

"My God, Ashur, you had her trapped in a corner, bleeding out…she wasn't a threat!"

"No but she would have been," he said. "The first thing you need to get through your head is that if you let your guard down, they'll have you by the throat. And you know, *they* won't make the same mistake."

Rose stared Ashur down. "How many people have you killed while they begged for their lives? And don't give me that same bullshit. Do you ever let any of them go?"

"As a rule, no."

She chewed on her lip. "Except for me, huh? Have a soft spot for teenage girls, you perv!?" She stepped forward and shoved him over her boot—a move he had taught her. He fell to the floor and lay there, staring up at her. "Huh? Explain that! I had a gun on you the whole time we met. You never made a move!"

"You were hurt and scared."

"*She* was hurt and scared. I'm willing to bet a lot of the people you kill are hurt and scared. So why am I still here!? What made me different?"

"You look like my daughter!"

All the anger and disgust and fear drained out of Rose's face. "W-What?"

"You look like my daughter," he repeated.

She was still for a moment, likely searching for a way to articulate her feelings. She settled on giving him a bloody nose with the heel of her boot.

"Feel better?"

"No," she said, voice hoarse. "You really are fucked up, you know that?"

He got up. "We don't have time for this. Lock it down. Let's do the job."

"Yes, sir. Very good, sir. Where to? This place looks empty."

Ashur rubbed his nose on his sleeve, but it continued to bleed. "It is, for the most part. First place anyone would've looked for medical supplies."

"Then why the hell are we here?"

"To get what the idiots missed," he said. He explored the immediate area and found a large map of the hospital's layout on the wall. He began studying it. "Run out to the bike, grab your rucksack and that jerry can of crude-fuel."

"What the fuck for," she said. "Sir."

"Just do it."

She started in on him. "How about you take it, and shove it up—" He grabbed her and slammed her into the wall next to the map.

"Okay, okay, Ashur," she said, hushed in a frightful awe. "Don't hurt me." Her arms were up to protect her face.

His breath was heavy, blood running over his lips. "We will deal with your issues, later. Right now, go…"

"Okay…I'm sorry."

"Just go."

She went. He continued to study the map of the floor plan. When Rose returned with the gas and her rucksack, she stood at his side without a word. "Are you all right?" he asked.

"Don't worry about it."

"I didn't mean to scare you so badly."

"I get it," she said. "We can talk about it later, when we're safe."

He nodded distantly. "It's regrettable. I forget you're a kid sometimes." He put a hand on her shoulder. "But I can't afford to treat you like a kid. Not out here."

He took one last look at the map and then they started off down the corridors. They passed through the ICU and reached an annex just outside of a waiting area. Two elevators and a stairwell sat before them. Ashur opened the door to the stairwell and found only darkness. He pulled a small flashlight from his pocket and gave it to Rose. Then he drew his gun and they started into the basement, wandering down the levels, through a morgue. Their path was black, save for what Rose illuminated. She took her time as she swept the moonbeam across the cobweb covered body drawers. Some lay open and empty, inviting the weary passersby.

"This place is creepy," she whispered, and then, in the spirit of the ominous atmosphere, carried a tune. He had heard her whistle the song before.

Something possessed him to join in towards the end, adding the lyrics. "*The miller still drowns in his dam, and the weaver still hangs by his yarn, and the little tailor, he skips through hell with broadcloth under his arm.*"

She halted. "My mother used to sing that to me," she said. "I can still hear her voice, how soft it was—the warmth of it, you know. But I'd lost the words. It's a weird song to sing to a child."

He shrugged. "My mom sang it to me, the song about three thieves. Back in the day they'd look for any reason to put you in prison. I guess it was her way of trying to teach me not to steal."

"Did it work?"

"Not really."

"Weird," she said. "It worked for me. What are we doing down here?"

He took the flashlight from her and scanned the new area they had passed into. It stopped on a white door. "We are looking for a drug storage room." They walked over to the door. There was a keypad lock on the knob, as he had expected there might be. "*Now* we are looking for…a boiler room, perhaps."

They found the maintenance room a level down from the white door. This room was also locked, but with a padlock. Ashur pulled from his belt, locksmiths' tools—a tension wrench and picks. He had the door opened in under two minutes. They entered the room and found a pair of backup generators on the far wall.

"Where'd you learn to pick locks?"

"Johnny taught me when I was about your age. I'll teach you sometime," he said. "Give me the fuel." She handed it to him. "The keypad lock on the storeroom door is electronic. When the power's off, they don't open. But old hospitals like this have backup generators," he explained.

"And that's what the gas is for?"

"You got it."

In a few minutes he had the generator up and running. Lights flickered to life and Rose shut off the flashlight.

"We don't have long. Let's go." The duo hastily found their way back to the drug storage room. Ashur examined the keypad lock.

"So how do we get around this one?"

"Power's been out for a long time. The keypad might've reset itself. If it did, all I have to do is put in a default code and it might open." Ashur punched in some variation of one through five, and then again. The tiny red light on the pad stayed red and when Ashur twisted the knob the door didn't budge.

"What now?" Rose asked.

"There's more than one way around this. If all else fails, we can remove the hinges. But that'll take forever and a day." Ashur stepped back and used the butt of his rifle to smash the keypad. The casing cracked and its guts fell out. "People tend to forget something about electronics, cut to their basest level, they are one thing. That is, on or off." He ripped the small circuit-board from the device, leaving nothing left besides a few colored wires. "We strip it out and we complete the circuit." He twisted a few of the wires together. On his third try, the little light changed green. They opened the door and went inside. The storage room was stocked with drugs and Pyxis SupplyStations.

"Neat," Rose commented.

"Clean the shelves and let me see your short sword."

Rose unsheathed her sword and gave it to Ashur. He pulled out a list and matched the chicken scratch with the labels on the vials in the cabinets. She watched him as he used her sword to shatter the glass on the locked Pyxis cabinets. When he was done he handed it back to her. She took off her rucksack and began sweeping supplies into it.

"I'm not a chemist, but isn't most of this shit going to be expired?"

"Yes," confirmed Ashur. "But a lot of it it doesn't go bad. It only becomes less potent."

"And it's still safe to use?"

He nodded before bumping a vial of something. It fell to the floor and shattered. Neither of them noticed.

"So…why'd you get so drunk the other day?" she asked while dumping a tray of bottles into her bag. "It worried me. I've never seen you that bad."

He stopped scavenging needles for a moment, and then continued without looking up from the process. "It's a family matter."

"I'm not family?"

He came over to her and dropped a few bottles of morphine pills into her rucksack. "It was my kid's birthday," he said.

Rose's curiosity drifted away and she became soft-eyed. "Oh." A moment later she added: "I'm really, very sorry for kicking you in the face."

"Don't be," he said, returning to scavenging. "It was a good kick."

Rose's tone changed. "That's sweet," she said. "Truly. You have a way with words."

A trap went off a few floors up, shaking dust loose from the ceiling. They wrapped up and exited the room, moving back up the stairway. Upon reentering the elevator annex, a volley of gunfire landed around them. Ashur and Rose found cover on either side of the archway.

"Cease fire!" a voice shouted.

Ashur poked his head out and saw a fire team of four men organized in a wedge formation, all dressed in black tactical gear. They planted themselves towards the back of the waiting area and all of them carried automatic carbines, with the exception of one whom carried a much bigger light-machinegun. Ashur brought his head back in.

"Who's out there?" Rose whispered to him from the other side of the threshold.

"Cheyenne Company dog soldiers."

"Mercenaries?" she asked.

"The very worst."

"Come out with your hands where we can see them!" a voice commanded.

"We're just scavs," Ashur hollered back.

"Then you have nothing to worry about," the man promised. "We just wanna make sure everything's green here. Sorry about the gunfire, but I ordered my men to shoot on sight. When we came in and found six ghosted raiders, we figured a clan was here."

"No gangs. It's just us."

"You two cleared out those dregs?"

Ashur hesitated for a moment. "Yeah. It was us."

"Nice work. And did you get the power back on too?"

"I did."

"Damn…I'd like to talk to you face to face. We could help each other. Why don't you come on out?"

"What'd are we going to do?" Rose asked.

"I don't know."

"Listen," the commander bayed. "We haven't verified if the rest of this area is clear. So the longer we have to wait, the more risk I'm putting my men at. So until we know that you're not a threat, we have to treat you as one. If you don't come out now we're going to be forced to open fire. And we don't wanna do that. So what's it going to be?"

"The area's clear," Ashur told him.

"Sorry, but we can't just take your word for it. I'm going to count backwards from three. After that I'm lighting you up."

He began counting down. Rose looked to Ashur.

When the commander reached one, Ashur shouted, "Don't shoot! I'm coming out."

"Hands first," the man ordered.

Ashur stuck his hands around the corner, followed by the rest of him.

The commander was massive, six foot four with arms like tree trunks. He was dressed in the same all black Cheyenne tactical gear as his men, with the exception of a boonie hat rather than a helmet. Cheyenne Company was much more decentralized than Aegis Armed Forces, but perhaps more deadly because of it.

Operating as independent cells, they moved in small fire teams and did not bother wearing clunky, metal combat armor. Cheyenne's main tactic was stealth. The other portion of their deadliness came from the matter that they would put a bullet in a man's head if he looked like an easy target. They had a reputation for slaughtering whom they wished without reason, even Rangers. Their only exceptions were other Cheyenne Company cells.

"Your friend too," the commander said.

"Don't worry about her. Worry about me."

"Your friend too," he pressed.

Rose stepped out.

"Cute friend," one of the mercenaries corrected his commander. Ashur saw the way the group's attention changed when they saw Rose.

"What's your team doing here?" Ashur asked, palms still up.

"We needed some medical supplies," he told them. "Now if you would be so kind as to put your guns on the floor and kick them over."

Ashur thought of his beautiful, prized rifle skidding across the floor. "That's going to be a problem," he said.

"How come?"

"Do you know who I am?" he asked.

The man shook his head. "Who are you?"

"Ashur Stanton, at your service."

The fire team stood there, guns still shouldered. None of them moved.

"Who?" someone said.

"Ashur Stanton?" Ashur asked. No one said a word. "Well, shit. Here I was thinking I was famous."

There was the sudden sound of crinkling in the ductwork above. Most of the group looked up in wonderment.

"The hell's that?" a merc asked.

"Probably rats," Ashur offered. "I saw one when I was over at the living quarters."

The squad turned their attention back to Ashur and Rose.

"So what's in the pack?" the man in the boonie hat asked.

"Oh you know…sundries," Ashur said, taking a very slow step backwards. He was looking for a way out but these guys were not letting their guard down.

"Is that how this is going to go?"

Ashur stared the commander down.

"Fine. Taylor, Johnson, get their gear."

Two of the men on the line broke off and started towards Ashur and Rose. One man circled around Ashur, taking a good look at him while the other stood in front of Rose, likewise taking a look at her.

"What's your name, sweet thing?" Taylor asked her, getting unnecessarily close.

"Rose."

"Rose? I think that's a pretty name," Taylor said. "You wanna know what else I think? I think you're going to give me that pack, without a fight. Then you two are going to hand over your weapons to my friend there. Then I think me and you are going to have a little quality time."

"You want to rethink the last one," Ashur said flatly. "Actually all of that is a terrible idea. Just stupid really."

Johnson—who had been strolling around Ashur and observing him—promptly punched him in the stomach. Ashur cradled his abdomen. With his head lowered, he noticed something on Johnson's vest. Right above where Cheyenne Company was written in bright yellow, he saw another pair of words crossed out: **Shyan Company**.

"Don't count coup yet," he said laughing. "I'd be more afraid of you guys if you could spell your own name."

"Hands up," the commander broke in.

He put his hands back up. Taylor relieved Rose of her guns and the pack she wore. He opened it and shuffled through its contents.

"Found what we came for," Taylor told his CO before tossing the pack to him.

"Time for your guns," Johnson said to Ashur. "That's a nice rifle. Where'd you get it?"

"That one's a long story."

"I'm listening."

Ashur shrugged. "Well you see, I was running a caravan to Medway with a couple of guys. We got ambushed by some small-time wannabes, slaughtered my men. They all wore black gear like you guys.”

“Is that so?”

“It is. I spent a week in the blacklands, hunting them down.” Ashur lowered his hands and used them instead to help with his storytelling. He also began to wander slightly from his spot. “See what I would do is I would wait for them to make camp. Then when they went to sleep, I’d execute whomever they put on night-watch and drag him into the darkness. But then I’d leave, wait for the next sun fall. I took one every night. It was like an old slasher movie. Anywho, the leader of the team was carrying this rifle.”

“Really.”

“Former Sheriff Mansell of the old Ranger Syndicate gave it to me as a present for wiping out a raider clan.”

“Who’d you say you were again?” the commander asked.

For a murderous gang, Ashur thought they asked a lot of questions. The squad seemed legitimately interested in him. Perhaps the commander intended some type of working relationship.

“Ashur Stanton?” Ashur said. “Of the Stanton Brothers? Ranger legend? Pillar of Tavern Springs and professional XP? Any of this ringing a bell?”

The ducts above them once again came alive with motion.

“Wait a second,” Taylor said. “I think I’ve heard of you. Aren’t you a bar boxer?”

“Well not by trade,” Ashur said.

“Hey yeah,” Johnson joined in. “This guy’s got that huge bounty on his head. Ashur Stanton, master-at-bars of Tavern Springs. The Whiskey Warrior!”

The squeaking in the ducts grew as the fire team had a good laugh at Ashur’s expense.

“Some big ass rats,” the commander remarked.

“They’ll take your head off,” Ashur informed him.

Not a second later did a highwayman drop down out of the ceiling and bury a hatchet into the commander's skull. This ended the team's laughter. When they turned around to shoot into the creep, the duo made their move. Rose flicked open her butterfly knife and planted it firmly into the back of Taylor's neck. Ashur drew his handgun and dropped the two remaining, sidetracked mercenaries. They were wearing vests and helmets, so Ashur was forced to aim for the neck and base of the skull. When the gun smoke settled, five bodies lay on the ground. Then the hospital's power cut out.

Rose reacquired her gear and they began to pick what they could from the soldiers of fortune. "I don't know about you, but I've had enough adventure for one day," she said and then went cold, catching sight of blood. "Ashur, you're hurt."

"Huh?" He looked down at his right arm. A long hole was gashed in the upper sleeve, near the shoulder, and the fabric was beginning to run dark. "Damn it. This was my favorite jacket," he said.

"What do I do?"

"You stay calm." He stood up and removed his rifle and jacket. Blood was running down his arm. "It's only a graze," he said as he sat down against the wall. "Won't even need sutures." Rose took off the carbine she had stolen and then removed her rucksack.

"What am I looking for?" she asked, franticly rummaging through it.

"My medkit, bandages, gauze, antiseptic. Any of that."

He began applying pressure to the wound. She brought over some gauze and cotton medical bandages. She fumbled with them and some of the gauze fell from her grasp. "Damn it!" she cursed.

"Take a breath. I'm the one who's been shot."

She steadied herself while he began patching up his arm. When he finished fiddling with the dressing, he stood up, put his jacket back on, and grabbed his rifle. They returned to the task of picking the dead mercenaries clean. It was unfortunate really, the squad had so much worth taking that most of it had to be left behind.

Chapter 20

"Lemme see the hands!"

"Do we have to do this every time I pull up?"

"I will shoot you dead, Stanton!"

"Last thing you *shot dead* had been hit by a truck."

"It were still kickin' though."

"It was missing a leg, Captain."

The gate rolled up and they entered town. It was eventide now. The sun grew orange and low, casting the damaged town in an unflattering light. This was nothing new. Tavern Springs looked unflattering in any light, no matter the time of year. They soon arrived at the city's main medical clinic. Graffiti here:

Officer, your use of force is far less precise than you have been led to believe

> **Why don't we just unionize
> the entire lower class?**

That's what we're doing you idiot. Keep up.

Once off the bike, he handed Rose the rucksack and told her to go in and ask for a woman named April.

"Why don't you come in with me?" she asked.

"I've had enough of medical facilities for today."

She scoffed at the front. "Come on."

"No thanks. The good doctor, April and I, we don't get along. She doesn't like me."

"Why's that?"

"I think it's because she's met me," he said with his distinctive smirk.

"Don't be a bum. Come on."

They entered the clinic, walking past a pair of sentries that stood at the door. The waiting room was typical: chairs, a coffee table, a few magazines, all in front of a counter with a clerk and a triage nurse. They walked through the waiting area and Ashur opened the door to the interior of the center. The clerk stood up and told him that he was not allowed back here, but he dusted him aside, telling the clerk that he was here on city business. He and Rose continued down the hallway of exam rooms, the clerk hounding them the whole way. The hallway ended in an expanse filled with desks, computer terminals, and clinic staff. April was one of them. She broke away from the nurse she was talking to an approached the group.

"I tried explaining to him that he's not allowed back here but—"

"It's all right," she said. "Thank you. I'll handle it."

April was a woman of fair complexion, a rarity with the sun being as unforgiving as it was during the day. She wore cyan scrubs with a clean-pressed, white lab-coat over top. She was smooth-skinned with charcoal hair and glowing, blue eyes. She bore a resemblance to his wife. Not only that, but she sounded like her, felt like her—they even had similar mannerisms, with the exception that she would not receive him. This was where the tension between them stemmed from. As soon as he saw her, that familiar deathly numbness came upon him.

"I brought you a goody-bag," he said. Rose took off the rucksack and handed it to the woman. "Got everything you could dream about in there."

"How thoughtful," she said, handing the pack over to a nurse. "Who's this?"

"I'm named Rose," she said with a slight, Victorian curtsy.

April blushed at the gesture. "It's nice to meet you. I'm April, the head medic. We appreciate the supplies."

"Anything to help, Ms. April."

April tilted her head, taken with Rose. "What a mannered young lady. That's not something you see these days."

Rose smiled and looked away. "Thanks."

April then moved her gaze past the girl, to Ashur. The bloodstain on his sleeve had only gotten bigger since it was bandaged. "What's happened to your arm?" she asked.

"It's good, doc," he mumbled. "Clean bandages taken right from the supply we gave you."

"That's not what I asked you. What did you do to it?"

"It's a graze."

There was a moment of silence as April glanced between the two in front of her. "I'd like to take a look at it. You never were much good at patching up your own wounds."

"That really won't be necessary."

"*Ashur*," Rose said. "She's a doctor. Let her look."

He flicked his fingers in a nervous tick. "Yeah…sure."

"Room number eight is empty, I believe. I'll see to you in there. Rose, you can wait in the foyer if you'd like."

"Yes, ma'am."

They started down the hall, diverging at exam room eight. April guided Ashur to the examination table where he removed his jacket, afterwards rolling up the sleeve of his T-shirt, which had also been tattered and bloodstained. She closed the door, got supplies together, and then set up next to him. "You shouldn't be bringing her out there with you," she said while carefully cutting away the old dressing. "You're going to get her killed."

He said nothing.

"How long has she been running with you?"

He didn't answer.

"Ashur."

He inhaled sharply, like he had forgotten to breathe. "Just over eight months."

"Eight months? Are you and her…at an understanding?"

He gave her a ridiculing look.

"No. Of course not," she answered and then examined the abrasion. "You've sent people in here with worse, but we're going to put some rubbing alcohol on it for good measure. I know. It's your least favorite kind of alcohol." She picked up a clear plastic bottle and unscrewed the cap. Turning the bottle upside-down, she let a cotton ball soak up the isopropyl and then began dabbing it on Ashur's graze. The wound was wrapped up in expert time—service with a stoic silence. She cleaned up the supplies and wheeled her chair directly in front of him. Slouching over, she dropped her elbows onto her thighs and rested her chin in the palms of her hands. "You know, when your enthusiasm and bloodlust go, there's not much left of you. It's kind of…disarming actually."

"Did I just squeeze some pity out of you?"

"You've always had my pity," she said, taking his hand between her own two and kissing it. "And my thanks." This breathed a bit of life into him.

"But, above all, I've had your contempt," he said, made bitter by this impulsive show of affection. "Because I'm the barbarous sort. And you're straighter than the rest."

The smile she forced was pretty despite its pretense. "No. I'm no straighter than the rest. And you're not the barbarous sort. I'd detest you less if you were. You know what to expect from that kind. It's because you so naturally walk that line between civilized and barbaric that I find you loathsome," she explained. "I travelled with you for months, Ashur. Can you imagine what that's like? Sleeping next to someone who you know would snap your neck if that's what it came to? And I remember the leaner parts of our journey, where my death would have helped you along. And I *was* awake those nights you watched me, contemplating that very fact." She lowered her voice slightly. "Do you know how frightening that is?"

Ashur was quite for a long time, eventually letting his hand slip from her grasp. "What do you want me to say? That I'm sorry the things I did? Would you even try to believe me? We've all done monstrous, unforgivable things in order to get where we are. The only difference between us is that I carried you here. I did those thing so you didn't have—"

"You would have done those things regardless. You didn't carry me here. I followed you. You strung me along with scraps like I was a stray animal. The only thing you did for me, was show me the kindness of not killing me when I got too close. And in a fucked up kind of way, I'm thankful. Truly, I am. No, the real difference between us, between you and the rest of us, is that you keep going back out there. Are you looking to die?"

He perked up, as if someone had called his name from across a crowded room. "What?"

"What?"

"What did you say?"

She hesitated a little. "I asked you…if you wanted to die."

He glazed over for a moment before resting his hand on her forearm. "I can't live in here. I can't fix machines or till the land. I've seen it happen. There's no illness. There's no injury. Some people go to sleep, and then they just don't get up. And I know the only reason that's not me is because they're in here, and I'm out there. Fighting. So I just…keep moving."

She crossed her arms sheepishly and clucked her tongue. "I'm sorry. We get on to this every time. It's why I never see you anymore, isn't it?"

He stood up to leave. "I think we can leave it at that."

"Actually, I'd like to talk about Rose."

He was silent.

"Don't drag her into this," she said. "She's either going to end up like you, or die somewhere along the way. And she's too good for that."

"I'm not dragging her anywhere," he said. "She's pushed me to teach her at every turn. Kid wants to learn how to take care of herself. And I've enjoyed teaching her. You don't like it, you can talk to her. She won't listen to me."

She nodded. "Okay." Then she did something that shocked even Ashur. She stood up and hugged him, quite sincerely. And then walked out, leaving him to catch up. Rose was waiting there for the two of them, happy-go-lucky.

"That's that then," April said. "I will see you guys around."

"Bye, April," Rose said.

"Goodbye, sweetie."

Ashur's only farewell to April was shoddy eye contact. They stepped out of the door and immediately one of the sentries grabbed Ashur's arm. He yanked it free of the man's grasp.

"Don't touch me."

"Sorry, sir, but Mayor Vanderbilt told us to send you to him the moment after you delivered the medical supplies."

"Then I'll go see him. I don't need a ride."

Part 3
No Replastering. The Structure is Rotten.

The evening was turning down to night. Ashur and Rose rode through the city streets, enjoying the cool air and buffeting wind. In moments, they would arrive at the mayor's palace, though Ashur thought it was odd that he would request his company so late in the day. It was more like Vanderbilt to wait until the next morning's sunlight, and then send for him. On the other hand, the city was still recovering from the raid and the storm.

"I'm sorry about your jacket," Rose said.

"I think it looks fine with a touch of color."

The bike slowed to a stop in front of the mayor's castle. When they got to the gate, the sentry informed them that Vanderbilt was meeting with some Company hotshot, and that it would be appreciated if all weapons were left at the gate, so as not to startle the businessman. The duo obliged and removed all visible weaponry.

After that, the sentry said, "You don't mind if I walk you guys to the door do you? I was about to go in and get some water."

The three of them began up the primrose path to the mansion. Stacey opened the door when the buzzer sounded, but did not greet them, only stepped back to make way. Once in the rotunda, which was unusually dark, Stacey led them farther away from the door. That was when the lights came on and they learned of the trap. A small army had appeared out of thin air—sentries, Stacey, and two Rangers, dressed in their dusters and cowboy hats. Vanderbilt stepped out from one of his many hallways and greeted Ashur and Rose. "Hello, you two. I have something regretful to tell Mr. Stanton. I am sorry. I really am. But I'm afraid your services are no longer worth the trouble they cause me. I thought I ought to send you out with a golden handshake. So…" Vanderbilt gestured to the Rangers.

"Ashur Stanton, you are hereby placed under arrest by the authority of the Ranger Syndicate."

Ashur put his hands up and eyed Vanderbilt.

"Don't take it personally, Ashur. It was only business after all. And if it makes you feel any better, I may lose a few nights' good rest looking for your replacement."

The Rangers stepped forward and one of them pulled out a pair of handcuffs. Rose moved in front of Ashur, shouting at the Rangers in defiance.

"Jett, get her out of the way," one of the Rangers barked— the one with the massive handlebar mustache. Jett grabbed her and dragged her to the other side of the rotunda, out of their way. The Ranger that was not tending to Rose put Ashur in a pair of cuffs before searching him. He found all his hideaway weapons.

"Vanderbilt."

"Yeah, Ashur?"

He smiled. "It was nice to finally meet you."

"You always were a pleaser. Take him out of here."

The Ranger started pushing Ashur towards the door and the circle of sentries parted to let them through.

"Wait!" Rose's called out, on the verge of tears. "Wait, please! Let me see him one last time, please."

Jett looked at his friend and he nodded. She was released and rushed over to Ashur.

"Rose—" She grabbed a wad of his shirt and pulled him down to her height. Pressing her lips to his, she forced his mouth wider with her tongue, progressing into a deep romantic kiss. Seconds later, he was pulled from her.

"We're going to get out of this," she said, out of breath.

"You can celebrate by paying for my next drink."

She nodded. "You can count on it."

The Rangers pulled him along and they left the mansion. Outside, they put him into the back of a Ranger SUV and started down the road, slightly faster than the limit. The late night uptown lights roared past—Lakeside Supply, Whiskey Breeze, Ashur's enclave, the depot.

"So, you're Jett. And who are you?" Ashur asked.

"Shut up," the man said.

"Aw come on. I can't know who's bringing me in?"

"No."

"I use to be a Ranger myself, you know?"

"Yes, we know," the mustached Ranger said. "Fairytale Grimm. How'd you get a name like that?"

"I'll tell you how if you tell me your name," Ashur said.

"My name is Ta'xet."

"Ta'xet? That's a weird fucking name, man."

"It's a First Nation's god. How about yours? How'd you get that beauty?"

"Ever hear the one about the Wolf and the Beast?"

"Sure. We've all heard it," said Jett. "Bunch of nonsensical dribble."

"You'd be surprised. Talk to Deputy Sloan about it, or former Sheriff Mansell if he's around. They'll fill you in."

"You're not…" scoffed Ta'xet.

"But I am."

"You can't be," said Jett.

"Believe what you will."

"So it's like a play on Grimm's Fairy Tales right?"

"Yup," Ashur said. The truck progressed down the main road that led out of town. Ashur thought he would be staying the night in the town jail before they went off, as the sun was nearly gone and it would be an unnecessary risk to get caught in the badlands after dark. "Whoa, what's going on? No overnight stay in the jailhouse? We're going straight through to Medway?"

"No, Little Red Riding Hood, we're gonna go see Grandma. Didn't you know she was under the weather?" Jett said.

"That was clever," Ashur complemented.

"Shut up now. I'm tired of hearing your voice," Ta'xet said.

"Oh hey, while you guys are here, can you tell me what I'm wanted for?"

"We don't know," said Jett. "Sheriff Stone posted your bounty right out of the wild blue yonder. No one really cared why Stone wanted you. There was money to be got. But I've got to say, your Axehandle Hounds are some scary looking motherfuckers. Had half the Syndicate shitting their pants."

"Enough," said Ta'xet. "I'm tired of hearing both your voices."

"Only half?" asked Ashur.

"Enough!" Ta'xet repeated as they slowed to a stop in front of the main gate. The Captain of the Guard was waiting there to open it for them. Moments later, they were creeping through expansive ruins of the old Appleton metropolitan area.

Ashur had not planned to take this trip tonight. He had been readying himself for a breakout at the town's jail, not in a moving vehicle. Fortunately, for him, the Rangers' truck was not a squad car, meaning the back seats were not caged in. It was a short distance before Ashur made his first attempt at breaking out. "Hey, I have to take a piss," he said.

"Hold it. It's only like three hours," Jett said.

"I'll relieve myself in your SUV if you don't pull it over."

Ta'xet turned on the radio. Country was playing. "I don't care. Now shut up."

After that plan fell through, he began setting up for another option. He pretended to cough into his shoulder and spit the hand-cuff key, which had been in his mouth, down onto the seat behind him. Rose, the clever one, had managed to snatch it off of Jett's belt while he was in close contact with her, holding her back. About forty-five minutes later, the soft music and nighttime car ride had lulled Jett to sleep. From there, it was as simple as pulling the gun from Ta'xet's belt.

It was quick. Nothing but a few pops.

***

When Ashur returned to Tavern Springs, he drove straight passed his house and continued down the street to Whiskey Breeze. He had told Rose that she was expected to pay for his next drink, and she said that she understood. Ashur had pushed her here instead of back home because he knew that as soon as Vanderbilt found out he had gotten back into town—how long that would take was anyone's guess—his house would be the first place they would search. Fortunately, it was unlikely that more than a handful of sentries had known about the plan to sell off Ashur, as he had the support of his subordinates, and if something was going to happen to him, he would have heard about it.

He parked the SUV outside and entered the bar. Rose slept at the counter, her head on her forearms. Lulu stood behind the counter drying a glass, getting ready to close. A large smile broke out across her face when she spotted Ashur.

He walked up and nudged Rose by the shoulder. "Wake up, flowerchild."

She stirred and rubbed the sand out of one of her eyes. They were red and puffy. "Ashur?" she asked before finding her bearings. She sprang up and hugged him. "I was so worried." She searched for words. "What do we do?"

He looked at Lulu, whom was standing there with her hand on her heart. "Can we get a booth and some tea?" he asked.

"My doors are always open to you two," she said. "Make yourselves at home."

They made themselves comfy in their usual booth. The bar lay empty other than our duo and Lulu, as it was late on a week-night. Even the guard had gone home. All the chairs had been put onto the tables and the floors had been mopped.

"Do you have a plan?" Rose asked.

"I do. But you're not going to like it."

"Why not?"

"Because you're not a part of it."

"What?"

"I mean to say, this is where you and I part ways."

"No," she said, confused. "No. It's not."

"You come along with me, you're going to get yourself killed. There's no need for that. You've got a house here, and enough coin to last you a good long while. Take up a job here in town. I know April will help you. Go to her if you need anything."

"It's your money and your house—"

"And I'm giving it to you," he said.

"I can't believe you're actually trying this. You're going to abandon me?"

"I'm trying to keep you safe."

"Then don't leave me here!"

He banged his fist on the tabletop. "Rose!"

"No!" she shouted and stood up, placing both her hands on the table. "You're not listening to me!"

Just then, Lulu came out of the kitchen with a fresh pot of tea and two cups. The duo settled down and said not a word as Lulu poured them each a tea. "Don't mind me," she said, placing a small bowl between them. "I'm just here to deliver the cream and sugar." Then she returned to the kitchen. They started up again.

"You need to understand what you're doing," Ashur said, taking a sip.

"I understand perfectly. It's you who isn't getting it. If they can't catch you, who do you think they're going to come after? The Cadre knows about me. The Rangers do too. Like it or not, you've already wrapped me up in this. So you can't leave me here. You'd be leaving me to die."

He did not respond and they sat in silence for a time, drinking tea. They would occasionally make eye contact for a split second before looking away. A few minutes later, Rose made a play and offered her hand out on the table. Ashur's eyes flickered back and forth between Rose's face and her hand. "Give me your hand," she said finally.

"I'm not holding hands with you after that kiss. That's weird."

"Give me your fucking hand," she said again. Her voice was shaky. He gave her his hand. She tried to say something but stumbled on her words and instead turned to look off in the distance. She took her time and straightened herself out, after which her attention returned to him. "We need each other. Let's figure it out."

Chapter 22

The streets outside Vanderbilt's mansion were well lit at one in the morning. A sentry watched over the entryway, not far from where Ashur had left his motorcycle. It was not the same guard that had been on duty a few hours ago. This one looked to be twenty-something with an orange beard and broad shoulders. Rose stepped out of the shadows and moved towards the entryway. She stopped in front of him, crossed-armed and meek. "Hey," she said.

"Evening, miss. Something I can help you with?"

"Actually, there is. I'm a little nervous about getting home this late. I was wondering if you would walk me. I'm about five minutes from here."

He thought about it for a moment, scratching at his facial hair. "I don't know. I'm really not supposed to leave the gate and at this hour it may be difficult to get another man to watch the front."

"I'll do you a favor," she muttered softly.

The offer caught him off guard. "Oh…okay." He slung his rifle over his shoulder and asked her to lead the way. She started off down the road, the sentry following close behind. Ashur was waiting around the first corner. Once the guard was dealt with, he took the assault rifle and gave Rose the revolver he had. The duo walked up the Breakers' pathway, past the Roman statue, to the door, which was illuminated by the porch light. The door was locked, as Ashur had figured it would be.

He stared at Rose, as his lock picks had been confiscated by Vanderbilt. "You have any bobby pins?" he asked in a whisper.

She reached into her hair to pull out a few. "Wait," she said. "Shouldn't the sentry have a key on him?"

Ashur stared at her blankly.

She left to get the key.

When they entered, the main rotunda was dark, with the exception of one conjoining hallway. It was the same one they had been led down when Rose first met Vanderbilt, though this time around there was only silence, no fluttering music. They crept down the passageway, treading softly. Ashur did not know which room he was looking for, but when the door on his right opened, and a shapely figure stepped into the hall, the course of action became clear.

He rushed Stacey and checked her in the chest with the rifle he had stolen. He pinned her to the wall and cupped a hand over her mouth. A muffled cry began slipping through the cracks in between his fingers. Rose took Stacey's sidearm and opened the door that she had just come through—a vacant pantry. Ashur dragged her inside. He dropped the rifle and put her up against the wall. Rose closed the door behind them as Stacey continued to writhe against his grip and murmur into the hand around her mouth.

"Shhh…cooperate and I'll let you live," he told her. As a response, she bit his hand. He took her gun from Rose and put it to Stacey's head. She stopped very quickly after that. "That's better," he said.

"How'd you get here!?" Stacey asked.

"Took the bus. Now, I'm going to ask you some questions. Answer them."

"I'm not helping you work your way out of this one."

He did not hesitate to break her nose with his elbow. The shot set her back about five minutes. "I do not have time to play games, Stacey. The next one is going to shatter your larynx, so you better speak up while that's still an option."

Her pupils constricted and blood flowed freely over her lips. "Go ahead and break it. Let me suffocate, but I'm not going to help you." She spit blood in his face.

He exhaled wearily. He took that moment to give her the up and down. Tonight she wore a green military sweater, the kind with the patches on the shoulders and elbows. The sweater appeared two sizes too small, flaunting her curves, and allowing for a not so modest sliver of skin to show around her waist.

"I don't get how someone so ugly could be so pretty."

"W-What...?" she said, stumbling for words.

Stepping away, he placed her pistol on one of the pantry shelves. Rose kept her gun trained on Stacey in his absence. A couple of seconds later, he was towering over the woman. With only momentary deliberation, he reached down and began undoing her belt. "You're really going to make me do this," he said. She stammered, thereafter grappling at his hands, trying to get a hold on them. When she did, he brought her arms up and pinned them to the wall with only one hand.

"Your job or your decency, pick fast." He reached down and clumsily finished his work with her belt. When it was off, he let the band of leather fall to the floor, thereafter returning to her waist, fiddling with the button on her pants. At a decibel level that would give the neighbors something to talk about, she let out a scream for help. He hushed her with a hand over her mouth, and one around her throat. She made whimpering sounds and continued writhing against Ashur. She bit him again, this time drawing blood, and then tried to knee him in the groin. They took the confrontation to the floor, with Ashur ending up on top of her, her hands pinned above her head. "Give me what I want, or let it happen."

"You're bluffing," she said before looking at Rose. He glanced back and found her standing a few feet away. She was silently watching all this with wide eyes, a gun still drawn but pointed in no particular direction. He returned his attention to Stacey.

"Rose, sweetheart, why don't you step out for a moment? You know, watch the door or something."

Rose blinked. "Huh?"

"Yeah, go on. Raid Vanderbilt's fridge if you like," he said. "The old man's probably sound asleep at this hour, with his tiring work and all." He started back at the button on Stacey's pants. Rose had her hand on the door by the time he had Stacey's pants halfway down her thighs.

At that moment, Stacey gave in. "Wait. Wait. Wait," she said in a broken voice. He stopped and Stacey looked to Rose again, finding no comfort in her likewise fearful expression. Stacey closed her eyes. "Okay. You win, Ashur. God, you win. Just…don't."

He leaned in and whispered, "I appreciate the cooperation." Then he got up off of her and stepped away to retrieve her pistol. She pulled up her pants and redid the button before getting off the floor. "Now I'm going to ask questions, and you're going to answer them."

Stacey kept her eyes closed. "Okay," she said.

"Good. Where's Vanderbilt?"

"He's asleep."

"Good. Where is our gear?"

"It's in the garage."

"Okay," said Ashur. "Who else is wandering around out there? Kitchen staff, butlers, maids?"

"Everyone is in their rooms as far as I know."

"All right then." He moved towards Stacey and grabbed her by the upper arm. "We're going for a short walk." The trio left the room. Ashur kept hold of her the entire trip to the garage. Upon entering the expanse, the lights flickered to life. His bike had been brought in. They descended the small staircase and Ashur found his and Rose's gear on a table at the far end, near extra Plexiglas shields. He let go of Stacey and told Rose to keep a gun on her. Once he had his inventory back, he traded places with Rose, letting her do the same. "The Cougar got a full tank of gas?" he asked Stacey.

"I don't know."

"Miniguns stocked?"

"I don't know, Ashur. That's not my job."

"Do you know where Vanderbilt keeps the keys?"

"In his room. In his wardrobe"

"And where is his room?"

She hesitated. "Ashur, please."

"Where?"

She fought with herself for a minute. It was smeared across her face, right there along with the blood. She gave in. "It's up the stairs, head right, it's at the end of the hall—the suite."

Rose finished with her things and came back over to them. He returned his gun to his underarm holster and told Rose to keep a gun on Stacey. She did so. After he had verified the whereabouts of Vanderbilt's room in more detail with Stacey, he unsheathed his hunting knife. Stacey made a repressed flinch at this.

"Don't let your guard down," he told Rose. "I'll be back with the keys."

"Why do you need the keys?" she asked. "Can't you just hotwire the car or something?"

"An expensive piece like that? No. At least, not in the timeframe we have." He exited. Rose kept the muzzle of a revolver trained on Stacey.

"He's going to kill me you know," she said to Rose. "He hates me and he's a heartless monster and he's going to kill me."

"He won't kill you," she said. "I'll make sure of it." Stacey didn't seem convinced and began looking around with shifty eyes. She watched Rose, looked at the gun she held, looked at the distance between them. She was analyzing, and Rose caught on. "Don't make it worse. Even if you were to able gain the upper hand here, if Ashur comes in and you have a gun to my head, he won't hesitate to put you down. Don't give him a reason to do it."

"Rose…"

"Just stay calm and play along," she said. "He'll let you live."

Ashur reentered the room. His knife, which he still held in his hand, dripped with blood. He could have easily cleaned it off, but he had not. He had left it dirty to terrorize Stacey. This was proven a moment later when he cleaned the blade on her sweater.

"Congratulations," he said while finishing with her top. "The ballots are in. You're the new mayor." She said nothing, eyes glued to the floor. "Ready to go, Rose?" he asked, sheathing the knife. She nodded. He turned to Stacey. "I've killed a lot of people today, Stacey," he said as he reached into his jacket.

"Ashur, no!" Rose yelled.

"Calm down," he said and pulled his hand out of his coat, revealing a pair zip ties. "I was just going to rope her."

Stacey and Rose expressed their relief. Stacey especially, who, upon seeing that she was going to live, eagerly stuck out her wrists. He opened the garage door and secured her to a decorative fence in the yard. "Rose and I will be out of this town in fifteen minutes," he said. "But until then, you need to stay quiet. Do I need to use duct tape?"

"No," she said. "I'll keep quiet."

"For fifteen minutes?"

"Yes."

He stared her down.

"Ashur, I promise. I swear to you, I'll stay quiet."

"I believe you." He gestured towards his own nose. "Would you like me to…?"

"Yeah. Fine. Just do it."

He cupped a hand over Stacey's mouth before properly setting her nose. She whined through his fingers for a second before recomposing herself. He removed his hand. "Should heal all right."

"Can you guys just go now?"

"In a moment. I've got one last thing I need to do." He returned to the garage and moved his bike's saddlebags to the trunk of Vanderbilt's prized Mercury. He returned to his bike and studied it. "Goodbye, old girl." He kicked it over. Shortly thereafter, the Cougar pulled out onto the sunless streets of Tavern Springs. He exited the vehicle and started back up the driveway, passing Stacey. In the garage, he found a jerry can of octane and began pouring it over the classic cars, with a few splashes on the walls and floor. When the can was empty, he pulled out a matchbox and struck a light. He watched it burn for a few seconds before flicking it into the Bel Air convertible. He waltzed out of the garage and back onto the driveway, a wicked heat following him.

"What are you doing!?" Stacey asked.

"Finishing what the revolution started. I'm burning down the Breakers." He continued down the driveway, towards the waiting vehicle. "I wish I could say, 'It was nice knowing you,' Stacey. But it wasn't. Best of luck in your new life. Take care of this town for me." He got in the car and sped off. They were back on the road, skipping town.

"Did you just light the town hall on fire?" Rose asked as they rounded a corner, the tires squealing.

"I did," he confirmed. "He burns me. I burn him."

"Why?"

"As a distraction."

"And you really think she's going to keep quiet?"

"I'm hoping for the whole, Stockholm Syndrome thing."

"Okay. You can explain exactly what that is later. The other thing I wanted to know was…" Her voice fell. "What the fuck, Ashur?"

"The pantry with Stacey? It was a scare tactic. We needed information."

"Mission accomplished! She was petrified. And it scared me too."

"I had already broken her nose. Would you have rather sat there and watch me break her fingers one by one until she told me what I wanted to know? And if you were so concerned with it, why did you start to leave the room when I asked you to?"

"I…I just didn't know what else to do. I've always done what you told me. I trust you."

"And she caved at the sight of you leaving and we got what we needed."

Rose looked out the window. "Jesus Christ," she said under her breath. "And did you *have* to kill Vanderbilt?"

"No. I didn't. But this world is the way it is because of men like him. They made me and thousands like me into killers. As far as I'm concerned, he did it to himself."

They flew through Tavern Springs thanks to the absence of traffic. In only ten minutes, they were hurtling through the rangelands, closing in on the main gate. Upon reaching the checkpoint, the duo found a near army of sentries blocking their path. From what Ashur could see in his high beams, there were at least forty men. He skidded to a stop as soon as he could, leaving a deal of breathing room between the car and the blockade.

"Should've gone with the duct tape," Ashur said. Stacey had obviously gotten free and radioed ahead to the gate. The situation looking grim. He was preparing to spool up the miniguns when the gate began to crawl upward. There were a few shouts and a few muzzle flashes—the crowd had dealt with those loyal to the orders. After that, the wall of sentries parted, and he took his opening. They sped off into the black of night, pursued by no one. After another twenty minutes of driving, the adrenaline began to level off, and Rose asked where they would be staying for the night.

Chapter 23

The muscle car stopped in front of a wide, metal, two story building. It was surrounded by a towering barbed-wire fence that had rusted through long ago. There was something written on the wall here, tucked away from the sun. The artist had used too much paint, causing rivulets to stem from every letter, as if it had been written in blood.

Everything is Okay. Trust Your Gov't.

The history of the building is as follows: It began its dreary life as the crowning achievement of government oppression—a DMV. It then degenerated into a minimum security reeducation center before finally retiring as a RAUC station. All of this, of course, was before the global holocaust.

Ashur shut off the car and got out. Rose followed in silence. They began shambling towards the low-brow structure before them.

"What is this place?"

"During the revolution it was a Riot and Urban Control station," said Ashur. "After that the Rangers used it as an outpost. Now it's a derelict."

"Why'd they abandon it?"

"After the Rangers got bought out by the Company they had little use for Interior positions. I was apparently the only person to have sense enough to convert it into my own personal way station." They walked around to the back door and then Ashur began fumbling in the dark for something.

"What are you doing?"

"We may be from different worlds, Rose. But we've got one thing in common. We're both latchkey kids." Ashur continued searching but wound up unable to find the key. "Someone's gotten inside," he whispered, now noticing the cinders from a nearby campfire. He pulled out his handgun and crept up to the door, slowly turning the knob. The door clicked and swung inward, creaking loudly. It was silent at first. Then from the walls of the black room echoed a low growl. There was a blur and in a moment Ashur was pinned underneath a vicious wolfhound.

His owner stood in the doorway, a long-barreled revolver in his hand. "Moonraker," he said. "He's not a chew-toy."

Rose rushed at the dog and bowled it over. "Get off!"

The mongrel stumbled a few feet before finding its bearings. It barked at them.

She drew her short sword and brandished it, to keep him at bay. "What the fuck, man. Call him off!"

Jackstraw eyed her suspiciously. The dog closed in.

"Jack!"

"Moonraker, stand guard."

The dog circled them, its head hung low. Ashur sat on his knees, catching his breath. Rose saw his gun laying nearby and hurried to pick it up. Moonraker cut her off and barred his teeth. She stepped back.

"Good evening, Ashur."

"Evening, Cousin. You've found me."

"I—a world-class tracker—found *you?* I mean it's not like your house is built into the side of a mountain or anything. Everyone knows where to find you. They just don't know how to get by your militia. Why do you think I met you at Medway?"

"I assume you're here for the bounty."

"Ouch. Right in the character," said Jackstraw. "You think family means I'd sell you out for a miserly five-hundred platinum?"

"Wouldn't you?"

"I mean I would, but everyone knows the Rangers aren't good for it. So why bother with all the fuss?"

"You've come to help then."

"Curiously enough, neither. Remember how I said I was living in temporary housing? I was looking for a cheap place to stay and I remembered you mentioning you had a safe house out this way a few years back so I took it upon myself to see if it was still standing. So, no. I didn't come to help. But seeing as you're here now I may as well pull your feet out of the fire for the umpteenth time."

"Says the vagrant mooching off my emergency rations."

He dug something out of his ear with his pinky. "Moonraker, at ease." The wolfhound returned to his master's side, giving his hand a lick.

Rose sheathed her sword and walked right up to Jackstraw. Laying both hands on his chest plate, she shoved him. "Fuck you, you asshole."

"You wanna?"

Ashur got between her and Jackstraw. "Rose, cool off."

They went inside and made themselves at home. The main room was dark and standardized in design. The whole building sagged with government regulations and reminders of the world that had been—propaganda posters and starred flags. Jackstraw led them into the section Ashur had made into a safe house. There was a small kitchen, six cots, and an equipment locker all of which had been stocked to maintain a group for nearly two weeks.

"I've eaten most of the ramen and beanie-weenies," said Jackstraw before sending out a frightful shutter. "I'm down to the Spam."

"Have you used all my ammo as well? And my money?"

"I plan on paying you back."

"You do have twenty gold and five sliver pieces."

"Well see, there's a funny story about that." He directed their attention to the giant, shredded teddy bear in the corner. "I left Moonraker alone with it while I was making some food in the kitchen, and well…yeah."

"Why did you come here without collecting the twenty pieces?"

"I needed some lunch, and I had to check on my dog. They wouldn't let him in at Medway. I was going to go right after. But in hindsight, everything's twenty-twenty, ain't it? It's a shame how that works. At any rate, I'll work off my rent."

Ashur's muscles slackened. "Family's family, right?"

"So what's the story with the bounty? It must be bad."

He brought his cousin up to speed with the situation. While doing so, he flipped through his key ring and found the one for the locker. By the time Jackstraw knew everything they knew, Ashur had found a bottle of booze he had stored long ago. He did not bother with chairs or glasses. Instead, he sprawled out on the cold, tile floor and began taking long draughts from the bottle. Rose walked over and swiped it from him, spilling some on him in the process.

"Hey. What the hell'd you do that for?" he asked.

"I need you here," she scowled.

He grabbed her wrist and pulled her to the ground with him. She wound up in his lap, where he reclaimed the bottle and took another swig. "What for? We're safe now." He shoved it back into her hands.

She pondered for a moment, let out a breath, and then took a draught herself, reeling from it shortly thereafter. "Why do you drink this stuff?" she asked, coughing.

"For the fine taste," he replied.

Jackstraw placed himself in a chair and lit a cigarette. As he did this, Moonraker sat by his side, at attention, watching Rose and Ashur. "Rough day, huh?"

"I wouldn't want to relive it anytime soon," said Rose, crawling out of Ashur's lap.

"And how," said Ashur.

Jackstraw converted half of his cigarette into ash with a single drag and then barked an order at his wolfhound. The dog, now free from his duties, sulked across the room to study Rose before leaving to finish off the giant teddy bear.

Ashur and Rose stayed on the floor, trading the bottle back and forth in silence. It was not long before Rose decided to hold onto the booze, if only to keep it away from Ashur. When that happened, a stillness set in and he grew near to passing out. "I didn't need to kill her," he said suddenly, running his fingers through his hair. "The woman in the hospital. I shouldn't've killed her." Jackstraw was on his second cigarette when this occurred. "Vanderbilt I won't lose any sleep over, but her…her and all the other people."

Rose looked Ashur over for a moment. "You did what you thought you needed to."

"I fucked up," he corrected. "It's all I've ever done. It's funny really. I spent my whole life surviving for the sake of surviving. It was only at the end of the earth that I realized it was for nothing." He laughed. "I've been dead all my life. This whole damned world has. But, for whatever reason, I keep on going, till the creek rises or fate grant again the courage for suicide." He made a pass at the bottle.

She kept it away from him. "Don't talk like that," she said, taking a swig.

"What is it that you're looking for from this line of work? 'Cause this right here, it's what you're going to get."

"I want what you want, more or less," she said. "Adventure with a bit of heroism."

"Yeah I'm a real hero."

"The Ranger medals in your drawer, those old military accolades you have stashed in your safe, the defender of Tavern Springs. You might have everyone else fooled into thinking you're a merc, but I know you. You're not mean-spirited. You're not evil. That's why you're so fucked up inside. Because you wish you hadn't but if you hadn't you wouldn't be here. You're not alone there, but you've been through the wringer more than most."

"There are other ways to help people that don't include strong arming. You belong in a school, or April's clinic. Not out here with us. The life of an XP is going to ruin you."

"Well, I'm here now. I couldn't turn back if I wanted to."

"Yeah? And what about down the road? What are you going to do when I'm not around to drag you into trouble?"

"I guess I'll have to go out and find it on my own." She got up and stowed the half empty bottle of booze in the locker. "You're done for the night, okay?"

He nodded. "Get some rest." After that, she picked out a cot and began making herself cozy. Moonraker, who had been enamored with her since they met, jumped in and curled up with her. She wrapped her arms around him.

"Would you look at that," said Jackstraw. "I've never seen him take to someone like that. He rarely even cuddles up to me."

***

Ashur sat on the curb drinking a cherry Coke. His bicycle lay not far from him. Johnny was nearby, leaning against the trunk of his high school junker. Ashur was fifteen. Johnny was nearing twenty. He had come to get Ashur from the park and bring him home. In the distance, sirens flared.

"You know what I could really go for?"

"What's that?"

"A candy bar," said Ashur.

Johnny scoffed. "You going to lift one of those too? Like you did that soda?"

"Maybe."

"You know if they catch you, my mom isn't going to vouch for you."

"They better not catch me then."

The distant sirens grew and a number of squad cars flew by, tailed closely by a brigade of fire trucks. No ambulances. The teens watched the emergency vehicles careen down the street towards downtown St. Louis. A large spire of black smoke rose from the city to join with the rest of the smog sky.

Johnny turned from his spot and walked to the driver-side door of his car. "Would you be able to make your way home from here?" he asked, popping the trunk.

"I guess so. If I have to. Why?"

Johnny returned to the back of the car. He moved the floor mat, revealing the compartment where the spare is normally stored. From it, he retrieved an assault carbine and a clip of ammo. He checked the breech before inserting the magazine and priming the weapon.

"Holy shit, Johnny. Where'd you get a gun?"

"I know a guy." After standing the rifle up against the bumper, Johnny brought out a bullet proof vest and put it on. Then he grabbed a few more clips. "You go on home now. I'll see you a little later."

"You're not going into that are you? Are you insane? You're going to get yourself killed," Ashur said. "What am I supposed to tell your mother?"

"Tell her that I had to work late with dad at the dealership." He closed the trunk. "You shouldn't be so quick to condemn my choice. You're getting older. It won't be long till you'll have to decide which side you're on…a conqueror or a freedom fighter."

***

Ashur had beaten the sun this morning, as he did on many occasions. He brushed his fingers through Rose's hair as she slept, watching her. Their cots were close together. He noticed his cousin was awake, his legs hung over the side of his cot. He was drenched in sweat, panting hard. "You all right, Johnny?" he whispered.

"I'm fine. It's just this God damn dream. I keep having it."

"Which one?"

"The one of the New Age." He caught his breath and came over to sit next to Ashur. He saw him playing at the girl's hair. "She's not Abigail," he said.

"Don't you think I know that?" Ashur asked flatly.

"It's just…it's not like you to stick your neck out for anyone. Even me. Honestly I'm a little jealous."

"Tell me about your dream."

"I'm standing in the middle of this salt flat, grains between my toes. And there's nothing around me, in any direction, except for what had once been an island. It's jutting up in the distance, out of the ground like a tower. The journey to it takes me hours it seems, like wading through an acre of mud, but I get there and I climb up to the shoreline. All the grass has died and there's this old, red-skinned man there. He's crying. He's lost his sight. He can't see. He begs me to tell him what has become of the world. 'What do you see?' he asks…and do you know what I tell him? Do you know what I *always* tell him?"

Ashur pulled his eyes off Rose and shook his head.

"I say to him—I say, 'My dear old man, you haven't lost your sight. This is it. Welcome to the last corner of the Earth, the land of nothing.' And then I wake up."

Chapter 24

The pacifying hum of an acoustic guitar fluttered about the air along with a number of other instruments: flutes, saxophones, basses. People played here in the market commons for tips and applause. Unfortunately for them, they were so many that their sounds, along with many other sounds, blended into a collective mass of cacophonous and indistinguishable noise. In fact, the number of part-time musicians in Irongrass was so many that it had become something of a tradition to throw a bass player out of a window when a party grew dull.

Irongrass worked a little different than most towns. There was no "mayor" here. In his place stood the despotic baron and his serfs. There were other factions, like the sentries, the work orderlies, the normal townies, but for the most part, Irongrass was founded on serf labor, slave labor. When the Green Bay coastline shrunk, it revealed iron deposits that had been hidden just below the water's edge. Because of this, Irongrass was rather industrious in the production of steel and machinery. Most people—those being the serfs—lived out of disused Grand Global shipping crates, one stacked on top of the other, on top of the other. Other parts of the town were built from the old tankers and ships left in port, now uncomfortably rusting on the floor of a salt bed.

Jackstraw knelt down and scooped up a handful of dirt, letting the soil slip through his fingers. It had been tainted to a ruddy crust by the smelting plants, just as the rest of the town had been. Even the sun looked red under all the pollution. "The Great Lakes used to be the world's greatest source of clear water," he said. "Did you know that?"

"Did the Collapse end that?" Rose asked.

He dusted his hand off on his pant leg. "No. We did that long before." He stood up and focused on the speck that lay on the horizon, near the new coastline—what was left of an island. He thought a moment and then scoffed.

"What is it?" she asked.

"A spare thought."

In the weeks following the run from Tavern Spring, the trio hadn't made much progress in securing Ashur's freedom. They lived on the fringes of the Interior, out of Ashur's way station, selling what they could scavenge from the rubble, taking odd jobs. At the start of it, the emergency money Ashur had stashed at the way station helped, but five weeks later, with Ashur unable to access his money back home, the trio was having trouble keeping their heads above water. Ashur was stuck at the station, unable to show his face in any settlement while Jackstraw and Rose investigated the bounties. Their victories were routine, but nonetheless, they were a long ways away from cleaning up the mess.

"I think we've picked up a tail," said Rose.

Jackstraw nodded. "Pug nose in the checked button down. Good eye, Red. You're learning quick."

"It's a habit of mine. What do you want to do about him?"

"We'll proceed to the theater, shake him on the way out." They returned their attention to the commons market and began towards their goal. The streets of the commons were cluttered with kiosks and stands, vendors selling produce and dry goods. As they walked, pieces of people's lives were peered into: a lover's quarrel, a fruit man making a sale, a sentry on patrol with his buddy, one side of an argument, still photographs of emotion. Jackstraw, having spent his more recent years as a tracker, was keen to this daily phenomenon, and had, on numerous occasions, used it to his advantage.

The duo entered a vaudeville theater on the fringes of the commons. It had once been a yacht named *Xanadu*, most likely owned by one of the old world's finer members, but now, beached and retrofitted, it saw new life as a place of entertainment. **Sad's Café** flickered in neon above the entryway.

It was sparsely populated and clouded with opium smoke. Those that were there were more enthralled with their own conversations than with the comedian on stage. He stood shifting back and forth, laughing at his own jokes.

Jackstraw and Rose approached the bar counter, finding behind it, as one would expect, a dirty barkeep in a black apron. "Anything for you?" he asked.

"Are you Sad?" Jackstraw asked. The man stared at them blankly. "Let me rephrase that. Are you the owner of the place?"

"Yeah I'm Sad. What do you care?"

Jackstraw gestured to his badge. "I'm John Brown from the New Saint Lou Trackers' Guild. This is my associate Marigold Fleur. We have a few questions we'd like to ask you." A number of patrons at the bar counter turned their attention to him.

"I don't think so," said the barkeep.

"It will only take a minute of your time."

"I'm not going to answer any of your questions. You guys are phonies. Now get out before I throw you out."

"Phonies?" Jackstraw asked. "What do you mean we're phonies?"

"Well, John Brown and Marigold Fleur—terrible aliases by the way—there's no central authority on bountymen. Sure as hell no New Saint Lou Trackers' Guild. You're wearing police armor, which makes me certain you weren't a cop in the world before.

What's more, the badge you got clipped to your hip there is a fire department piece. Now get out."

"All right. I'll cut to the chase. Baron's got a deal with the Company. Everyone knows that. They've got a monopoly on liquor and dope. It seems, however, that you've taken it upon yourself to stick it to the man. So unless you take a moment to answer a few simple questions, I'll have you shut down."

"You haven't got any proof," the barkeep said.

Jackstraw smirked. "The baron's an inquisitor. They don't need proof. One anonymous tip and he and his men will tear out the walls of this place until they either find what they're looking for or there's nothing left to tear down. Your choice."

The barkeep eyed the faux detectives and then his patrons before jerking his head. "In the back," he said. The duo followed him through the kitchen and into a storage area that had been added on to the yacht with a pair of Grand Global shipping crate. They were stacked to the ceiling with illegal booze and opium.

"How'd you know he was crooked?" Rose asked after seeing the contraband.

"Everyone's crooked," remarked Jackstraw.

"I must say I'm impressed with the how easily you called us out. You're a sharp man, Mr. Sad. Very observant."

"Nah it's the other way 'round. You guys ain't as sharp as you think. What's with the whole investigator routine anyway? Who you trying to show up?"

"From what I've experienced," said Jackstraw. "Most people are more cooperative when a sense of formality is impressed upon them. That's all."

"So what do you guys want?"

Rose pulled the door behind her shut and secured the latch. "Just a moment of your time." The crate was dirty and rancid. The walls appeared yellow but, because of the poor lighting, could have been any number of colors on that end of the spectrum.

"Who do you get the contraband from?" Jackstraw asked.

The barkeep scrunched his brow and reeled in distain. The reaction added a few more chins to his already flabby face. "You guys must be crazy," he said, shaking his head, his jowls wobbling. "You think I'm just gonna up and name my guy?"

"I'll save you the trouble," said Rose. She pulled out a sketch Jackstraw had done of an older, white male and held it up. "Rupert Ransby. He supplies you, and a number of other merchants in town. We want to know where we can find him."

"How am I supposed to know? I don't keep tabs on people, that's what we have you trackers for."

"Do you know where your shipments come from, Mr. Sad?" asked Jackstraw. "Or do you prefer not to ask questions?"

"You think it's easy running a club here in serf country? I gotta turn a profit. And with the Company's business regulations strangling me, I don't care if he's stealing from the town med center."

"It comes from New Valley," said Rose. "Stolen booze off of murdered caravaneers and Rangers is cut with bathtub gin and wood alcohol before being sold to upstanding citizens such as yourself. I suspect the opium trade works in a similar manner. People find you with goods from dead Company men and you're going to swing."

"It would be in your best interest to help us out here."

"Honestly," said Mr. Sad. "This guy's a spook. I leave a payment where he specifies and a few weeks later I find my shop stocked with booze. I've met him once."

"And how does he specify the drop spot if you don't talk to each other?" asked Jackstraw.

Mr. Sad sighed heavily. "A girl of his. She comes to the bar, trades a slip with the drop location for a Cuba Libre."

"This girl, she got a name?"

"Ancilla."

"Ancilla?" repeated Jackstraw.

"Yes, sir."

Jackstraw thought for a moment.

"What?"

"Nothing. What's she look like and when's she stopping by next?"

"Uh, Latino, serf rags, petite, black hair down to her ass."

"And when can we find her?"

He hesitated. His eyes flickered from Rose to Jackstraw. "I can't tell you that."

"Can't or won't?" Rose asked as Jackstraw moved to the stack of contraband. He grabbed a bottle, undid the cork, and took a draught.

"If I tell you, and trouble comes about, they'll kill me."

Jackstraw put down the bottle and pulled a hatchet off his belt. "Do you know why they call us hatchet men, Mr. Sad?"

Mr. Sad's scrunched brown and worry lines progressed deeper. "N-No."

"Tell you what, you tell us what we want to know, and you don't have to find out."

A few minutes later, Jackstraw and Rose had the information they had come for and Mr. Sad had only one broken finger. They thanked the proprietor for his cooperation. "Oh," Jackstraw asked as they left the storage room and entered the kitchen. "Does this place have a back exit?"

Mr. Sad nodded and readily showed them the back hallway, eager to be rid of them. Jackstraw exited the room, into the after-noon sun, and walked directly into the end of a Ranger's service revolver. As the hammer clicked back, Jackstraw went for his six-shooter. And because of the slight angle he was at when the bullet hit his riot armor chest plate, the ricochet caught Rose in the arm and put her on the ground next to him. As he sprung up and brought out his gun, the barkeep, Mr. Sad, clubbed him over the head with a meat tenderizer.

Jackstraw awoke in that back alley hours later, upon a pile of garbage bags. He noted the evening sun and the dried blooded streaks on the side of his head. It was pounding. Pulling himself up, he stumbled and fell back into the dirt. There was no sign of the Rangers or Rose. His gun was missing too.

When he found his bearing and figured out what had happened, he hopped in his sandrail and raced across the wastes, towards Ashur, and towards the Rangers.

Chapter 25

The sheriff's office was roomy and matched the description of some corporate CEO's. The sheriff himself was on the heavier side and wore a distinct, slightly larger badge, similar to that of Deputy Sloan's, but more grandiose. He rested comfortably in his executive leather chair behind a rosewood desk.

Ashur wasted no time in knocking a lamp off of it. "Let me see her!"

"And I want my gun back," Jackstraw joined in. "It has sentimental value. It's non-replaceable."

One of the Rangers in the room walked forward and attempted to place a hand on Ashur. He threw an elbow back and struck him in the face. The sheriff waved an authoritative hand, demanding silence. "It was just a lamp," he said. The Ranger moved back and stood next to his friend, by the door. "I'll give you a minute with her, and then you and I are going to sit down and have a little chat about why we're here." Sheriff Stone used the radio clipped on his duster to call for Rose Waters to be brought into his office. A short time later, the door swung open and a Ranger walked her into the room.

When she spotted Ashur, she threw her arms around him, hurting herself in the process.

"Are you okay?" he asked.

"I did get shot," she said, wincing. "But it's been cleaned out. I'm going to be fine."

He noticed her cracked lip. "What happened?" He reached out gingerly to touch it, but she grabbed his hand.

Her eyes flickered away. "Nothing."

He put his finger under her chin and brought her eyes to his. "It's not nothing," he said with a smile. "I hope you kicked his ass."

She held his hand to her cheek. "Well I'm not just going to give up."

"Good," he said. "I'm going to fix this. Just give me some time. We'll have you out of here. Until then, cooperate for me. Don't agitate them."

She nodded. "Okay."

The Ranger took her out of the room. Thereafter, the sheriff told the two others to leave. They abided, leaving Jackstraw and Ashur alone in the room with the sheriff.

"You better not lay another finger on her," Ashur said.

"I assure you, so long as you honor the agreement we're about to make, no further harm will come to her."

"You're holding the wrong girl hostage, lawman."

"Ashur—may I call you Ashur?"

"No."

"Grimm?"

"I'm not one of you anymore."

"Oh but that's where you're wrong, Grimm. When you leave this room, you will be a Ranger. You will be working for me. And you will be sincere about it."

"What do you want?"

"I want a problem solved."

Ashur crossed his arms. "What is it?"

"The raids. They've become quite the disturbance."

"They didn't seem to be a disturbance when Wellshire was burning to the ground."

The sheriff scratched at his chin. "Wellshire was a small, poor settlement. But if I had seen the problem would advance this far, I might've sent some men out there. They're raiding not only Irongrass and Tavern Springs, which obviously causes problems with the Company's caravans, but they've now started raiding Medway itself. The Rome of the blackland, and it's being raided by untouchables."

"So this is what I'm getting," Ashur said. "Someone is raiding settlements, which really only concerns you because the Company is losing money. Now that the raids have spread to Medway, I'm guessing the townies and the mayor are peeved because the Rangers aren't doing their job. So you guys are in over your head, and you've kidnapped the only person I care about so that I'll help you."

"Yes, Grimm, that is the situation in a nutshell. And if you can figure that out so quickly, you should have no problem figuring out a plan of action. I'm sure I'll have your full cooperation, and I don't expect you to bring down the whole operation by yourself of course. You'll have the Syndicate's help. Anything you need."

"I need my gun back," Jackstraw mentioned.

"Keep your men. They're useless to me."

Sheriff Stone reached into a drawer and placed a Ranger badge in front of Ashur. "I'm growing weary of this attitude of yours."

"You know where they are," he said, taking the badge. It was a deputy's piece, like the one he had in his drawer back at home. "Why don't you take your men and march on New Valley?"

"I'm not one to run into a fight blind."

"So you're saying you're short on intelligence?" asked Jackstraw.

"I find out who's behind this and then I call in you guys. Is that what you're asking?"

"Assassination is more what I had in mind," the sheriff said. "If they fall out of rank, we can defend our trade again. We need you to kill this Cadre character. You do that and you can go back to living out of your hut as a scavenger. But I expect you to do everything within your power to bring these men to justice, because if we fail, you fail. Is that understood?"

"Let me make something perfectly clear," Ashur said. "If anything happens, if you don't hold up your end of the deal, or this doesn't work out…" He took the photo of Sheriff Stone's family off his desk and memorized their faces. "It'll be your blood." He set the picture down and turned to leave.

"One last thing," the sheriff said and then made use of his radio again. A Ranger entered the room. "This is your handler," the sheriff said. "Thorn."

He observed the Ranger. He was scrawny, nearly a foot shorter than him, and had a face full of Vandyke. "You're giving me a handler?"

"Like I'm happy about working with a washed-up drunkard."

"Please, Thorn," said the sheriff. "It's best we start off on the right foot."

"Yeah well, we've got a thorn in our right foot," said Jackstraw.

"This man will be at your side and keep you in check until this operation is over with," the sheriff said. "You will listen to him and act as his partner. Or else…"

"Or else your little girlfriend gets it," Thorn finished. Ashur turned to the man and did something far more insulting that punching him: he took the back of his right hand and smashed it across the Ranger's face. Sheriff Stone halted the confrontation before it progressed any further. Thorn stood there, stroking his Vandyke, as if he was worried that the hit had messed it up.

"You're a war hero, Grimm," said the sheriff. "But this is not war. This is business. Don't let that slip your mind. Now go, all of you, and do your jobs. Stanton's, your weapons are waiting in the armory."

They left the sheriff's office complex and came into the star-shaped courtyard. Grand Citadel Dakota rested right on the edge of Medway, providing buffer against the scablands. It was a large complex of several newly constructed buildings, linked together with tunnels and pathways. The place was alive with Rangers running training routines, vehicles transporting equipment, and newly arrived or pre-departure Company caravans. Ashur hadn't seen the Rangers so productive since the days of the old syndicate. With all the raiding and political pressure, the sleeping giant had finally been pushed into action. And he was their vanguard—the tip of the spear.

Chapter 26

It would soon be nightfall. Ashur and Jackstraw were on the road way to New Valley in Vanderbilt's car. Ashur had never been but he had heard stories, none of them were pleasant. Jackstraw on the other hand had a bit of experience in the town. In the distance it sat, a towering super prison. Many like it had been built during the failed revolution, and many of them still stood today. With miles of chain linked fence, guard towers, and concrete cell blocks, it was a veritable fortress. They arrived at a gate, watched over by only two legionaries. The Cadre's soldiers were generally dressed in the same government issued riot armor Ashur had once worn. The only difference was the branding on the back: **New Valley Correctional Facility**.

"What's your business here?" the cleaner guard called.

"We want in," Ashur answered. Both he and Jackstraw wore bandanas to cover their faces. "What's the hold up?"

The legionaries looked at each other, and then back at vehicle. "I don't recognize your car, where are y'all from?"

"Newaukee. We heard this was the spot up here. I hope we weren't mistaken."

"You weren't mistaken. Come on through."

Ashur pulled the car into the checkpoint. They got out and stood before the men, saying nothing. From where they were, it was clear that the parking lot was decorated with crucifixes. Many of them had people nailed to them.

"What brings you up the coast?" one of the legionaries asked.

"Looking for work."

"I'm sure you'll find plenty of it. But before we let you guys through, we need your weapons. It's, you know, procedure."

Ashur shifted his gaze between the two of them and then pulled his Winchester off his back. But when one of them reached out to grab it, he smashed the stock of the rifle into his face. The hit knocked the man out cold, and his friend was left standing there, unimpressed.

"I may be new, but I'm not stupid," Ashur said.

The legionary examined the car for a moment, noting the miniguns. "Go on through."

They moved on and found a spot in the parking lot, afterwards entering the main administrative building. It was now a market and trading post. The place was packed, cellblock to cellblock, with drug dealers, weapon runners, slave traders, saloons, brothels, and auto garages. This was home to the dregs of society, the fiends and the scum.

Down with the Toad of Nazareth!

       Open the gates of the asylums and prisons!

Unscrew the locks from the doors!

Unscrew the doors themselves from their jambs!

   The anarchist's bomb

   Or the policeman's baton?

   We've made our choice.

        No Forbidding Allowed.

In time, Ashur and Jackstraw found their way into a hostel called The Rough Landing Inn. It was sparsely populated and filled with smoke. The bottom floor was more or less an opium den. The dope peddler at the counter bayed at them but they kept walking. They were here on Jackstraw's intuition, following a lead. In the back corner, surrounded by a pair of young women, sat a familiar, lanky figure. As they passed through the smoke, Ashur recognized him—the Dirty Danworth. The duo sat down in the booth, across from the racer.

Jackstraw held out a pair of sliver pieces. "Evening ladies," he said. "Why don't you go get something good from the peddler…for about twenty minutes."

The girls looked at Danworth. He assured them that he would be here when they got back, so they left. "And what can I do for you fine gentlemen?"

Ashur pulled down his bandana, revealing his face. "It's me, old friend," he said before making his identity scarce.

A wide grin broke out across Danworth's face. "By Jove, the balls on this guy. How are you doing? And who's this?"

"This is my cousin Johnny. And we need some help."

Danworth reached across the table and shook Jackstraw's hand. "Nice to meet you," he said, afterwards sliding a peace pipe across the table. "Help yourself."

Jackstraw eagerly snatched up the pipe but did not protest when Ashur took it away and gave it back. "No thanks," he said. "We're on the clock."

"So what do y'all need from me?"

"We need information on the Cadre," said Jackstraw.

"I don't know how much I'd be able to help you with that. He keeps a close-knit cabinet. They act as his arms, run everything now. He used to give speeches when he was rising to power. But nowadays we rarely see him."

"Have you been present for any of these speeches?" asked Ashur.

"I was. Only a couple though. He wore an old ballistics mask. I've heard tell that his face is fucked up, but even behind that veil, he's quiet the orator. Rallied the people preaching a code of order and great military conquest, and above all, he brought this city into its golden age, and for that the people love him."

"And what is this code like?"

"It's pretty basic. If someone pisses you off, tell a legionary and they organize a fight. If you kill anyone outside of a fight, or if you cheat, you get crucified. That's it."

"Really? What about other crimes?" Ashur asked.

"Someone steals something from you, assaults you, insults you, maybe you just don't like the way they look at you, then you tell one of the Cadre's men. Then you fight, bare-knuckled."

"Does anyone know where the Cadre keeps himself? He has to hang around here somewhere," said Jackstraw.

Danworth shrugged. "Warden's building I guess. No one but the legionaries are allowed in or out of that. But if you're thinking of sneaking in, I would give that up right now. You'd be walking into a gallows, or a crucifix more like."

"Well, there you have it," said Jackstraw. "Mission's a bust. Let's get lit."

"Your commitment to our cause is noted."

"Hey, she's your kid."

"Which makes her part of your family."

"Yeah," said Jackstraw. "Except I don't really think she likes me."

"Your powers of deduction are marvelous, detective."

"Wait a minute," said Danworth. "Y'all talking about the little red one?"

Ashur nodded. "Ranger's got her. If I don't do something about the Cadre, I'm not going to see her again."

"Those dirty bastards," Danworth said, dropping his voice into a whisper. "You mean to tell me they took that kid as collateral and sent you here, by yourself, to axe the big guy? That's utter suicide. Ain't no way you're gonna get out of here alive even if you could get close enough to take the shot."

"What's our most realistic option here?" asked Ashur. "How could we request an audience with the Cadre?"

"Requesting one isn't the hard part. It's being granted a meeting. You'd have to be someone mighty important."

"You mean, like a famous death racer?"

Danworth smirked. "Now, you know I'm sympathetic to you and your cause, but I don't wanna end up like the boys out in the parking lot. Big guy won't take any issue crucifying me, even with my stature. So keep scheming."

Ashur interlaced his fingers. "What about our story from being from Newaukee?" he asked. "Let's say we're ambassadors from a gang there. We do have our handler tied up in the trunk of the car. A Ranger would make a great gift. Or we could say we're reporters from Radio Free doing a story and we'd like an interview."

"He's shied away from the public eye this long," said Jack-straw. "I doubt he'd be interested in getting his name out there. Posing as ambassadors may get us close to him, but then what? He's in a tower. Maybe we can wait around till his next speech and I'll pick him off. Any idea when that's supposed to be?"

Danworth shrugged. "No clue. From what I've seen, he announces them the day of."

"I doubt we have that much time to kill."

"What if I just fight him?" Ashur asked. "Can I do that?"

Danworth thought. "There's no rule against it. But why would he fight you if he could just have you hauled off and crucified?"

"Because we won't give him any other choice."

The rally began with a gunshot. Ashur stood alongside Jackstraw and the Dirty Danworth, scraping together the courage to brave the crowd. They were on a small stage in the busy market of the city. Normally, the platform saw use by basement musicians or snake oil salesmen, but today it would be the point of origin for a rally which would push New Valley into disorder. The rushing market's attention quickly shifted towards the stage. Most everyone had a gun out in response to the discharge.

"People of New Valley," said Ashur. "I'd like your attention please. My name is Ashur Stanton." Anyone who hadn't been paying attention after the gunshot was grabbed by the name. He now had the market at a standstill. "And before you go slinging a bullet, I'm here of my own free volition. You won't make a cent off my head. But listen up and you'll get a good show. I'm new here to this town, and I like what you've built. I've heard a lot about your new leader, the Cadre. I hear he gives some great speeches, and that he's only got half a face. How does New Valley feel about his leadership?"

The crowd that had gathered gave out three solid cries, chanting in unison.

"Has he not been a fair leader? Has he not been a distinguished leader? Has he not instilled a code here by which you can live free of law, yet defend your property and clan mates?"

The crowd cheered again.

"And since this is the case, should your fair and distinguished leader be exempt from this same code that he has impressed upon you? Should he not live by the rules of his people? Any man—no, any leader excused from the authority of his own decrees is not a man. He is a god. And let me tell you something about the end of the earth. There are no gods here."

The marketplace became uproarious with the cheers of the mob.

"Are you willing to live under a godhead? Under a delusional idol?"

"No!" said the people.

Ashur pulled off his left glove. "Any man can challenge any man. That is the code. Then in the spirt of this code, let us put the Cadre to the test. Let me hold him to the same standards he holds you." Ashur threw his glove at a nearby fire team of legionaries. It landed a few feet in front of them. "I challenge your leader, the Cadre, to a duel. He wants me dead, let's see him do it himself!" The crowd went nuts. One of the sentries picked up the glove and rushed off through the bellowing horde.

Ashur left the stage and, followed by a mass of onlookers, moved from cell block to cell block, announcing what he had just done. Everywhere he went he gathered more and more ruffians. He made sure that if the Cadre said no, there would be a riot to answer for. Ashur made it to the fourth cell block before a team of soldiers arrived to confront him.

"So?" Ashur said. "What says the big guy?"

Ashur's glove landed at his feet. "He accepts your challenge."

Chapter 27

The ring was Cell Block C. Three stories up, people hung from the balconies, waiting. Each level was packed with crooks, thieves, and killers. Jackstraw and Danworth stood nearby, on the bottom level. All the tables had been pried away from the ground to make ample space. The convicts, as it seemed, formed the actual ring.

Ashur strode out before all of them. "Well?" he yelled. "Where is he?"

On cue, the crowd parted. Down the alley of spectators lumbered a dark figure. The Cadre bore a full set of riot armor, the ballistic mask included. It had eye holes and nose holes with six vertical slots over the mouth. The only other thing he wore was a leather jacket. It was human hide. He looked like the last horseman of the apocalypse.

A referee strode out between them. He addressed the Cadre. "Sir," he said. "Your armor is forfeit. Disarm." The Cadre began with his gauntlets and leg pieces. Nearby aids took possession of them. His left arm was scorched. Ashur looked to his cousin the moment he knew who he was fighting. Jackstraw was sheet-white. He had figured it out as well.

"At the dawn of the New Age, there roamed an untouchable band of raiders, feared by all and afraid of none," spoke the Cadre. "The leader of this gang was the fiercest, most ferocious corpse-maker the scablands had ever seen. The Great Beast of the Lakes was the name set upon him, and nightmares gathered in his wake." The last piece of armor to come off was his helmet, the mask coming with it. The rumors were true. He had half a face.

The first punch landed. It sent Ashur reeling back. The crowd cheered. "Come here to die?" Garwood asked before delivering a frightening kick to the thigh. It put Ashur into a kneel. Garwood drove a fist into his cheek before he could right himself. It sprawled Ashur onto the floor. "Because I mean to put you in the ground." The crowd roared. Garwood stepped back to allow Ashur to get up. He didn't have to. He could have dropped a knee into Ashur's chest and beat him to death. But that wouldn't have made for a good show.

Ashur stood up. His tongue was bleeding from the last hit. "What have you done?"

"The world's a sandbox, and I'm—"

"The world's dead."

"Then I lay claim to its corpse!" He came at Ashur. Ashur deflected the hit and kneed him in the ribs a few times before pushing him off. They circled each other and growled. "What was it you said to me before you went in search of your family? Before abandoned us in Chicago?" asked Garwood. Ashur came at him with a haymaker. He ducked it and replied with a head-butt, closing in on Ashur as he stumbled away. "We are not foot soldiers." He swept Ashur's legs out from under him, knocking him onto the concrete. "We're the appointed warlords." He placed his foot on the side on Ashur's neck, pinning him to the ground. "We are the coming law." He began applying pressure. "What I can't figure out is why you had a change of heart." Ashur gritted his teeth and strained. He tried to get a hold on Garwood's boot. "What? You lose your wife and kid and go soft? You barely saw 'em! You were a visitor to them. A holiday treat. I was more family to you than anyone. And you scorched off half my face. Like, what the fuck, man?"

Ashur got a grip on his boot and twisted. Garwood drew his foot back and nailed him in the stomach. He rolled over.

Garwood stepped away and let his opponent to catch his breath. He locked eyes with Jackstraw and shook his head slowly. "You choose to stand in the way of progress?"

"Trampling people isn't moving forward," Ashur said, spitting up blood.

"That's not how you felt twenty years ago. Now you have an army standing guard over a town of nobodies. Why?" The crowd had grown deathly quiet, no doubt in awe of their ruler's command.

"You're curious as to why I choose to protect people while you choose to rule over thieves?"

"Warriors," Garwood corrected. "Fighters. People with spirit. Admirable men!"

"All the admirable men are buried." Ashur bolted from where he was on the ground and shoulder-checked Garwood. He wound up on top of the god-king and began laying into him with punches.

Garwood laughed with each blow. "I want to know, Stanton. I want to know what changed."

Ashur paused his assault. "We protected those bastards while they trashed the place. Look at what we did."

Garwood grinned. "It's beautiful," he whispered, tears in his eyes. Ashur attempted to drop an elbow into his throat but he blocked it. They rolled and separated. "Your aim is to work off your portion of the debt? That's noble. At this rate you'll be done in four hundred years."

"I'll die trying."

"So you got a second daughter, to make right for the first one you killed?"

Ashur hit him with an uppercut. Garwood took a half step back and retaliated. He grabbed Ashur's head and made connection with his knee. Ashur dropped to the floor. His vision blurred.

"Don't beat yourself up over it," said Garwood. "I had just as much a hand in it as you did. We all did our part. No one is going to hold you to account for the things you've done." He started to help Ashur up. "And as soon as I kill you, there'll be no one to hold me to account for what I am." Garwood got him up and let him wander across the ring.

He leaned on Jackstraw. "If you've got a plan B, you might want to consider it," was all he said before letting him back in the ring.

He fumbled towards Garwood and began clinching on him before he could swing. Once he had some energy back, Ashur ducked under his arms and got him in a sleeper hold. The first thing Garwood did was gouge at the eyes. Ashur released him and struck him in the back of the head. Garwood responded with a spinning back-fist. They returned to clinching.

"On the advice of my council, I'd like to attempt a secondary course of action. I request an audience."

Garwood got a hand free and jabbed him in the ribs a number of times before he could draw him in close again. "Let me hear it."

"The plague that is the Ranger Syndicate, I'm looking to burn them to the ground."

"Why would you do that?" Garwood panted.

"They have my kid."

***

The posse had moved from the ring, to the warden's building. The place was now a penthouse. There were posh animal skin rugs, retro lava-lamps, record players, and modern paintings of the blackland. Ashur was receiving medical attention. Jackstraw stood nearby. Danworth, however, had wandered off to resume his life of debauchery.

"I don't like this," said Jackstraw. "He could kill us at any moment."

"He could have killed me in the ring," Ashur said, studying the slave-girl that was putting stitches in him. She avoided all eye contact. "But he didn't. He's decided to hear me out."

The Cadre kicked the door in. "Yes I have!"

This startled the nurse. She lost grip on the needle. "Shit," she hissed, meeting gaze with Ashur. She knew exactly what was going to happen next.

Garwood grabbed her by the back of her shirt and hauled her off of him. She landed on her ass a few feet away. "You can finish that later," he told her. "I still haven't decided if I am going to throw him off the balcony or not." One of the nearby legionaries helped her to her feet. She left the room. Garwood grabbed a wooden chair and spun it around so that the backrest was towards Ashur. He straddled it. "You've got two minutes to tell me why I shouldn't kill you."

"I'm here under the direct orders of the sheriff. I'm a Ranger at the moment. An honorary one. I can walk right into the Citadel, right up to him, and ice him."

"So why didn't you?"

"The same reason I didn't sneak into your building and ghost you," Ashur said. "There's an army waiting. And I would very much like to get out alive."

"I'm not seeing an obvious course of action here, Stanton. Clock's ticking."

"Raid the place. I need your army, to hold off their army. I walk in, get my kid, ice the big guy, maybe a few of his deputies, leave a few doors open for you. Then I take off, and you guys have your opportunity to strike. That's what you've been waiting for right? An opportune moment?"

Garwood turned his head to look at a man in the corner—one of his generals. The man said he would be happy to lead the raid. "Let me see," said Garwood. "I send my army to burn Grand Citadel Dakota. You get out of there. And then what? What is there to stop you from coming after me?"

"Or you me?"

"Okay so you and I have a little truce," he said, pointing his finger back and forth between Ashur and himself. "We glass the Rangers. And then we go back at it. Is that it?"

"Or you could throw me over the balcony into the yard, find your own way to bring down the Rangers. But I was just there. And they're mobilizing. It's now or never."

Garwood picked at the burnt half of his face while he thought. "I can't see your hide making a good jacket. It's so full of scars. But your girl's. I bet she'd make a pretty throw."

Ashur resisted the urge to look around the room at all the animal rugs and tapestries, realizing what they were. "Do we have a deal or not?"

Garwood stood up and put the chair back where he had gotten it from. "We have a deal."

Chapter 28

Ashur, Jackstraw, and Moonraker entered a small courtyard fenced in by rubble. They had come in search of Dixon and his men. The Aegis Compound was a fort tucked away in the Interior somewhere. All mercenary companies had to live out in the scablands. The Rangers considered private military contractors illegal, and most towns had a natural fear of them.

As dawn broke, the sun's orange glow struggled to pierce the dilapidated cityscape. **There Never Was Anything Great About It**, was the only piece of graffiti left standing in the rubble. The main feature of the courtyard was an old office building and the entrance of an underground parking garage. A matte door had been erected after the Collapse. The top of the office building and much of the sides were gone, but the center support had held strong. Because of this, the second floor now acted as the structure's roof.

They approached the building and found a woman asleep on the floor near a pile of embers and her pack. Their presence startled her awake and she sat up, turning away from them to reach into her bag. They had their handguns trained on her in an instant. "Pull your hand out of the bag nice and slow now," Jackstraw said. She did as he instructed, bringing out a knife. "Toss it," he said. She complied, then put her hands up and turned to face them. It looked as though she hadn't washed in months. Her skin was dark from grime. Her hair was black and brittle.

Jackstraw put his dog at ease.

"Pack up your things," Ashur said. "Move along. This wasn't a good spot to make camp."

"What?"

"You're sitting on top of a paramilitary compound," he said and pointed to a CCTV camera that was fixed in the corner of the wrecked building. At first, she was confused, but as the garage door to the compound began scrolling open, she made the connection. Her eyes went wide and she grabbed her pack, leaving her bed roll. She pushed past them and sprinted through the courtyard, towards the road. She didn't get there.

Two armor clad men burst forth from the compound and grabbed her. They wrestled in the dirt. She screamed and fought back, biting one of the men in the hand. He pulled back and struck her across the face. The blow sent her into a stupor, giving the other man the time to tear off her shirt.

"Let her up," Ashur called over, halfheartedly.

"Fuck off," one of them returned. "Go find your own."

Jackstraw raised the hammer on his long-barreled revolver. "Should I?" he asked Ashur.

He drew a weary breath. "That's your call, man," he said and trudged off towards the compound. "I'm not going to do a damn thing." Jackstraw stood there deliberating for a moment before following his cousin.

They were just about to pass into the garage when one of the mercenaries gave them attention. "Hey! You can't go in there," he said before taking note of who he was. "Stanton?" The merc nudged his friend who was still fighting with the woman. "Look at this."

The second man did a double take and dropped what he was doing. "He's got money on his head."

No one moved. Ashur and Jackstraw still had their guns drawn, and an attack dog on guard. Dixon's men, on the other hand, were caught quite literally with their pants down. Ashur met the woman's gaze and mouthed the word "Run" while nodding. She scattered. The mercenaries didn't notice. Once she was out of sight, he spoke up. "Ranger's already got me. They'd open up on mercenaries the moment they spotted you anyways."

The tension dissipated. "Dixon is in the compound," one said, searching in the distance for his prey. "What do you want with him?"

"I got a job. I'm thinking about hiring Aegis."

The warriors led them into the den. The top level of the compound, was used as a garage for Aegis's numerous trucks, cars, armored fighting vehicles, and one monstrous structure that was covered in a tarp. The second level was a storage area and workshop. There were ammo presses, work benches, a lathe, pallets of explosives, spare parts, and weapons. The third level down was the heart of the operation: barracks, mess hall, firing range, gym. One of the mercenaries branched off into these sections as they walked down an immense hallway, leaving the other to lead them the rest of the way.

"Dixon's pretty irked about Wellshire," he said. "We all are. I don't know how happy he's going to be to see you." The mercenary knocked on a door. The door opened just a crack and an eye glared out at them. It took note of Ashur and softened. Dixon opened the door and stepped into the hallway. He was dressed in jeans, a stone grey T-shirt, and a new eye patch.

"This is a surprise," he said as his man walked off. "What brings you here, and who is this?"

"This is my cousin Jackstraw. We'd like to have a sit down. I've got a proposition."

Dixon motioned for them to follow him and continued down the hallway. "Your face is fucked up something awful," he said as he led them into the command center. A man was sitting in a chair watching a wall of CCTV screens. He greeted his boss without looking up. The room was cluttered with papers, journals, and reports. One end of the room was covered in dusty maps that no one had looked at in years. "Let's hear this proposal."

"I'm bringing down the Cadre," Ashur said. "And the Rangers. All I need is some backing. Thought that might be you."

"You know, that's a real temptation, and no one wants to bring down that bastard more than I, but in case you haven't heard, I lost most of my firm to him. I've got nine men at my disposal. If Aegis Armed Forces ever bounces back, it'll be a year or two."

"I may have a squad or three of men comparable to yours at the ready, but I'm going to level with you, Dixon. I can't see me and mine coming out of this, and judging by what the Cadre did to your company, I'd say the same for you and yours."

"Not a powerful selling point," he said.

"We're circling the drain here. You sit in your hole and sooner or later I know the Cadre will sweep on through and finish you off. You don't have a year or two. So you got three options: you can pack up, set out for the Southland or Newaukee or Traverse, and wait for the Cadre to catch up. You can lie down and die. Or you can make a Hail Mary at payback, leave this world the way you came in, kicking and screaming. It would be a travesty for an Irishman to die a subtle death, a coward's one at that."

Dixon was sent into a silence. He leaned back on a console and placed a hand on his chin. Soon though, he began to nod. "An attempt. I owe my men that much," he said, snapping his fingers at his man to hand him the nearby microphone. Depressing the button, he said, "This is your chieftain speaking. Yis to the barracks, rank and file." The man that had handed the microphone to his boss ran out of the room, down the hall. Dixon, Jackstraw, and Ashur followed at a normal pace. When they got to the barracks, each man stood in front of his bed at attention. Dixon stood before his men at the same kind of attention, and began to speak. "My faithful companions," he addressed them. "As ye have mourned, I have mourned. As ye have grown weary, I have grown weary. As ye have felt indignity, so too have I felt indignity. But today, that changes. These men behind me have come to bring us out of our shame. I have asked things of my men, many, many things, and now I ask yet another. But let it be known, should ye accept the challenge, you will ne'er lay eyes on your home again. I ask of you this, assist me in avenging our fallen brethren! Or die trying! Who stands with me?"

All at once, and without hesitation, his men shouted, "I do!"

Dixon bellowed, "The great Gaels of Ireland are the men that God made mad!"

And in unison came, "For all their wars are merry! And all their songs are sad!" There were a few cheers and whoops before Dixon put his men at ease.

"Looks like you're not the only poet-warrior here," Ashur said to Jackstraw.

Dixon called one of his men over—the one that had been watching the TV screens in the command center. "This is our sapper, Specialist Miller," he said. "He and I have something mighty to show you." They started on their way up to the first floor. "So why are you taking on the task of bringing down the Cadre, and the Rangers?"

"The Cadre and I have a history. He won't stop until I'm dead. He won't stop until he runs this patch of dirt," said Ashur. "As for the Rangers, that's just a bonus."

"And you?"

Jackstraw hesitated. "I won't be coming along for the ride."

Ashur stopped in his tracks. "What?"

"You said it yourself. We're not coming back from this. That ain't me."

Ashur ran a hand through his hair. It had grown out a bit in the past few months. "You're just going to jump in your sandrail with your stupid dog and go back to St. Lou?"

Jackstraw shrugged. "Yeah. Pretty much."

"How many men did you lose to him?" His voice echoed throughout the parking garage. "Eighteen? Twenty?"

"That was ten years ago, Ashur."

He came up on Jackstraw and shoved him. "They're still fucking dead!"

Jackstraw pushed him back. "Yeah but I'm still standing."

"What's it worth to you? You got a dog, a shack…nothing. Do something right for once in your miserable fucking life…brother."

Jackstraw did not respond. They carried on to whatever Dixon wanted to show them. They reached the first floor and stopped before a large machine covered in a tarp. Specialist Miller and Dixon undid a few ties and the tarp slid off.

Ashur smiled like an idiot at the thing. "Does she run?"

Miller nodded. "She runs."

Chapter 29

Jackstraw walked up to Ashur, his dog alongside. They were in the courtyard of Grand Citadel Dakota. The place was a beehive. "Last charge is set," said Jackstraw. "Dixon has the goods. Ready when you are."

"Now we wait for the—"

"This is Comanche," the radio in Ashur's ear buzzed. *"We are in position."*

He held the button on the earpiece and tagged their message as received. Ashur was patched in with the Cadre's men. Jackstraw was patched in with Dixon's—the wildcard. All was going according to plan. Ashur and his cousin began across the expansive star-shaped courtyard of the fort, casually making their way towards the sheriff's administrative complex. As they neared the guarded entrance to the building, Ashur detonated the charges he and Jackstraw had laid at the entrances and other weak points. It doubled as a signal to the lurking army.

The dust and shale had yet to stop raining down when the fort's civil defense siren began wailing. The beehive of Grand Citadel Dakota became a hornet's nest. Rangers sprinted to their battle stations, preparing to repel the oncoming raid, the guards in front of the office complex were no exception. In the same breath, a legion of Rangers burst forth from the building. They watched the building empty out, standing to the side as the hundreds scrambled for the fight.

Once the number of cowboys coming through the doors had thinned, the team entered. There was a flood of incandescent lighting. The floor was tile, the walls were white plaster, the desks were metal and laminate all lined up in rows. It was a proper office building. The only security the building boasted was the now missing door guards, past that, there was maybe a couple of straggling Rangers, nothing intimidating.

They got onto an elevator and the doors rolled closed. Soft jazz was playing. Jackstraw pushed the button labeled 7. They made it up to the third before the elevator stopped to let someone on.

A Ranger stepped into the threshold and held the doors open. "Going down?" he asked.

"No," said Jackstraw and pointed up. "We're going up."

"Oh," said the man. He stepped back and let the doors close. The jazz continued. Ashur and Jackstraw looked at each other. The lift chimed at the seventh floor and they exited. The floor had an open design. There was a receptionist's desk, a small waiting area, a break room, and a number of work desks littered with papers. The sheriff's office door was on the back wall.

A lone Ranger sat at one of the desks. He stood up and started towards them. "This is a restricted area," he said. "I need to see your clearance."

Jackstraw set his dog on the man. The mongrel tore the man's throat out. They moved passed as the dog continued to maul the shrieking man. They pushed on through over turned chairs, half-finished hot drinks, and flickering, monochromatic terminal screens. They stopped at the waiting area, just before the door to Sheriff Stone's office.

"*Oh, Sheriff Stone*," Ashur called in a sing-song fashion. "It's your three o' clock." He drew his hand gun and kicked in the door. The sheriff was behind his desk, rushing to put bullets in a revolver. When he saw Ashur, he stopped. The gun was set on the desk and he leaned back.

Jackstraw entered the room behind his cousin, and likewise brought a gun to the appointment. "Hands up," he ordered.

The sheriff complied. Right then, there was an explosion on the outermost buffer of the Citadel. The sounds of war began to fill the air. The battle was underway. "I don't understand," Stone said, mouth left open as if out of breath. "This is you?"

"You see, it turns out that the Cadre is an old army buddy of mine," said Ashur. "Sure we've had our differences: I blew off half his face with a frag grenade, he put a bounty on my head." He pointed to his face. "Prettied me up some—your healthy squabbles. But when I told him I was looking to burn you, well he couldn't help but join in."

The sheriff was left unable to speak. Jackstraw holstered his gun and got some water from the nearby office cooler. Moonraker wandered in right after. Jackstraw downed a cup and then poured a second. He used it to wash the blood off his dog's snout.

Ashur watched this as he let the lawman process everything. "I'll cut to the chase," he said finally. "Bring me Rose."

The sheriff sat up and eyed him, dutifully quiet.

"I thought you might say that," said Ashur. He picked up the photo of Sheriff Stone's family from off the desk. He swept the revolver and bullets onto the floor and set the photo dead in front of him. "Johnny, could you check in with our friends at Aegis for me?"

Jackstraw held the radio receiver that was clipped to his police armor. "This is Jackstraw. I'm here with the sheriff and Ashur. We'd like to get a confirmation on those goods you picked up." He let go. What came back through the radio sent the sheriff to a different place. Hearing his wife crying and screaming for help, this was no longer a game of strategy for him.

"I think you understand me now," said Ashur, cocking his gun and aiming it at him. "I will kill your wife. I will kill your daughter. I will kill *your infant son*."

The sheriff's face was priceless. He stared at the family picture before him—a still of happiness. His hand trembled as he reached up to the radio on his duster to call for one of his jail guards. He instructed for Rose to be brought up. The jailer confirmed the order and dispatched a man with her. Stone tagged the message as received and then turned to his captors.

He started to say something but Ashur put a tight grouping of three rounds into his chest, silencing him. It knocked the sheriff's hat onto the floor. He stood there, his mind a million miles away, gun still trained on the corpse. "Get to the rooftop and pop a flare," he said. "Make sure everything is in order." Jackstraw collected his dog and left the room. Ashur took the photo off the desk and dropped into one of the room's chairs. The frame was dirty now. "Iustitia omnibus, lawman," he said. His mouth was dry. The battle outside continued raging. His hope, his entire plan rested on the armies crippling each other. Once he was done here, they would lead an assault on Garwood's fortress, leaving both factions leaderless and drained.

He set the picture down and returned to the elevator to wait for the jailer and Rose. By chance, it wasn't long before the lift arrived. He stood with his gun pointed at the door. When it opened, there wasn't much the jailer could do. His hands went up.

"Ashur!?" Rose said, wide-eyed and smiling. It had been nearly two weeks since they had seen each other. "I knew this was you."

He stepped forward and held the door open. "Grab his gun for me."

She relieved the jailer of his sidearm and tossed it out of the elevator. Thereafter, Ashur ordered the jailer to remove her handcuffs. She pushed the lobby button and walked out underneath Ashur's arm. He let the door slide shut.

"What happened to your face?" she asked suddenly, reaching out to touch it. "You haven't taken up bar boxing again, have you?"

He grabbed her hand and led her away. "We've got to go." They made for a service stairway and climbed up to the rooftop. The sunlight strained his eyes. The air conditioners and exterior duct-working gleamed. In the distance, bullets raced and mortars burst like the hearts of little suns.

"What's going on out there?" she asked upon seeing the battle.

"War," he said. "I started a war." He could see Jackstraw on the other side of the roof. When they got there, Jackstraw told them that the extraction was two minutes out. Ashur left them there and went back to mine the door. He used a frag grenade and the door's handle. A flare burned on the cement floor when he returned. Rose went to ask why they were on the roof but she was cut off by the sound of an approaching rotary engine. Off in the distance, a Blackhawk helicopter closed in on the Citadel.

Rose bounced up and down like a child on Christmas. "We have a helicopter!?"

"I pulled out all the stops for you, kiddo," said Ashur. As it descended towards the building, the skirmishing between the Rangers and the Cadre's men ground to a halt. The whole battlefield watched the helicopter touch down on the roof. The side of the vehicle brandished the same brass, circular shield that everything Aegis did. The sound of the rotors washed away the world and the team boarded the chopper. The miniguns from Vanderbilt's car had been fixed to the sides, allowing for door gunners—two of Ashur's Axehandle Hounds. He had returned to the Springs to rally them. When he explained the situation and his plan, the majority of them joined him, seeing that they would have to fight the Cadre off sooner or later.

No moves were made on the chopper at first, likely out of utter shock, but as the team finished boarding, the helicopter began taking small arms fire. By the time the fire grew concentrated enough to warrant a response from the gunners, they were horizon-bound.

Rose was absolutely ecstatic the entire ride back to Dixon's compound. Ashur actually had to pull her back into her seat a number of times. She would not stay put. "I'm sorry," she yelled over the rotor. "This is just so cool." With the sheer speed of the helicopter, it was before long that they descended towards the Aegis complex. The engines were cut and the crew disembarked. A large number of vehicles and personnel stood nearby, silently awaiting instruction. Most were Ashur's expeditionary force, some were Dixon's Celtic themed mercenaries, and all were battle-ready. Ashur plodded across the courtyard to a medical technician and exchanged a few words with him.

Rose wandered around the helicopter, smiling ear to ear. "This thing is badass," she told Jackstraw. He was inclined to agree. She climbed into the passenger seat and made herself comfortable. "Hey," she said to the pilot while looking over the buttons on the console.

"I uh…hi," he replied.

"What?"

"Should I be talking to you? Boss's daughter and all."

She laughed. "Oh it's fine. Tell me how this thing works."

"Flower girl," Ashur called, waving her over. "Come here."

"Sorry," she said to the pilot and exited. Before closing the door, she added: "Don't go anywhere. I'll be right back."

She was nearly thirty paces away from Ashur, the full breadth of the courtyard. She saw that Ashur, Jackstraw, the soldiers—everyone was watching her. She furrowed her brow and started off. When she stopped before him, she tensed as if poised to run. "What is it?" she asked.

He held out his hand to her. "Come here."

She mindlessly extended her hand to him, looking over her shoulder at the legionnaires that surrounded them. Everyone was so quiet.

He pulled her in for a hug. She stood with her arms at her sides for a moment before she realized what was happening. She brought her arms up, hesitated, and then hugged him back. He changed his grip to cradle the back of her head and she nuzzled into his chest.

"I missed you too," she said. They stayed like that for a time, the whole courtyard watching. At some point, he held out his hand and a medic placed an automatic syringe in it. When the time came, he jammed it into her thigh. She pulled back to look him in the face.

"Oh?" was all she said. Her breathing grew clumsy almost immediately. She became heavy and began to slip from his grasp. He took a knee and brought her down, holding her. The last thing she said to him before blacking out was, "Why?"

He sat in the dust with her. He knew she wouldn't have let him go willingly, would have done everything in her power to stop him. And had she put up a fuss, had she begged him to run away, he would have listened. He couldn't allow that. Garwood had been his man. The Cadre was now his burden.

Jackstraw and his dog stood over them now. "You didn't say a damn word to her. You didn't even let her say goodbye."

"What do you think this is?" he whispered, as if afraid to wake her.

Jackstraw lit a cigarette. "She didn't know that." He spoke from the corner of his mouth, his teeth touching. "Leaving her on the side of the road like you found her. She's going to hate you."

Ashur reached up to wipe his nose with the back of his glove. "I hope she does. Anger's easier than grief."

Jackstraw took a drag. "You really don't see us coming back from this."

A black van pulled into the courtyard and stopped near the helicopter. Ashur's sergeant approached him. "Sir, we need to move before the Cadre's army can return to New Valley."

The yard stood idle.

"Take her," he said.

The sergeant waved a man over. He took her and began carrying her into the compound. "And the sheriff's family?" the sergeant asked, gesturing to the black van. Dixon and another mercenary got out of it. They began towards the group.

Ashur pointed to the compound. "Find a man or two to stay behind. Take everyone back to the Springs when this is over." The sergeant passed on the order.

Dixon took over from here. "This is it, gentlemen! Charge for the guns." The soldiers made haste. Most of them proceeded to the nearby armored cars while Ashur, Jackstraw, his dog, and a couple of gunners got into the helicopter. Dixon would lead them from the ground while Ashur and his cousin came in from above. The mercenary leader jumped into the passenger seat of the Mercury Cougar as the rotors of the helicopter spooled up. The driver honked twice and the attack convoy rolled into the wastes, towards New Valley.

Chapter 30

The children raised their hands to the dim fire, searching to find some warmth from the cold night's air. Their father returned and placed another log in the fire, sending out a cascade of embers that quickly died off. "Where was I?" he asked.

"You were going to tell the tale of the Wolf and the Beast," said the son. "The second part."

"Ah, yes. The Wolf and the Beast. Let's see, how to begin…It was this man, this packless wolf, who brought about the end to the reign of the Beast. He sniffed out the clan and confronted them in their own den. He sauntered in, slaughtered them as you would sheep, and then he sauntered away."

"But not the Beast," said the daughter.

"That's right," said the father. "The Beast, though badly injured, survived. He spent years in the shadows, gathering his strength. His former clan of ten grew to thousands. During this time, a sickness fed upon the Rangers. They became corrupt, a shell of their former selves. This is when the Beast attacked. He burnt towns. He took slaves. He shut off the lights."

"But then what happened?"

"The Wolf reappeared, this time with a pack under his pilot. He stuck a dagger in the Rangers' side and used them as bait, drawing the Beast's army away from the den. Then he and his bunch moved in on the king of thieves. The battle was fierce and hot, but when the dust settled, the Beast was slain, once and for all. The demon's clan scattered into the wilderness, leaving the Ranger Syndicate in shambles. This is when the present syndicate took form, loyal to the people and once again respected. The Rangers rebuilt themselves into a force for good, as they had been in the past. And all grew quiet in the wasteland."

"It's my favorite story," said the boy. He looked to the Ranger deputy whom had been listening to the folktale along with them. It was also her favorite. "Where's the Wolf gone to now?" he asked her.

The woman shook her head. "He gave all he had to give that day. He's moved on now."

The children leaned in and murmured to each other. Then the boy asked: "Do you think he could still be out there? On the prowl for killers and thieves?" They had misunderstood.

She smiled one of her sudden, shy smiles at the children.

"Well I like to think he is," she said, looking out into the distance. "Somewhere."

The End